NE

Beach Rental

Double Winner in the 2012 GDRWA Booksellers' Best Award

Finalist in the 2012 Gayle Wilson Award of Excellence

Finalist in the 2012 Published Maggie Award for Excellence

"No author can come close to capturing the awe-inspiring essence of the North Carolina coast like Greene. In her debut novel, Greene seamlessly combines hope, love, and faith like the female Nicholas Sparks. Her writing is meticulous and so finely detailed you'll hear the gulls overhead and the waves crashing onto shore. Grab a hankie, bury your toes in the sand, and get ready to be swept away with this unforgettable beach read."

—*RT Book Reviews* 4.5 stars, Top Pick

Beach Winds

Finalist in the 2014 OKRWA International Digital Awards

Finalist in the 2014 WisRWA Write Touch Readers' Award

"Greene's follow-up to *Beach Rental* is exquisitely written, with lots of emotion and tugging on the heartstrings. Returning to Emerald Isle is like a warm reunion with an old friend, and readers will be inspired by the captivating story, where we excitedly get to meet new characters and reconnect with a few familiar faces too. The author's perfect prose highlights family relationships that we may find similar to our own and will have you dreaming of strolling along the shore to rediscover yourself in no time at all. This novel will have you wondering about faith, hope, and courage, and you may be lucky enough to gain all three by the time *Beach Winds*' last page is read."

—*RT Book Reviews* 4.5 stars, Top Pick

Kincaid's Hope

Finalist in the 2013 GDRWA Booksellers' Best Award

Finalist in the 2013 Gayle Wilson Award of Excellence

"A quiet backwater town is the setting for intrigue, deception, and betrayal in this exceptional sophomore offering. Greene's ability to pull the readers into the story and emotionally invest them in the characters makes this book a great read."

—*RT Book Reviews*, 4 stars

"This is a unique modern-day romantic suspense novel, with eerie gothic tones—a well-played combination, expertly woven into the story line . . . She rode the wave of excellent writing in her first novel with the same complex writing style, which easily draws the reader in."

—*Jane Austen Book Maven*, 5 stars

The Happiness In Between

"*The Happiness In Between* overflows with the warmth, healing, and hope Greene fans know to expect in her uplifting stories."

—Christine Nolfi, bestselling author of *Sweet Lake* and *The Comfort of Secrets*

The Memory of Butterflies

"*The Memory of Butterflies* is an emotionally gripping tale of a mother's love and the secret so great it threatens to destroy her world. Grace Greene masterfully captures the beauty and isolation of Cooper's Hollow and enriches it with deftly created characters that tug at your heartstrings. A beautiful story, beautifully told."

—Christine Nolfi, bestselling author of *Sweet Lake* and *The Comfort of Secrets*

"The power of a mother's love can overcome everything . . . until secrets and betrayal threaten what means the most. In *The Memory of Butterflies*, Grace Greene weaves a captivating tale of loss, love, and forgiveness."

—Patricia Sands, author of the Love in Provence trilogy

wildflower heart

ALSO BY GRACE GREENE

Emerald Isle, NC Novels

Beach Rental

Beach Winds

Beach Wedding

"Beach Towel" (short story)

Beach Christmas (Christmas novella)

Beach Walk (Christmas novella)

Virginia Country Roads Novels

Kincaid's Hope

A Stranger in Wynnedower

Cub Creek

Leaving Cub Creek

Stand-Alone Novels

The Happiness In Between

The Memory of Butterflies

The Wildflower House Novels

Wildflower Heart

wildflower heart

THE WILDFLOWER HOUSE SERIES

Grace Greene

This is a work of fiction. Names, characters, organizations, places, events, and incidents are either products of the author's imagination or are used fictitiously. Any resemblance to actual persons, living or dead, or actual events is purely coincidental.

Published by Lake Union Publishing, Seattle

www.apub.com

ISBN-13: 9781542040600
ISBN-10: 1542040604

Cover design by Caroline Teagle Johnson

Printed in the United States of America

Wildflower Heart *is dedicated to those who survive and thrive despite rocky starts and to those who help us grow our lives in positive and loving ways. This book is about overcoming—with love. It is about learning to invest the best of who we are into everything we do. Most importantly, this book is dedicated to my sister, Jill Jinnett, who listened to my stories when she was a toddler and is still—and always—my first reader and my expert on all things Cub Creek. She is smart, an honest advisor, and ever willing to help me grow in craft. I am greatly blessed. Thank you, Jill.*

In memory of Elaine Suzanne
Troy—she is greatly missed.

PROLOGUE

- *Wildflowers are tough. They root in unlikely, often hostile environments, yet they manage to grow and bloom.*

- *Wildflowers are fragile. Careless or deliberate acts can easily destroy them.*

- *Wildflowers grow where the seeds find themselves. They must succeed or perish. If they don't grow, no one notices. It's as if the seed or the flower never existed.*

- *Wildflowers are beautiful for a season. Some may be beautiful for seasons to come. The wildflower will never know the difference because it either is or isn't. Only the bees and the butterflies—or a human heart—may feel the lack.*

—Stitched by Kara Lange Hart at Wildflower House

I never considered the truth about the existence of wildflowers as I hid in my father's home and threaded my embroidery needles to stitch the rich red shade of poppies or the purple-blue hue of delphiniums into the taut canvas. It wasn't until later—after the move to Cub Creek—that I understood. For most of my life, I had lived in shades of gray. I'd rooted where I'd found myself and had been only slightly more self-aware than those lovely but hapless flowers.

Long ago, the essayist and poet Ralph Waldo Emerson said, "Earth laughs in flowers." There was precious little laughter in my life. I had learned in devastating ways that life could be messy and inconvenient. Colorful thread and an embroidery hoop were much safer.

In my heart, though, when it came to life and living, I knew the perfection of a fine copy was a drab substitute for the real thing.

CHAPTER ONE

My father, Henry Lange, was the unofficial automotive and tire magnate of a large portion of the mid-Atlantic. He devoted his life to his work, having started his business in one small corrugated-metal building on the east side of Richmond and growing it across three states. He stood tall and dressed well. His words and his manner carried authority. Business suited his skills and talents. Objectivity and logic ruled his world. The nurturing of biological creatures like his only child, his daughter—me—he left to his wife, my mother.

Mom was there for me. She did the best she could. I never doubted that. She was home when I was and always asked how my day had gone, what I'd learned, and whether I'd made new friends. Usually, a snack was waiting for me at the kitchen table. I'd sit with her, telling her stories about school, my teachers, and so on. She stared into the distance a lot, occasionally turning to me with a smile and touching my hand. I knew she wasn't always listening, but I told her about my day anyway—sometimes truth, sometimes fiction—because I sensed that was what she wanted. If, when I came home, she was still wearing her nightgown and robe, I knew I'd be fixing supper. If she had dressed for the day, then she'd cook or call in pizza or something. Either way, we had that interval between school and supper together. It was our time.

We lost her when I was fourteen.

Lost? *Euphemism alert*, I chided my adult self. The truth was that one day I came home from school to find a piece of paper on the kitchen table. A coffee cup was set on top of it like a paperweight. No snack. No Mom.

A solitary dusty rosebud was in the coffee cup. The bud was crafted of wax. I knew where it came from. Mom had had a brief adventure as a contestant in a beauty contest when she was a teenager—she'd told me about it a few times—and had received a bouquet of red wax roses and a plastic crown. The roses had fascinated me. They looked real. Mom had explained that the appearance of perfection was what gave things away as false.

It was odd to see that bud in the ceramic cup. I moved the cup aside and picked up the paper. It was a note in Mom's neat writing wishing Dad and me well, saying in essence, "So sorry, Kara, to leave you and your father this way, but I don't belong in this life. Let your dad know I made my decision."

I blinked, then refocused and read it again more slowly.

My heart refused to accept the words. Nausea bent me in half as my stomach spasmed. I closed my eyes and fought it off. I outran it. I raced along the hallway to the garage door, yanked it open, and stood on the threshold. The interior was dim and empty. Her car was gone.

I dashed back down the hallway, up the stairs, and into her bedroom. I pushed aside the closet door. The door rattled on its tracks as it slammed into the wall. Not all of her clothing was gone, but what was left was no longer so tightly squeezed together. Next, I pulled open the dresser drawers. It was the same. Items remained. Much was gone. She'd taken what mattered most and abandoned the rest.

Including me.

It's okay, I told myself. *There's been a misunderstanding. She'll be back any minute. She'll ask herself what she was thinking of to do such a thing, and she'll turn around.* That overhead garage door was going to open—I'd hear the hum of its motor—and she'd emerge from her car slightly embarrassed. She'd tell me she'd had a moment, a big, bad moment, but had shaken it off and seen how foolish she'd been and had rushed back to me. She'd ask me to forgive her. She might even ask me not to tell my father. I would assure her that she was home again and all was well.

There was good reason to believe she'd return because she'd left about a year before. She'd been gone for two days, returning with a silly excuse about getting lost. Or maybe she'd said *being* instead of *getting*. I was never sure. Dad had been angry at her, but in his controlled way. I'd just been grateful. And I dimly remembered a time before that when I was much younger. Mom had been gone longer—maybe a week or two—and my Grandma Mary Lou had come all the way from Illinois to stay with me until Mom came home. I'd heard other kids talk about their grandparents in ways that made me glad my one and only grandparent was coming to visit, but it hadn't worked out well. No one had been happy about it—not my grandmother or my father—and neither would talk about Mom except to say she would be home soon. Finally, Dad took Grandma Mary Lou to the airport and brought Mom home. Funny, maybe sad-funny in retrospect, but I thought Mom would bring a baby with her. That had happened to other families on our block when the moms went away and grandmothers came to visit. But Mom didn't bring a baby home. She did, however, look happier than she had in a long time, and she'd hugged me and kissed me. I remembered that much, and so hope was reasonable.

I went outside and stood in the street looking both ways, wanting to catch a glimpse of her. Waiting and watching, I stood there until the January cold reminded me I wasn't wearing my coat, and my teeth started to chatter. Finally, I retreated back inside.

In the kitchen, I read her note for the third time. The paper had been torn from a notebook and then ripped in half across the middle. Her writing was neat and clear. No possibility of misreading the words. The table was otherwise bare. No other hints or clues except for the missing snack, so that meant she'd left early, perhaps right after I'd headed to the bus stop that morning. Hours had passed since. A whole school day. I had only a vague idea of how the states arranged themselves beyond the ones that immediately bordered Virginia, but by now, she could be that far or farther. Or just down the road setting up a separate life. At that point, I was out of ideas. I called Dad at work.

"Gone? Is that what you said?"

"Mom left a note."

"Can you read it to me?"

His question was simple, and his voice was even. No urgency. I tried to slow my heart to match his tone so I could find the calm, the breath I needed to speak Mom's written words, her goodbye words, aloud into the phone receiver. When the words ran out, I went silent. After a moment, Dad spoke.

"Are you okay, Kara?"

My jaw moved; my lips tried to shape words but failed. My chin quivered. My eyes burned.

"Fix yourself a snack. Can you do that?"

"Yes, sir," I whispered.

"After you eat, start your homework. I'll be home as soon as possible."

"But, Dad . . ."

"Yes?"

My fingers still clutched the note. Irrationally, I feared that if I did the wrong thing, there'd be no hope of going back, no hope of better to come. If I released the scrap of paper, would it vanish? Maybe crumble into a small heap of ashy dust with no evidence to show a message had truly existed? That a mom had been here and might yet return?

"What should I do with her note?" My voice was breaking. I barely got the words out.

"Put it on the counter, Kara. I'll know where to find it when I get home. I'll handle it."

I nodded. "Okay, Dad. I will."

But instead of fixing a snack or starting my homework, I stared at Mom's photo—a picture of her with her long, straight black hair that I loved to weave my fingers into. We were together at the park. I was probably five or six when the photo was taken, and we were both smiling. Dad wasn't in the photo. He was on the other side of the camera. It was spring, I thought, because there were vibrant banks of flowers behind us that looked like azaleas.

I took the framed photo from the fireplace mantel and carried it with me to the sofa, where I curled up with the throw pillows and pulled the sofa blanket over my head. I could smell my mother's scent in the blanket, and it gave me comfort.

Dad came home from work early. When I heard his key in the lock, I pushed the blanket aside. He stood by the sofa and stared at me briefly as if assessing my general well-being and was apparently satisfied. "We'll manage okay."

"Will we?" It all rose up, suddenly, swamping my calm. "Mom's gone, Dad. *Gone.* We have to tell someone. Get help. Find her. We should call the police."

"Kara." He sat on the edge of the coffee table and leaned toward me, gently putting his hand on my shoulder. "I did that already. I called them after we spoke. They are coming over to talk to us and view the note, but they won't search for her, not for forty-eight hours, at least, and probably not even then because she left by her own choice."

"What about Grandma?" She'd visited that time when I was little. I got a card from her on my birthday; otherwise, nothing. But even if she wasn't much of a grandmother to me, Mom might be driving to Illinois right at this very moment to visit her.

"I called Mary Lou immediately in case she'd heard from your mother." He shook his head. "She hadn't. I'm not surprised. They don't get along."

"We have to do something."

He sat on the arm of his chair near the sofa. "Kara, we know your mom hasn't been well . . ." He cleared his throat. "She hasn't been happy in a long time." He paused and waited, gathering his words again before resuming. "We do what we can to help the people we care about, but they have to want it too. It's no good trying to force someone to stay who doesn't want to be with you. You understand?"

No, I didn't understand. Maybe my lack of understanding was due to me being fourteen. But deep inside, Dad's words rang true. Mom hadn't been happy. Her thin smile had only lived on the surface, on her lips. It hadn't reached her eyes in a long time. My instinct and pain couldn't reconcile with logic. I wanted to find my mother. If I couldn't do that, then I wanted to scream. I looked at my father and knew I couldn't do that either. I pressed my face back into the pillow. I heard Dad sigh and stand. I moved the pillow down a couple of inches so it covered only my mouth.

Dad eyed my backpack leaning against the coffee table. I'd propped it there when I'd first come home, before I knew my world had changed.

"You need help with the schoolwork?"

I shook my head slowly. Mom was gone, and Dad was worried about my homework? My brain felt all jangly inside, as if the sharp edges of my thoughts wanted to come together but were too fractured to fit.

"Kara? Your homework. Focus. Do you need help?"

I didn't shake my head again but gave only a single nod. I muttered into the sofa pillow, "No. It's not hard. I can do it."

"Good." He picked up the newspaper and sat down in his special chair to bury himself in the pages. "Let me know if you do need help. We'll order in pizza—the usual—after the officer stops by. We'll manage, Kara. Try not to worry."

Try not to worry. Impossible, of course, but how like my father to reduce a catastrophe to the drama level of a pepperoni-pizza order and sum up a life-altering event with an everyday phrase. As I hugged the pillow and dug my fingers into it for control, I observed him reading. His large hands gripped the sides of the paper in a firm grasp, but I perceived their slight tremor and the barely there shaking of the paper. Alarm nibbled at me. If Dad could lose his cool, then any awful thing was possible.

Dad shook the newspaper once with a rough but controlled movement, as if the problem were in the newsprint and not in his heart, and the paper settled back into place. After that, he gave every appearance of calm. I tried to imitate his composure. I wanted logic that could be applied to today and comfort, too, about the future—to feel that comfort as a certainty. Gradually, the sharp, tangled feeling in my brain eased, and my breathing felt more normal. After a few minutes, I did feel less inclined to fly into a million tearful pieces.

A detective came to the house, viewed Mom's note, and spoke quietly with me, and then he and my father walked outside to finish the interview.

I saved my tears for the cover of night. I drenched my pillow and then fell asleep. But my sleep was that of an emotionally exhausted child and far from restful. For the next few days, I skipped school and walked miles through our neighborhood, even crossing under the interstate overpass to check out nearby hotel parking lots looking for Mom's car or any sign of her. When the school called the house, I happened to be there to grab the phone. I put on my mother's voice and told them Kara was a little under the weather and would be returning to school on Monday.

A few days later, when Dad came home from work, I tried again, asking him the questions that continued to bubble and boil in my head. We were in the living room again with me on the sofa, my schoolbooks nearby, and Dad just settling into his chair and smoothing out the newspaper. It was his routine to come home, pick up the still-folded newspaper, sit with a cup of coffee, and settle in to reading. He read it page by page, all the way through. Always.

I interrupted. "Dad?"

"What?"

"Why do you think she left? Was it me?"

He looked up, staring forward, then frowned, all but confirming my fear. I sank back against the sofa, pulling a pillow onto my lap, wishing I could drown inside the soft cushions. Just disappear. Like my mom had done.

"No."

The word was spoken so softly I wouldn't have heard it if the furnace had chosen that moment to click on.

"No?" I whispered back.

He folded the paper and set it on the arm of the chair and stood. He walked over to the fireplace. He stared at that photo of Mom and me on the mantel. He ran his hand across the top of his head in a quick gesture, then shoved both of his hands in his pants pockets. "No, Kara. Not you. Things were . . . well, difficult between us. She wasn't happy. Whatever it was that she needed, I couldn't give it to her."

I waited.

He must've felt the questioning silence because he added, "That's all I can tell you."

"Why didn't she take me with her?"

It was an honest question, and I had to ask it, but it hurt him. His shoulders curved inward as if warding off a blow.

I rushed to add, "I didn't mean that I would *want* to go with her." Maybe I would've wanted to go with her. I wasn't sure. But it hurt not to have had a choice. "She's a mom. Moms don't just leave, right?"

Dad turned to face me, but it took a few seconds for him to meet my eyes. "Kara. Don't worry about that. You were the best thing your mom ever produced in her whole life. I don't know why people . . . especially people like your mother . . . make the choices they do. Emotional people like your mother, I mean. But what I do know is that you are the best thing that ever came, or will come, from her. The best decision she ever made as a mother was *not* to drag you into her . . . to take you away from your home. I give her credit for that."

There was a lot of meaning within those words that I couldn't catch. I knew it was there, but I was fourteen. These were adult mysteries, some of them messy, and I didn't want to hear them. Not now. Maybe later. But I had to ask one more question.

"Where is she? Do you know where she went?"

"No. Hopefully, somewhere sunny. Winter has always been a hard season for her. I wish her well. I hope she finds the life she thinks she wants."

"Like Dorothy?"

"Dorothy?"

"With the ruby-red slippers. She decided there was no place like home."

"From *The Wizard of Oz*?"

"Yes. She clicked her shoes together and made a wish and came back home."

"That was a story, not real life. Don't waste your hopes on her coming home. She's gone, Kara. She won't be back."

Dad picked up his newspaper and eased into his chair.

The subject felt closed. Into that silence, I forced one more question. "But if she did return?"

He shook his head no, then focused on his paper.

I stood and walked to the window. What if she was driving up the road at this very moment? What if she was on the last of her gas, riding on fumes, afraid she'd run out before she made it home . . . ?

Dad saw me. Like a mind reader, he said, "She's not coming back." He spoke in that same careful, word-by-word way that he always used when tackling a difficult personal subject—which he only ever tackled if he couldn't find a way to avoid it. "I wish I could spare you hurt. I understand this is an adjustment." His eyes focused on me again as another thought arrived. "Are you lonely or afraid between when you get home from school and I come home from work? Would you like a sitter?"

A sitter? I was fourteen. I didn't need a sitter and was horrified at the idea. At times, a little company might be nice, but a *sitter*?

"No, thank you. I'm fine."

"If you need help with your homework or schoolwork, you'll let me know?"

"Sure."

"Okay, then," he said. His eyes lingered on my face for a long second or two.

The shadow of worry—not quite worry but only the shadow of it—left his eyes. I knew he appreciated my answer because it relieved him of having to make a fatherly decision that might cause a fuss.

I didn't believe my father had ever been afraid of anything, except perhaps of being a father and maybe a husband. Yet I trusted him. I knew he wouldn't leave. His head was forever in work and business, but he always lived up to his commitments and responsibilities. Maybe he had friends at work with whom he enjoyed something more like friendship or fun. He never said. As for me, I knew a few kids in the neighborhood, but we didn't hang out. School was fine, and I had friends there, but the truth was I was a loner and mostly okay about it. Maybe being content with solitude and naturally independent made the transition to one parent easier for me.

Over the next weeks and months, I wondered how I'd feel if Mom walked back in the door. If she came home and apologized for leaving us, could we go back to normal? Could I trust her to stay?

Dad and I did okay. We sorted out our roles. I cooked the meals and washed the laundry and kept up my grades. Dad attended to business and paid the bills. We managed.

Mom didn't come back. I thought she might drop me a postcard or send a birthday card, but she never did. It was as if someone had picked up a pencil and erased her from our lives.

Then one day, about two years after she left, I learned she'd never come home, ever. I was sixteen when Dad, once again, came home early from work. He motioned to me to sit on the sofa. I did, and calmly, not showing that my heart was trying to climb up into my throat and choke me.

"Kara," he said, "I'm sorry to tell you this." He reached out, and his hand brushed mine before dropping away. "Your mother is gone. Deceased, I mean. She died in Ohio. The police there contacted the authorities here. They came to the office to tell me."

My mouth opened. I intended to ask how or what or why, but I couldn't ask any of those things.

Dad said, "Probably went in her sleep. Her . . . they said her heart stopped."

He'd ended so awkwardly that I waited, thinking he had more to say. He didn't.

I asked, "What about her funeral?"

He looked aside and then down at his shoes. "Her mother is handling it."

Feeling breathless, I managed to squeak out, "We're going to Illinois?"

He shook his head. "No, Kara. She . . ." He coughed and started again. "Mary Lou asked us not to. She is keeping it very simple."

I stood. That choking feeling in my throat turned to queasiness and then nausea. I ran from the room. I didn't vomit, though. I knelt on the bathroom floor and shed a few quiet tears, then huddled in the dark for a while. At some point, Dad knocked on the door and asked if I was all right. I called out yes. And I was okay. Truly. I'd done most of my mourning and crying back when she'd left. This was no more than a final farewell and acceptance.

By the next day, I was back on track. Life went on. But even though I knew the truth, it was a rare day that I didn't come home and hold my breath as I entered the kitchen. Hope died hard. Even in the face of reality.

When I left for college, I didn't grieve for what I was leaving behind. I'd learned that from my father—not to be overly sentimental, to keep everything in perspective and in its proper place, and to never look backward. *Don't dwell in yesterdays. Live in the now.* Frankly, you didn't miss hugs and kisses you'd never had. You didn't even know they were missing.

~

I met Niles Hart in college. He had a handsome face, good hair, and a charming smile. We fell in love in statistics class. After we completed our economics degrees, we married and moved to Northern Virginia, where we had a cute apartment and good jobs waiting for us. My job was in project management for a tech firm, and Niles worked in the accounting department of a start-up tech business. We both loved being part of the teeming traffic and the super pulse of life in the DC beltway, where even jobs like ours could seem exciting.

I was a businessperson like my dad. I was content to function within that business environment. Niles liked the energy of a start-up. In that way, I thought Niles was a lot like my dad, too, because he was willing to work hard to achieve his goals. That wasn't necessarily true—not for either of us. But it took me a few years to learn how badly I'd misjudged.

Dad attended my college graduation and gave me away at my wedding, and he paid for both without complaint. Beyond that, he was rarely an on-the-scene part of the life Niles and I built together, which was natural enough. Niles and I were newlyweds. By the time the newlywed newness had worn off, our habits had been established. Dad was busy with his business. Niles and I were advancing in our jobs.

We exchanged phone calls from time to time and visited on occasional holidays, but we were each absorbed in our own lives many miles apart.

In my mind, Dad continued doing what he loved most—running his tire empire. I had Niles. We'd each gotten fresh starts. Dad no longer had to worry about my well-being, and I happily put my childhood heartaches behind me.

It all worked well until the accident that nearly killed me, and my whole world, once again, turned upside down.

CHAPTER TWO

After six years of marriage and six years of the workday world, Niles and I had settled into a routine, which to my mind wasn't a bad thing, but I sensed restlessness in him. Sometimes in myself too. I blamed it on him mostly, even though I knew it took two to make a marriage good. We each, separately and together, had to choose our happiness or unhappiness.

I stood in front of the full-length bedroom mirror admiring the slim black dress and my short haircut. My dark hair fit my head almost like a cap, emphasizing my hazel eyes. My father's eyes. I owed him a call. Or he owed me one. It seemed to me that it shouldn't be this hard to stay in touch. But that took two, too.

I shook my head. No negative thoughts tonight. This evening, Niles and I would recommit and find our energy again—that lovely energy we'd created in our first years together. The love was still there between us; I knew it was. Something that had been so intense, so very real, couldn't be allowed to wither and die.

In no way did I view our marital trouble as history repeating itself. My parents' marriage had failed, but that was different. I didn't have my mother's emotional problems, and as it turned out, Niles was nothing like my father. Niles was busy and passionate in his interests and ambition but not focused like Dad. We didn't agree on everything, and sometimes our goals were at cross-purposes, but those were small things. This evening, we would put aside petty disagreements. Tonight was about us and our anniversary—and my special news.

My perfect little black dress with a silk skirt and lace on the bodice worked well with strappy heels. I took another quick look from the back and was satisfied. Never a beauty, but I was attractive, and tonight I was glowing. Niles stood behind me and fastened the diamond pendant he'd given me on our first anniversary around my neck. The back of his hands, warm and sure, brushing the nape of my neck, warmed me. I reached up and pressed my fingers to his briefly, and then he was done. Our smiles met in the mirror.

My phone rang on the dresser. I glanced down at it.

"It's Victoria," I said. "She's been calling a lot lately." In fact, the frequent calls had become annoying. I added, "It's as if she has something on her mind."

His voice was suddenly harsh. "Like what?"

"That's the problem. She can't seem to get to the point."

I reached toward the phone. Niles intercepted my hand, gently taking it in his.

"Don't answer it," he said, his voice now persuasive. "She probably wants to complain about her mother or her job or something. We're running late."

"We're in plenty of time. Besides," I said, patting the necklace, "I'm ready." I picked up the phone, but the ringing had stopped. "She probably wanted to wish us a happy anniversary. I'll call her back tomorrow."

"Forget Victoria. Let's go," Niles said.

I hesitated. Now what? His persuasive tone was gone. His voice had that "let's go and get it over with" tone. *No*, I told myself, *don't jump to conclusions or read hidden meanings in his words*. Especially if it was over Victoria and her phone call. I forced a smile and said, "I'll be right there."

"I'll get the car started and meet you out front."

We'd moved from our first apartment into this town house two years before. It was roomier, and more importantly, it had room for one more. I smiled to myself as I shrugged into my coat and tucked my purse under my arm. We were on schedule, with plenty of time to make our reservation. Niles got like this sometimes; that's all it was. I refused to descend into sniping. This was our anniversary, and I had news to share. Good news, as far as I was concerned. I hoped he would agree.

Niles drove us to the restaurant. His car was fancy and shiny—a Lexus. Niles saw his car as almost an extension of himself. He drove his fancy wife in his fancy car to a fancy restaurant with fancy people—and he liked that. To be honest, I had enjoyed that, too, in the past. Less now, though I didn't know why. Despite how well I was doing in my career, I was experiencing discontent. But my father had taught me persistence and to stick with the plan. *Make it work.* If I'd thought something was worth doing once, then it was still worth doing. I needed to get my head back into the right space and keep moving forward. Besides, maternity leave was a normal part of doing business now. Pregnancy and motherhood wouldn't hurt my standing in the work universe. It was commonplace, even among executives. I anticipated Niles's arguments—that we couldn't afford a child; that it was expensive living in the DC environs; that the world was going to crap, and it was wrong to bring a child into it; and all that stuff. Some of it was valid, but some of it was just what people said when they didn't want to change their status quo.

But life was often about the unexpected, the unplanned, right? A smart project manager allowed for that too.

I glanced at Niles, suddenly reluctant to talk and uncomfortable because the right words wouldn't come. He sat there, staring straight ahead as he drove—not unusual considering it was dark and rainy. But there was something rigid about the set of his jaw and that fierce stare ahead, as if he might have read my thoughts and was already angry. I hadn't shared my news yet, not with anyone. I had to tell him first. He would be happy about it. Oh, he might be dismayed at first, but he'd be happy once we got that first "surprise" out of the way.

The restaurant was an upscale place amid fancy shopping in McLean, Virginia, not far from the corporate headquarters where I worked.

Niles asked, "You okay?"

"Sure. Why?"

"You sighed."

"Oh." I smiled at the streetlights, traffic lights, in the dark night. The light rain gave everything a little extra glitter. "I'm good. You?"

"Of course."

In those two terse words, I heard that he wasn't good at all. "Are you sure?"

He flashed me a quick smile that didn't last as long as his sentence. "I told you I was."

At dinner, when the waiter reached for my wine glass, I waved him off. "None for me."

Niles said, "Why not? You enjoy wine."

I bristled. "I do. But not tonight, thank you." Then I hesitated. Maybe this was the moment to tell him? An opportunity. Maybe I could put this evening back on track at this very moment by sharing the news of the pregnancy.

"Suit yourself." Niles pushed his chair back an inch or two. Every movement, even his bored glance around the room, communicated that he no longer wanted to be here.

He was annoyed. Generally annoyed, I thought. Sometimes he got that way. So, no, I didn't tell him. Instead, I tried to change the negative direction of the evening by mentioning the trip we were planning.

We'd decided to forego gift exchanges and put our money toward a special trip we wanted to take. We talked about Paris a little and about whether we should start in the eastern Mediterranean and then go on to Europe or the other way around. Niles's posture eased a little. It felt like he came back to me in those moments, becoming himself again, yet the conversation seemed stilted. Insincere. It hurt my heart. Somewhere between the main course and dessert, my stomach soured along with my mood, and I decided this evening was not the time to tell Niles he was going to be a father. Tomorrow would surely be better.

As we walked to the car, I pulled out my keys. "I'll drive."

"I'm not drunk."

He was annoyed. I didn't think it was about the driving but more about looking for a place to hang his annoyance—and I was the handiest person available.

"No, you aren't drunk, but you drank a lot of wine."

"It's just wine." He laughed, but the sound had a harsh edge.

"Don't worry. I'll be careful with your car."

"Happy anniversary to you too."

I cast a quick sideways look at him, but he wasn't speaking to me. He'd addressed that remark to the universe or the night.

"Suit yourself, Kara. If you want to drive, then by all means, take charge."

"I will." We climbed into the car. I turned on the windshield wipers. The drizzle was light, and the night was especially dark. The streetlights, the neon business signs, the car lights—they threw reflections everywhere, creating a certain disorientation, so I ignored Niles's noises and finger tapping as I concentrated on exiting the parking lot and merging onto the main road. Traffic wasn't bad this time of evening, but it was never light up here in Northern Virginia.

"You do, you know."

Still focusing on the road, I asked, almost absentmindedly, "I do what?"

"Always want things your way."

A pickup truck passed quickly, throwing up spray. I tapped the brakes to slow a bit and allowed him to outpace me so I could see through my windshield better.

"Not true, Niles. I might say the same about you. It always has to be *your* way."

He didn't answer. I wanted to modify how those words had sounded. I added, "That argument is as old as marriage itself. We each get our way, and at other times, we don't. Marriage is give-and-take, right?"

That was his chance. His opportunity to jump back onto our marriage train and bring us home—back together—as a team.

He said, "I agree. It's supposed to be like that in a marriage. It doesn't work that way in ours."

I closed my eyes, then forced them back open. I was tempted to pull the car over, park it, get out, and walk away. But it was raining. It was dark. We were still a few miles from home. Plus, dramatically braking, slamming the door, and running into the night would be childish and unfair. If Niles felt unheard or unappreciated, then we needed to discuss it. I still believed in us. Maybe he didn't.

This was a divided roadway, not an interstate, but traffic flowed on each side of the center islands. Where the road approached another major artery, the traffic increased. On this dark, rainy, desperately unhappy night, I tried to focus on the driving. We'd make it home, and then we'd talk. Really talk.

He said, his voice sounding strained, "I've wanted to tell you this for a while."

"Wait, please. Let's talk when we get home."

"Always your way, right? I don't want to wait. It's time to clear the air. I'm seeing someone."

The car swerved. I heard horns honking.

"What does that mean? Seeing someone?" I didn't recognize my own shrill voice.

"Someone who understands give-and-take. Who understands working together, sharing goals."

The tires hit a puddle, or maybe the rain had raised a patch of oil from the asphalt. The tires slipped. We nearly hit a railing before I regained control of the skid.

"Hey, what are you doing, Kara? Trying to get us killed?" He hit the dashboard with his fist. "You're like your father. You only think about yourself. Everything has a place, a compartment, a role, and anyone who steps out of it gets smacked down. Living with you is like being trapped in a box. A prison. Who can live that way?"

"My father? I'm not like him," I yelled.

"Oh, yeah? Well, maybe you're right. Maybe it's your crazy mother, but I wouldn't know since she ditched you."

My hand moved of its own accord, aiming for his face, but the angle was awkward. I missed. I was glad. My temper . . .

"Watch what you're doing!" He shifted in his seat and tugged on his seat belt.

"Me? Me?" That temper, my hurt, came roaring back even stronger. "You are the one who chose this moment to tell me you're having an affair . . . because you are, right? You aren't just *seeing* someone. Where? Hotels? Your office? In our home? In this car?" I saw his face. "In this very car. And you tell me on our anniversary!" I repeated, "Our anniversary!" The words flamed out of my mouth like weapons. I didn't care. This screaming voice belonged to someone with power. Fake power or real power—it didn't matter. Just the power to punch back. To return the hurt.

"Kara," he shouted. I realized I was looking at him. At Niles. I saw my husband's pale face, almost ghostly in the light of the dashboard and the reflected light of the vehicles and night lights around us. His eyes seemed lost, vacant in their dark, shadowed caverns. He looked like a stranger.

At Niles. I was looking at Niles. I should be looking at the road.

He lunged toward me, grabbing for the wheel, but I was already moving and trying to correct the car's trajectory as gravel churned under the passenger-side tires. Headlights came toward us, immense and brightly white. It had been only a moment of distraction, but Niles grabbed the wheel as I was trying to figure out how those white lights were in our lane, and then . . . that was it. *It.*

My memories were like vignettes or surrealistic scenes frozen in time—moments of flashing light and darkest dark accompanied by the sound of screaming and the hot, burning smells of metal and plastic and those of flesh and blood too. Those memories were the special little gifts that marked the occasion of my biggest error and later haunted me more than any true anniversary ghost could've done.

Thus, without deliberate decision or my conscious participation, the next stage of my life began.

CHAPTER THREE

The accident made the news because it closed a major artery in a heavily trafficked area of Northern Virginia for four hours while they landed the life-flight helicopter and then cleared the debris of our car and a semi from the lanes. Both the injured and the deceased rated a mention by the local TV reporter as video of the aftermath played, but the greater emphasis was on the disruption of traffic arteries rather than on the blood spilled from the human ones.

My sharpest memory was that of asphalt, gasoline, and hot metal. I remembered not opening my eyes. Perhaps I hadn't been able to open them. I did recall the emergency lights flashing against the thin flesh of my closed eyelids and imprinting there. A gap existed between that half memory and waking at the hospital. That slice of time happened without me being conscious, or my brain had mercifully chosen to set the memory aside.

My one consolation was that the headlights of the semi had been oncoming because the truck had been in the wrong lane, not me. But if I'd been focused on my job—that of driving—I might have seen the danger in time to avoid the collision. Maybe not. I'd never know.

Dad left his executive office in Richmond, at the largest of his tire and automotive facilities, and stayed at my hospital bedside for days. He held my bruised hand—the least damaged one—as I lay there, my head wrapped in white gauze and tape and one leg elevated due to a bad break. My other arm was in a cast. He broke the news of my husband's death as I cried. He blotted the tears on my cheeks with a tissue. He was there when I was moved to the rehabilitation facility and again when I was released to his care, not to mention being present on many days between. I appreciated his presence because he was my voice to the doctors and medical staff. He never made me feel like an inconvenience. He offered no overt expressions of sympathy or emotionalism in general and seemed to require none from me, so we did well enough together.

He handled the business end of my medical expenses, making sure the insurance company covered me and my car and that the other insurers met their obligations, like paying off on Niles's life insurance. He coordinated putting the items from my married life into storage and closing out the rental agreement for our town house.

When I was discharged from rehab, Dad brought me to his home on Silver Street, and because of the stairs, he set me up in the first-floor master bedroom. He'd already moved his personal items and clothing upstairs. I was surprised he'd put a few personal touches in the room, even managing to place my clothing in the proper drawers. And that photo of Mom and me . . . it was on the dresser as if it belonged there and had never been anywhere else.

Time and medications blurred most of my memories of the recovery, of the therapy and learning to walk properly again, reducing them to one indistinguishable series of events—like how you remember something hurt horribly but not the reality of the pain itself.

Dad never gave me a hug and rarely shared a smile or approving word, but he saved my sanity during that first year after the accident. I was grateful.

The authorities had asked me questions about the accident, wanting the details of what and how. My memories were spotty and unreliable. The doctors suggested details might come back to me over time, but I already remembered more than I wanted to. Mostly I remembered the brilliantly magnified headlights of a semi, huge and glaring. The image was stuck in my head like a malfunctioning light switch popping on when least expected. Each time the lights flashed on, they came with the grinding of glass and metallic screams, vehicles, tires, and more glass twisting and flinging its fragments across the highway in slow motion, as if it were all embedded in that blinding light. And I felt it all, all over again, each time. It started in my brain and seared its way down my body. The light-and-sound show eased over time, becoming less frequent, but it didn't stop.

One of the doctors mentioned the pregnancy in past tense. I heard him but turned my head away and closed my eyes. There was nothing to discuss. Nothing to say. It just was, and it was in the past.

And there was Niles. Or rather, there wasn't Niles, but only the memory of him and our life together remained. As the pain eased and my recovery progressed, memories made with Niles before that final, awful night crowded the emotional aftermath, fighting to stay remembered. Survivor's guilt? Maybe.

A few acquaintances visited me in the hospital. I had vague recollections of my boss and a coworker dropping by. At Dad's house, a couple of folks from the old neighborhood showed up. Most of my college friends hadn't been local, and they'd dispersed long ago to their adult lives around the world. Victoria came to see me several times. We'd both grown up in the Richmond area but hadn't met until college. Her hair was dark like mine, but longer, and she had curls. I envied those curls. My own hair was growing out fast and seemed in a hurry to return me to those college days when it had been as long as hers. Victoria liked to experiment with colorful highlights. Her voice was brash. Her laugh was loud. At times, her lack of volume control got on my nerves, but I never doubted her heart and good intentions. She'd been friends with both Niles and me beginning in our sophomore year. After graduation, she'd found a job in the beltway area, too, not far from us.

Victoria told me she'd visited me in the hospital. I didn't remember. So many memories hadn't survived the anesthesia haze or the pain meds, but I knew she'd come to the rehab facility. Seeing her at that point had been too much of a reminder of what I'd lost, and especially of Niles, so when I'd told her I didn't want to discuss him, she'd backed off. Even so, she'd continued visiting. I appreciated her loyalty.

After a few months at Dad's house, I was able to manage the stairs well enough. At that point, I insisted Dad take his bedroom back, and I moved upstairs.

Dad had bought this house after I'd left for college, so it wasn't the house I'd grown up in. No unexpected childhood memories lingered here, and none of Niles, either, except for our wedding portrait hanging in the foyer. He'd visited rarely. This house was as quiet as a museum and as relatively untouched, except for the dust. Managing the dust was on my job list, along with cooking and assorted kitchen and laundry duties.

The comfy overstuffed chair where I stitched flowers or read novels was the most lived-in spot. Near at hand, a small walnut cabinet held most of my needlework supplies. A stack of novels was discreetly fitted between it and the upholstered chair. My world. It was serene and well contained.

I zealously avoided the triggers that preceded the flashes and headaches. Sound sensitivity was one of the gifts that the accident had bequeathed me, so except for Dad watching an occasional sporting event, the TV remained off. I could tolerate some music, but I preferred silence. It was the same with artificial light. I did most of my stitching and reading beside a large window with natural lighting. I tried to explain the problem to the doctors and therapists, asking if the symptoms might be lingering effects of the head injury. They would examine the scar on the side of my face, pressing their fingers against it, and shine lights into my eyes. They'd tell me to be patient. To work with the therapists. I saw concern in their eyes, and maybe pity, as they offered assurance. I understood they were reluctant to speak the truth to me in harsher terms—brain damage. I stopped complaining, accepting that it was simple justice that I hadn't come through the accident unscathed. I bore a large part of the responsibility for the accident and for Niles's death. After more than a year, during which most of my injuries had healed, I'd learned to accommodate my disabilities. I stayed home and stress-free, and I did well enough.

The scars on my leg and arm would never go away, not totally, but could be covered by clothing. It was different with the repair to my head. Each time I looked in the mirror, I saw the scar. The ridge of flesh was a couple of inches long, near my temple, just in the hairline. My fingers found it anew every time I washed my hair or smoothed lotion on my face. The plastic surgeon had done what he could, but no one could turn back time, and no do-overs were being offered for the night of the accident.

Dad told me not to dwell on the past. The therapist said I should talk it out. But all the words in the world didn't ease my guilt or regret, so I followed Dad's example and stopped talking about it altogether. I grew thin and picked up embarrassing habits like nail biting. I had a series of workout tasks I performed to keep my leg limber and my arm from stiffening. The therapist suggested I take up needlework or adult coloring books—useful to keep my hands busy, with the added benefit of improving my dexterity and hand-eye coordination. I grew addicted to needlework. Dad never complained about the growing pile of colored threads, embroidery hoops, and pattern books.

Online shopping was my best friend. I could get anything I wanted without leaving the house. Dad would see me at the computer and ask, "Any luck with finding a job?"

"Not yet."

"Kara, come work with me at the automotive center. Something administrative to get you used to leaving the house again. You can ride in with me."

He meant it kindly. I did need to find a job and reclaim my life, but each time I did more than surf job openings posted on the web, I'd feel the headache setting in, the lights in my brain would start flickering, and I'd know nausea was imminent. I'd turn off the computer and lie down until the discomfort eased and my world became acceptable again.

One afternoon in April, I heard the front door open. Dad called out, "Kara?"

"I'm upstairs. Everything okay?"

He looked up. I was standing at the top of the stairs holding an armload of warm towels, fresh from the dryer.

"You're doing well now? Back to normal." He gave me an extra look, then added, "Almost."

I smiled. "Pretty much." I shifted the towels to secure one that was working loose. "I haven't started supper yet. You're home early."

He nodded. "We should talk."

What did that mean? "I'll drop these on the bed and be right down."

He walked away. His footsteps sounded in the hallway, changing in tone as he reached the tile floor in the kitchen. I went into my room and tossed the clean towels in a heap on my bedspread.

Dad wanted to talk.

He didn't often initiate conversation, much less invite me to a special chat. This one did feel special—which could be especially bad or especially good. I held the railing as I stepped down the stairs and carried my cane in my free hand. The muscles in my thigh resisted and tightened. I gripped the rail more tightly until I was safely down, then joined him in the kitchen. I hung my cane over the back of a chair but didn't sit.

He was standing at the table. Waiting. No coffee. No newspaper.

"What's up, Dad?"

"I told you that I was thinking of selling the business and retiring."

I leaned against the counter, putting most of my weight on my good leg, and crossed my arms. "You mentioned retiring. I didn't realize you meant now. You're barely sixty."

"It makes sense to do it while I can enjoy it. No point in procrastinating and missing the opportunity."

It?

"Dad, you are saying do *it* and enjoy *it*. You spend every waking moment working. I don't understand what *it* is."

He stared beyond my shoulder and smiled a little. "Something that has nothing to do with rubber or tires."

Coming from my father's lips, that was almost a world-class joke. This was serious. I pushed away from the counter and walked to the table.

"Tell me."

He shrugged. "I'm not sure where to start. I don't want you to think this is about you."

"About me? I'm certain you don't mean that the way it sounds."

He paused and frowned, then realized what I meant. "Of course not. It's only that I was thinking about retiring when . . . when the accident happened. I put it off."

"I see." I pulled out a chair and sat.

"No, Kara. I'm glad I was here and available. But I would've been regardless. This isn't about that. This is about plans I've had in mind for a while." He stood and went over to the counter I'd just left. He got a glass and held it under the faucet for water while saying, "I'm moving. I'm selling this house."

I stayed silent as he sipped his water. When he faced me again, he eyed me warily.

"Tell me more," I said.

"I want to get out of the city. I want to garden, do a little tinkering, some renovation."

"A garden?" I clasped my hands together on the table and forced them to relax. "The backyard here is large enough, if you want to grow something. Moving is a big deal. Not saying you shouldn't, but it seems like a huge . . . a big commitment for something I've never heard you talk about." I finished weakly, not liking the idea that I might be sabotaging his dream, perhaps a long-cherished dream, for my own convenience.

"I've given it lots of thought. I'm not looking forward to the actual move, of course."

I wanted to say something supportive. I tried, but the only words that came out were, "Move where?" I shook my head. "I'm sorry, Dad. It's very unexpected news."

"I didn't say much before now because I didn't want to rush your recovery. You had to be here for medical treatment, physical therapy, and all that, but you're past that now. The property I was waiting for recently became available. All in all, the timing is perfect."

I shook my head. "I can't believe I never suspected you wanted to be a farmer."

"Not a farmer, Kara. A gardener. Maybe have a small orchard." He added, "You don't have any sentimental attachment to this house, right?"

His question surprised me. I'd lived here now for more than a year. I had an attachment of sorts, but nothing that should stand in the way of my father living the life he wanted. He deserved to make his own choices.

I leaned forward and tried to show excitement and energy in my eyes and voice. "So where do you want to move? Do you need help? You said the right property is available?"

He pulled his briefcase toward him and opened it. From an interior pocket, he withdrew a photograph. He stared at it for a long moment, then passed it across to me.

Did I detect a slight shake in his hand? Hesitation? Unlikely, and yet perhaps my opinion did matter to him. I examined the photo—it wasn't recent—and tried to keep my expression bland.

The house was huge. Victorian? Old. I gave him a quick glance and then looked again at the picture.

The photo showed trees and neatly trimmed bushes. A wide front porch wrapped partway around the large house. Ridiculously large. With a turret. A fairy-tale house. One that could quickly become a nightmare house, a money pit. Just to paint that porch and the railings would be a killer. Replacing the roof would be . . . I stopped myself. None of that was really my business.

"Dad . . . why this house? It's massive."

"Not as big as it looks in the picture. It needs work—mostly cosmetic. Which is what I'm looking for." He smiled broadly. "It has a garden. The grounds were beautiful at one time, but they've been neglected. Lots of potential. It's only about an hour from Richmond."

"But to . . ." All I could imagine was my aging father rambling around this deteriorating house to the sounds of his own echoing footsteps, growing older and more lost every day, without his business to manage and occupy his time. "Dad, this doesn't seem like you. Are you certain?"

"I am."

It was his life, I reminded myself.

"What do you need me to do? Did you already make an offer? Was it accepted?"

He nodded. "Yes."

"What's the timing?"

"Closing is in three weeks."

Three weeks. I felt breathless. I would have to find my own place if I wanted to stay in town. I'd have to go back into the workforce. Was I ready for the physical and emotional stress of that? Did I have a choice?

I said, "Tell me what you need help with."

"It's time you lived your own life again, Kara."

I nodded. We were two bobbing heads nodding politely back and forth across the table rather than expressing what cried to be said. Now he'd spoken the literal truth: "It's time you lived . . ." and I was still bobbing my head. I sat up straighter.

"It's past that time. I appreciate all that you've done for me."

"I'm your father. Of course I help you. Are you afraid?"

"I'm apprehensive, but I've given in to that for too long."

"You'll know when you're ready. Come with me for now. I can use your help."

He wasn't pushing me out? My relief embarrassed me. "When are you putting this house on the market?"

"When I'm ready to move."

"And that will be when?"

He rubbed his jaw. "I need to complete the sale of the business. It will be wrapped up soon."

"I didn't realize . . . about the sale. It's that far along? You already have a buyer?"

"Of course."

"Did you tell me?"

"I told you I was planning to sell the business, but a sale isn't done until it's done. It's almost done now. We're signing papers. That's why I'm telling you now."

I rubbed my temple. The thicker skin of the scar tissue was there at the tips of my fingers. Unnecessary conversation had never been my father's strong point.

"This new . . . *new-to-you* house"—I forced a smile—"is already empty, right?"

"Yes. The people who owned it died last year. Their heir took a while to decide to sell it and then had to clear it out. But yes, the house is empty."

"You didn't say where it's located."

"In Louisa County. West on I-64. Exit on Route 522, then a few miles north. In an area called Cub Creek."

"Louisa County?" My voice rose on that last word, unintentionally, of course. "Who do we know in Louisa County? It's just woods out there. Trees."

"It isn't wilderness, Kara. It's convenient to the towns of Mineral and Louisa—and even to Charlottesville."

Wilderness. I shook my head and squared my shoulders. "Dad, this is a big decision, but I support you in it. If this is what you want, you've earned it." But in my head, I was thinking, *The deal's not done until the contracts are signed and money is exchanged.* Like Dad had said about the sale of his business—the same was true of this house. Maybe the sale would fall through.

"I'd like to see it, Dad."

"Tomorrow is Friday. I could leave the office at lunchtime. We can drive out there together."

"Sounds good."

He closed his briefcase and reached for his keys. He saw me staring. "I have to get back to the office. I may be late tonight."

"I'll put supper in the fridge for you. Call me when you're on your way, and I'll heat it up."

He stopped beside me and pressed a light, quick kiss on my forehead. It was uncharacteristic of him.

"Don't. I'll be eating out. Try not to worry, Kara." His footsteps echoed up the hallway to the front door.

His last words had been spoken so softly that I wasn't entirely sure I'd heard them. I could almost believe that I'd hallucinated the whole conversation, except I was still holding the photograph. The slick feel of it between my fingers made me uneasy.

About eighteen years ago, I'd sat at our kitchen table, a different table in a different house, but still my father's, and I'd read that note from my mother.

No wonder I felt uneasy.

Mom's departure had signaled a sort of restart to my life. The change in players, in circumstance, had required new routines. Marriage to Niles had been the next life restart—a welcome one at the time. Then the accident. Three false starts? Was this signaling a fourth?

I'd hidden in my father's house and avoided new relationships and commitments. Was heartless fate here for me again? Sticking its evil fingers into my life and upsetting the balance one more time? I could almost hear its whispery, raspy voice asking, "Ready for another spin?"

The scar on my face burned. I reached up and pressed my fingers against it. Better to give in to that than to bite off my nails.

I refocused. This photograph . . . it was impossible to tell the house's age, because the photo itself was old. This house would likely involve a lot of work, not to mention getting Dad's current house packed up.

And the storage unit in which Dad had stored what was left of my married life? I would have to deal with that eventually.

I felt exhausted and achy just thinking of it.

Had Dad thought he could handle a move himself? Or had he assumed I'd take it on? This move would take me further from what I *should* be doing, which was finding a new job and returning to the land of the living, living the life of a widowed thirtysomething woman. Early thirtysomething, I amended.

A little later, back upstairs, I folded the now-cooled towels. I was disheartened by the trembling in my hands that echoed in my chest and even in my head. Anxiety? I'd been hiding here too long. But knowing that, understanding my reaction was emotional and even reasonable, didn't blunt the impact.

I sat on the edge of the bed, clutching a half-folded towel. I pressed my face into the clean terry cloth, breathing deeply of the fresh scent.

My father had worked hard all his life. He'd supported me and had been there when it counted.

I had to repay the favor. I had to support him. Somehow, within that, perhaps I would find my own guts again, my courage.

Dropping the towel, I looked in my bedside-table drawer for the pill bottles. I hadn't needed a pain pill for a while. I had a variety of brown plastic bottles left over. I should've tossed them but hadn't as a just-in-case. My hand hovered over a bottle. Did I need the medication now? Really need it?

I heard Dad's voice in my head saying, "Take it if you need it, but be sure you really need it and don't just want it." It made him uncomfortable to see me taking the prescription pain meds.

Yes, my head was hurting, no doubt due to the unexpected news. I'd give it a chance to pass on its own. I slid the drawer closed.

Tugging one of the oversize towels across me like a blanket, I lay down on the bed and closed my eyes.

I dozed, but I was awakened by the jarring clash of metal and tinkle of broken glass as flashing lights assaulted my closed eyelids. All of this lived only in my head—I knew that—but it brought me to instant consciousness anyway.

The sound and visual disturbances had diminished over time, but frankly, it had been a year and a half. If they weren't gone by now, then they never would be. I didn't need modern medicine to tell me that.

I left the towels, still mostly unfolded, and went downstairs to the living room. I needed a distraction, and stitching would soothe me. The light was fading outside, but I could tolerate a lamp with a soft-white incandescent bulb. I switched it on. Dad's picture of the house—the house he claimed to want—was lying on the coffee table and caught my eye. I picked it up again.

Would I want to live here? Could I? There was plenty of room. Quite an understatement, in fact. Dad had said he needed my help. He wouldn't abandon me.

I stared at the picture.

The deal wouldn't fall through. I knew that. This whole thing . . . my dad and his declaration about wanting to be a farmer-gardener and renovator . . . Dad was never impulsive. If he believed this move would happen, then he had good reason to believe it, and it would.

Within a month, Dad would be living in that wilderness—a place called Cub Creek. Would I be there too?

~

The next morning, I pushed through the clothes in my closet. My standard T-shirt and yoga pants wouldn't do. I might run into more than field mice or feral cats. People, maybe. I'd like to look a little more put together. In fact, Dad had mentioned the real estate agent joining us there. I was thinner than before the accident. I chose a long straight-hemmed tunic and leggings. My hair had gone uncut for a year and a half. I secured it in the back with a clip. My hair was dark like my mother's and thick and straight. When I looked in the mirror, I saw her hair but my father's eyes. Somewhere in there, I was hiding—or trying to.

The clock ticked the morning away as I worked the threaded needle through the taut fabric to create the petals of a daisy. Finally, at eleven thirty, Dad called.

"Sorry, Kara. This meeting is taking longer than expected."

"Okay. I'll be here waiting," I said, stating the obvious.

"Why don't you meet me out there?"

For a moment, I couldn't breathe.

The last time I'd tried to drive, I'd had a panic attack. That had been a while ago. I was stronger now. Before the accident, driving had been simple, but the accident had changed many things.

Dad had been driving both our cars to keep them in good shape. He believed that one day I'd be working again, needing a car and using it for all the purposes of living. Belief. Faith. I had assumed that was true too. But performing an action was harder than letting an untried assumption stand.

"I don't know the area."

"It's an easy drive. You can't get lost."

No, I can't go out there alone. My heart is racing. My head will start pounding soon.

Aloud, I said, "I don't know the way. I'll get lost."

"No, you won't. The directions are simple. Nicole will be there between one and one thirty. By the time I get out of here and drive home to pick you up, we'll be late. Going directly, you have plenty of time."

I swallowed hard. I switched hands on the phone. My palms were damp.

He gave the directions, and they did sound easy. He added, "I'll be there about one p.m. too. If you arrive before me, just wait."

"Okay."

"You can't miss it, Kara. West on the interstate and north on Route 522. Turn just past Apple Grove and watch for the red mailbox with a flag hanging from it and a For Sale sign."

"Dad," I said, "I haven't driven in ages."

"You'll do fine. Trust me. I'll see you there."

I set my phone on the side table and massaged my temples.

Belatedly, I wondered, *Who's Nicole?*

Then I realized Dad had probably done this on purpose. Like tossing me in a lake to make me swim. Something like that. He'd waited until he knew I was dressed and ready to go before calling me.

Did I like being manipulated? No, but perversely, I felt rather proud. Dad would have done that only if he truly believed I *could* handle it.

The keys in my hand felt damp and clammy as I approached the door. I stopped by the sofa, and despite all common sense, I grabbed my project bag. It would've made more sense to grab a book or magazine in case I found myself waiting, but the needle and threads were my touchstones.

I made it out the door. I could do this.

The car started. I suppose some part of me believed, hoped, it wouldn't. I successfully backed down the driveway and didn't end up in the ditch, nor did I take out the neighbor's mailbox. Encouraging victories. I stopped at the stop sign and took another look at the photograph.

Ugly house. Ridiculously huge.

I warned myself not to make assumptions, good or bad, based on an old faded photograph. This was Dad's dream. I hoped only to be helpful, one way or another.

CHAPTER FOUR

After leaving the interstate, I followed Route 522 as it crossed rural, rolling countryside. It was undeniably picturesque. The appeal of the houses in those tidy country settings with their patches of forest and neat fences, especially to city people tied to office jobs, was obvious. The farther I drove, the more wooded the land became. When I left Route 522, the neat farms were gone. The area back here looked forgotten and derelict. Acreage denuded of trees stood alongside thick forests with vines and downed trees and sticker bushes. Each spin of the tires brought me deeper into what I had expected—wilderness. The narrow road sloped down to an old pockmarked concrete bridge crossing a creek. The creek looked as dark and uninviting as the unkempt and tangled forest.

I drove over the bridge, and the road rose again. Soon after, I saw the red mailbox and the **For Sale** sign. It showed the agent's name as Nicole Albers and listed a phone number. A small American flag hung, flapping, beneath the mailbox. As I slowed to make the turn, I also saw the sign had an addition slapped on it: **Under Contract**.

The driveway was camouflaged by trees and scrubby growth. Someone had thinned out the trees a while back, but the drive hadn't been kept up, and understory plants—mostly weeds, sticker bushes, and scrub pines—had taken advantage of the open space. It surprised me that no one had tried to make this driveway more inviting to prospective buyers. But then, they already had an eager one waiting, right?

The trees reached up and out, overarching the drive in a forbidding way. The rutted drive seemed to go on forever. How had Dad ever found this place? He'd said he'd been waiting for the right house to go on the market . . . had he meant this specific house? No question he must've been actively looking and working with a real estate agent—apparently Nicole Albers. And he'd never said a word.

The driveway wound around trees, and I watched carefully for potholes. The deepest ones had been filled in, but there might be more tire killers lurking ahead. But then, around the next curve, the view opened up, and there stood the house.

Its size left me speechless. Dad had had a lot of nerve to say the house wasn't as large as it looked in the picture. Honestly, how had he kept a straight face saying that? This place was massive.

If Dad had been with me, I'd have had plenty to say. Like, "Are you freaking kidding me?" It would take two days just to walk around the house.

Okay, not true—not two days. I pressed my hand over my heart. If armed with a machete to hack through the tangled growth I could see on the sides, a hardy soul might be able to walk the perimeter in two hours. Was that an exaggeration? Maybe, but not by much.

The grounds were neglected, and the house was too. This home had been stately in the long-ago past, and the grounds must have been well groomed and beautiful—a long, long time ago.

Woods framed the house and open yard area on either side, but between the tree line and the house, the weeds and scrubby growth had taken over.

It was a ridiculously large residence for one man who wanted to spend his golden years puttering around in dirt and sawdust and playing with paint chips.

Dad and his real estate agent hadn't arrived yet. I parked and exited the car, then climbed the steps to the porch and tried the door. It was locked. No problem. The list of why Dad shouldn't do this crazy midlife crisis thing was growing in my head. No time like the present to check the exterior—assuming I could find my way through the jungle.

The side yard was a tangle of greenery and stickers and giant overgrown bushes. I could hardly see around me. I picked out hints of architectural details, maybe a porch, lots of windows, but focused on making my way through. As I fought past a thicket and edged between two massive hollies and rhododendrons the size of a small house, the backyard view formed, seeming almost to assemble itself piece by piece.

I stopped, gasping.

Before me was a vast field of weeds—flowering weeds. Wildflowers in a swaying quilt of colors, shapes, and textures. As a mass, they raised their bright faces to the sun, gathered its rays, and reflected the light from bloom to bloom, ultimately bouncing it back to greet my eyes.

My light sensitivity? Maybe that was why my knees weakened and I stumbled forward. But the sensation wasn't painful. It was joyous.

Had this flower field been planted on purpose? Surely not. The arrangement looked random. Haphazard. As if someone had started with a plan but then walked away. It looked like a product of neglect.

Neglect wasn't supposed to be beautiful. Yet this was breathtaking.

Beyond the slope of mixed weeds and wildflowers waving in the breeze, the glittering water of a broad, sun-drenched creek snared my attention. The creek was wider than some small rivers I'd seen. I held my breath and heard the light wind moving through the tall, weedy grasses along the shoreline and the gentle slapping sound of water as it flowed by. All around me was color. The rough stalks of the flowers brushed against my legs and palms as I walked into their midst.

I was a guest among the wildflowers, sharing the glory. Their triumph. Ahead of me was the dark topaz-colored water of the creek. In my peripheral vision, I was aware of trees on either side of the yard and, among them, a few outbuildings, but that awareness held only long enough to dismiss them as unimportant.

Lifting my face to the sun, I closed my eyes. Now I could sense them—as an insect found flowers by sight or scent and was drawn to them. I smelled the earth beneath my feet and knew its residents, worms and beetles, were burrowing into the richness. The bees buzzed near me. The water had its own sound and scent . . . but I couldn't form any more words. The entirety of my surroundings rolled together in my mind, the senses, the sounds, the feel, and the smells. It was as if I left my body altogether.

The pain, the past, the regrets, the fear—they all vanished. I didn't know they were gone until they returned with a jolt.

I shuddered, suddenly back. Suddenly grounded again. The colors abated along with the rest. Now the weeds were just weeds. The wildflower blooms were less vibrant. A thin layer of clouds was moving in across the forest and the lake, and a more solid cloud bank had materialized in the distance. My skin tingled. I turned away from the slope and the water view and faced the house.

I'd traveled halfway down the slope. As I stared at the house, I heard strains of music, Copland's *Appalachian Spring*, on the breeze.

How could that be? The music was quickly gone. An auditory mirage? A gift left behind by the accident?

"Simple Gifts." That was the part I'd heard.

I stood quietly for a few long moments in case the music returned, but it didn't. The strong light hadn't sparked any visual disturbances; I was grateful for that. If I was to be treated to brief, unexpected strains of music, I could deal with that.

The back of the house had a covered porch. Steps led from the porch down to a concrete terrace fitted with an arbor . . . or was the word *pergola*? Maybe so. Thick columns supported a white-painted wooden construction that spanned the three open sides, but nothing hung from them. No flowerpots, no vines. The columns needed a good sanding and a fresh coat of paint.

Like the front yard, the back was a mess, except for the beautiful field of flowers. The overall house structure had good lines with no obvious sagging. To my untrained eye, the bones of the house looked sound. And absolutely rooted in reality.

Despite the music, nothing spooky was going on here. That musical gift hadn't come from this place. I remembered Copland's *Appalachian Spring* from years ago, perhaps attached to a movie or something. My own brain, in a moment of delicious clarity, had beheld the wildflowers and offered a connection.

Something else popped into my head, fresh from the depths of my memory. I'd had an interest in Ralph Waldo Emerson in college and had read many of his essays and poems. A phrase of his, long forgotten, returned to me: "Earth laughs in flowers."

Yes, I thought. *Yes.*

I turned back toward the wildflowers and laughed. A mowed path ran along both sides of the flower field, between it and the woods. The path ended in an open, grassy area down by the water. As I walked down the slope, I spied areas in the woods, half-hidden, with a bench here or a chair there. But it all looked neglected and overgrown.

The water wasn't a lake or a pond but more of a broad pool where the creek had been widened as it flowed along the open area of the property. It was plain brown creek water, but exposed to the sky. The sun glinted on the surface. The lazy, shimmering reflections were almost golden, giving that jewel-like effect. On the far side of the water, maybe forty feet away, were rocks and trees. A wild scene but beautiful in its natural state. A spotted fawn moved, and then I spied the adult animal, surely the mother, only a few feet away from it.

"Kara?"

Dad's voice came from a distance. At the sound of his voice, both deer disappeared into the brush and trees.

I turned back toward the house. Dad was on the back porch. Between us lay the field of flowers, and behind me the water sighed and gurgled. Beyond that, in my mind's eye, I saw the animals moving quietly in the woods, going about their day. I internalized that peace, feeling it, knowing it was momentary but real and alive.

"Kara?" he repeated.

"Yes, Dad?"

A woman had joined him. They both stood at the porch railing, staring down at me.

He called out, "Are you okay?"

I walked back up the path. When I was close enough to speak in a normal tone, I said, "I'm fine. It's beautiful out here, isn't it?"

My father, the master of underwhelming statements, said, "Nice view. It has lots of potential."

I smiled more broadly and said, "It's gorgeous. Did you know about the flowers?"

"Yes. I mentioned a garden, right?"

I laughed. Never mind how many tires and automotive parts he owned, my father was, in truth, the king of understatement. I saw the surprise in his face as I laughed. It was a look of pleasure, perhaps mixed with relief. He nodded toward the woman standing beside him.

"This is Nicole Albers." He gestured between us. "Nicole, this is my daughter, Kara."

Nicole said, "Pleased to meet you."

Dad added, "Nicole is my real estate agent and a friend. She found me the house we're living in now and then gave me the heads-up when this one was about to go on the market."

She was attractive. Blonde. Looked professional in a suit and silk blouse. From where I was standing, she looked a few years older than me. A few years younger than my father. Beyond that, I couldn't tell.

"Why don't you join us? Nicole will show us around."

I ignored Nicole. She was the agent. Selling houses was her business. My father's well-being was mine.

"Dad. The flowers are beautiful and all that, but this place . . . it's huge. How can you live here?" I waved my arms at the . . . edifice. *Home* was too cozy a word to fit. "Who would build such a . . ." I stopped short of saying *monster*. "Who would build a mansion like this out here in the middle of nowhere?"

Nicole said, "I'll tell you the house's history as I show you around."

I looked from Dad to Nicole and then back again. *Okay, Nicole*, I thought. *Have it your way. But I'll have my way too.*

"I'll be in soon. I'd like to take a longer look around out here while I can." I pointed at the sky. Clouds were massing, and the breeze carried the smell of rain.

"Come in when you're ready." He waved at the sky, saying, "But watch out."

He was right. The bank of clouds had acquired a sharp edge and seemed to be building, growing darker. I tried to focus on business. This was my time to look—to see it all now and add it to my list for Dad. Maybe it was warmth or the sun or the flowers, but that list was seeming less important.

The house was built of wood and painted white, now mellowed by age. The windows were wide and tall on both the main level and second floor. There were smaller windows at the basement level and even a few windows high above in the attic area. The chimney stacks looked very old but seemed trim and straight from this vantage point. I saw no cracks in the walls that might indicate a shifting or sinking foundation. But who was I kidding? What did I know about such things?

"Cosmetic issues," Dad had said. Sometimes it was hard to see beyond the cosmetics. Had he hired an expert to check the bones of the house? To inspect the utilities like heat and whatever else needed to be considered? Had his agent done that? I would ask him. As a businessman, he would respect reasonable questions.

A crawling sensation teased my flesh as a loud clap of thunder snapped overhead and a sudden bright flash came from behind. I jumped in a whole-body reaction. I glanced back. The dark bank of clouds had moved all the way in. A large wet drop plopped and splattered on my arm. I moved quickly, despite my limp, toward the covered porch.

I made it just as the rain began.

The drumming rain played the roof overhead like a musical instrument. Before me, the flowers swayed, almost dancing. Beyond the field, the water hit the creek, splashing with BB gun sounds, but I could see the brighter day already peeking from behind the leading clouds. It was a spring shower, sudden and gusty and already passing. The smell of rain, of fresh water washing the thirsty flowers and filling the earth, was almost overwhelming. I breathed in deeply, savoring it. I hugged myself, my hands grasping my upper arms, my face raised . . . with a feeling of people around me, here before me, whose eyes had seen this or similar vistas and who might even have watched the rain from a porch, perhaps this porch. I experienced a strange sense of commonality, and I wondered who I was.

I didn't feel like the person who'd left the house this morning. Even the memory of who I'd been before the accident seemed flimsy. Like a false front. I was standing on a porch—an old paint-flaking porch, sheltering from an April shower—and felt like I was standing on an unexpected, unimagined threshold.

The wind shifted, sending the rain slanting past the railing and onto the porch. I stepped back, just out of its reach. The door opened.

"It's raining," Dad said.

"It is."

Nicole stepped from behind my father and spoke. "I'm glad to officially meet you, Kara. Come in where it's dry."

Nicole Albers looked well put together, very much in control, and dressed for success. I read determination in her expression and posture.

In contrast, I felt slouchy and drab. She couldn't be more than ten years older than me, and in her, I saw a woman of business who dealt in reality, not in fears and what-ifs. Her no-nonsense gaze reminded me of my father's.

The wind gusted again, and wet drops splashed my leg and arm.

Nicole stood aside to let Dad and me enter the house and then pulled the door closed behind us, saying, "I'm sorry it's chilly and dark in here. The power is off."

The interior was dim, lit only by the daylight the windows allowed in. On a brighter day, and with cleaner windows and trimmed shrubbery, that would be substantial. On a cloudy, rainy day—not so much. We walked through a small room—Nicole called it a mudroom—and then into the kitchen. It was dingy. No one would want to cook in here. The walls were light blue but stained and scratched. Cleaning wouldn't make a dent in the dirt and discoloration. White cabinets were hung along two walls—lots of storage space but totally uninviting. This wasn't original cabinetry. Someone had tried to update this kitchen and had done a poor job.

I looked up. And up.

Nicole said, "These are twelve-foot ceilings. Amazing, right?"

"Yes." I imagined my father on a ladder tall enough to paint these ceilings and shivered.

The kitchen opened onto a small hallway with a set of stairs off to the left. Nicole gestured toward them.

"Those are the back stairs. They go down to the basement and up to the second floor and on up to the attic." She pointed. "Do you see that door?"

"Yes. Next to the stairs."

"It goes out to a porch on the side. You probably caught a glimpse of it through the growth when you walked around to the back."

She wasn't asking a question. Merely making a statement. And she walked on.

I paused to peek up the stairs. The stairwell was enclosed, almost like a closet might be. It was dark and narrow. Servants' stairs, I presumed.

"Kara?" Dad prompted and waved to me to rejoin them.

Down the main hallway, there were rooms on either side. Dad said, "That's the dining room there, with another small porch off of it."

I stopped in the doorway of the room opposite the dining room. It was a plain room with a door and a window. "What's this?"

Nicole said, "It was probably a classroom or office back in the day. But it would be useful as a bedroom—sort of a first-floor master. Not en suite, of course."

"A classroom?"

"The Kinney family built this house as a school for girls. Some boarded; some didn't. It was quite a distance into town back before cars."

"A school."

"A private school for girls. But that sort of educational opportunity, shall we say, was already on its way out, in large part due to the automobile. The Depression ended it here altogether. The folks who bought the house from the Kinneys were wealthy Richmonders looking for a country place. They made some nice improvements but weren't here often.

"This is the foyer. The parlor is over there." She pointed to our left. "The sitting room is in front of the dining room." She smiled at my look of doubt. "I know it seems overkill by today's standards, but the structure is sound, and it's roomy, with lots of potential."

The parlor, the room to the left, was a private room. It was octagonal with windows opening onto the porch, but with a door. The opposite room, on the other side of the foyer, was wide open to the foyer and gave it a feeling of space, of light. But both rooms were papered. Old stained paper. The repeated rows of cabbage roses in the parlor looked nightmarish. The landscape vignettes in the sitting room paper were a little more acceptable.

"Potential for what?" I asked, but my father and Nicole had already moved on.

Most of the interior seemed in dire need of wallpaper stripping and fresh paint. Each of the downstairs rooms had its own fireplace, but they were blocked off and painted. Decorative only, now. And unattractive.

I couldn't help noticing the interplay between Dad and Nicole as we walked from room to room. Was it my imagination that he touched her arm more than necessary? Or that the warm smiles she gave him echoed in her blue eyes?

Was I being hypersensitive? I felt rather soured by the interaction. It mixed with my mood about the interior of the house.

It would be all too easy for Nicole to sell my dad on a house she needed to unload. I reminded myself that real estate agents were all about yeses. The sky was the limit when an agent was enumerating selling points.

I said, "I see the fireplaces are blocked."

Nicole said, "Gas heat. The former owners upgraded the bathrooms and the heating system a few years back when they installed AC."

"The floors are a mess."

"They need cleaning. You can have them sanded and stained if you want, but they are in good shape, despite the dirt. I recommend having them cleaned first."

"No garage," I said.

Dad said, "There's an old carriage house. Did you notice it?"

"They updated it when they modernized. You could use it for a garage or add on a garage that attaches to the house. You've got plenty of acreage around this house. In fact, land is going fast out here in the county. We were lucky to get the offer in first." Nicole moved smoothly onward, waving her hand at the woodwork and the tall stained glass windows on the landing. "Here's the main staircase. It's a beauty. These windows were all the rage at one time. They are exquisite."

I followed them. Dad had his hand on Nicole's elbow as if she might be unsteady on the stairs. She wasn't. I wasn't, either, but I was more likely to need a steadying hand than the lovely Nicole. This annoyed me. Dad was probably fifteen years older than her. Maybe it was natural that he'd be attentive, perhaps attracted, to her. But I wasn't amused.

We reached the top of the stairs.

Nicole turned to my father. The light touched the side of her face, and I read fondness in her expression as she asked, "Is this how you remember the house, Henry?"

"You've been in here before, Dad? Of course you have. That was a silly thing for me to ask."

"I have seen it before, yes." He turned to Nicole as they walked into the master bedroom. I wasn't sure whether he was directing his next words to me or to her. "It was a long time ago."

How long had he been planning this without a hint or a word to me? Yes, Nicole had expressed Dad was lucky to get his offer in first. I was confused and stopped, letting the two of them go ahead. I went the other way to investigate on my own.

Here were the back stairs. I paused to peer up and down the narrow flights. Nicole had said these stairs went from basement to attic. There was a door at this level and probably at the other landings too.

"These stairs are close to the kitchen."

I jumped.

"Sorry, Kara," Nicole said. "Didn't mean to scare you." She moved past me and opened and closed the stairwell door as if demonstrating. "These stairs were convenient to the kitchen on this floor and to the bedrooms above. Being enclosed helped keep kitchen smells from making their way up to the bedrooms, controlled drafts, and so on. The doors would probably slow down the spread of kitchen fires too. As to the fire, that's just a guess." She smiled. "Would you like to go up there now? See the attic? It's empty, and it's been swept clean."

The window on the landing above offered some light to see by, but not much.

"I'll check it out later."

"Sure." Her smile never faltered. "Now where'd your father get to?" She walked off, calling, "Henry?"

There was no window at the landing below. The stairs ended in a dark well. I pulled my cell phone out of my pocket and used the flash-light app. Instead of going upstairs, I went down. Down past the first floor to the basement. Why? Because I could. I didn't need Nicole's permission or escort.

As I took those last steps with care, I recalled that basements were always the source of trouble in movies. Hauntings, dark secrets, ax murderers . . . but they were also where humans chose to locate their electrical panels and heating units. Which just went to show the scary stuff was all about the story, not a real-life thing, because if basements were truly dangerous, people would locate the tools that controlled the necessities of their lives elsewhere—like in the living room. And it was that logic that gave me the courage to twist that knob and stick my nose inside.

A cool breath of air touched my cheek and moved on. Nothing ghostly, but merely the change in pressure of opening and closing doors in spaces that weren't often disturbed.

There was a short set of three steps that went the rest of the way down, and my phone light didn't penetrate too far. The basement floor appeared to be flagstone. A large hulk of a heater stood on the far side. Shelving covered many of the walls. There were cobwebs, but not many. Someone had come through here and cleaned. There were surely spi-ders in hiding, but I wouldn't look too closely for them. To my right, toward the back of the house, I saw the doors to the outside. I didn't know their actual name, but I thought of them as tornado doors—just like the ones that guarded the entrances to shelters in every tornado movie ever made.

I was thinking that perhaps I had watched too much TV in my childhood.

Having gone this far into the basement, I decided I'd done enough. I'd seen what I needed to see and had proved I wasn't an overly imaginative hysteric. That was important to me because how could you live in a house like this if that was who you were? Nope. I had passed the test without even realizing a test was in progress.

Like my father, I was firmly grounded in reality. Despite the hard knocks of my life, or maybe because of them, I was a rational, logical person. And with that thought, I retreated back into the stairwell hallway and closed the door gently but very firmly.

Dad's voice came from a distance, calling my name, traveling through the vacant spaces and long wooden hallways. My name echoed as it went, and then he repeated the call.

"I'm here, Dad. Coming." I climbed the stairs to the main floor and stepped through the stairwell door into the short hallway.

So far, I'd found nothing beyond the reality of a huge house and unkempt grounds . . . but the wildflowers, the creek, and the stepped slope with echoes of a grander past were strong arguments in its favor.

I had doubts, but I'd been hiding at home for so long . . . there was an invitation here. A lot of work, yes, but as far as Dad was concerned, this deal was inevitable and welcome. Who was I to cast doubt?

~

In the morning, I awoke to *Appalachian Spring* playing softly in my head—the part of the composition that sounded as light and lyrical as a ballet. With my eyes still closed, I saw that field of white and gold and blue, sun drenched and waving in the breeze as if in tune to the music.

I hadn't consciously planned to go back to the house and the wildflowers right away, but by the time I'd showered and dressed, I understood that I was. This time, knowing how to get there made the trip seem shorter. Not short, but shorter. Dad wouldn't be commuting, but if I did manage to find a job or got tired of living in the country, I'd have to find a small apartment and move back to town. It was past time for me to get on with my own life anyway. When the time was right, Dad had said. And he'd said I'd know when that was.

It wasn't yet.

For the second day in a row, I drove away from my father's home on Silver Street and out to the country house. *Progress*, I thought. Mostly, though, I just needed to see it again.

The **For Sale** and **Under Contract** signs were still in place near the red mailbox. As I maneuvered up the dirt driveway, I vowed I'd persuade Dad to have it paved first thing and trim back some of the growth too.

I was struck anew by the size of the house, though it was already assuming more normal proportions in my head. Still very large. Very roomy and dim and chilly. No cars were parked in front of the house, exactly as I'd hoped.

The field of wildflowers amazed me again. This time I hardly noticed the weedy parts. My senses were focused on the colors and shapes of the petals and, again, the gentle whoosh of the breeze rolling up from the creek.

Standing here and seeing it up close, I realized the creek bank had been artificially shaped long ago. Grass filled the leveled area between the creek and the wildflower field. I could imagine lawn furniture here. Probably white wicker with plump, flowery cushions. The grass would've been a fertile shade of green and well trimmed. A tall sundial and a bench nearer the water were the only items actually here now.

There was potential in the house and grounds, as both Dad and Nicole said, but also a lot of work. Was Dad up to this kind of labor? Did he need to be? Not really. He'd done well in business, and he wouldn't sell it without making even more profit. His nature wouldn't allow him to do otherwise. So if he could afford to hire out the work, then he could put a hand in from time to time but mostly supervise.

This whole property, inside and out, had lots of nooks and crannies. There was a large shed along with the quaint old stone carriage house a few yards from the mansion. The buildings were half-lost in the overgrown lilacs, hollies, and unidentified bushes. But today wasn't about seeking out every possibility or finding every oddity. I simply needed to see it again. To see how I felt this time, when it wasn't so new to me, and without the distractions of other people.

I was oddly reassured. As for the financial risk? That was all on my father.

As I walked back up the slope, I acknowledged that my opinion didn't matter. The deal was done. The decision made. Had been, really, from the moment my father had chosen it, whether it had been yesterday or a month ago.

Mom hadn't taken me on her quest to find a new life. Dad was willing to share his adventure. And yes, I wanted to go along. At least for now.

When I reached the terrace, I stooped and grabbed hold of a straggly vine and gave it a yank. It resisted, throwing dirt and bits of loose concrete onto my shoes. I tried again and tore it free.

"Fair warning. My dad, Henry Lange, is moving in here, and he doesn't tolerate nonsense."

I brushed the bits of greenery from my hands and pulled my phone from my bag. I set the camera selection to panoramic. From the terrace, I slowly covered the property from one wood line to the other, encompassing everything in between, especially the flowers and the lake.

I returned my phone to my bag, then climbed the steps from the terrace to the back porch. Half-heartedly, I tried the back doorknob. I'd already checked the front door when I'd arrived. Everything was locked up tight. That was disappointing but also a good thing. Otherwise, anyone could wander in.

Leaning back against the porch rail, I looked at my father's new enterprise.

Dad would have his fun, with my assistance, and we'd make our mark on this house. It occurred to me that this was the third house we'd share, but making our mark together could only be said about this third house.

Yet another restart for me, and a fresh start for my dad too.

Even at this moment, if I wanted to, I could run in graceful slow motion through the flowers like some silly commercial. The butterflies and bees would take flight. I would be the disrupter in their peaceable kingdom. Me. Kara.

I smiled. Everyone needed to experience that feeling of potential. And silliness too. Who knew what tomorrow would bring in a house like this?

Our country house.

No, that wasn't right. A country house, yes, but far more appropriate to say a wildflower house.

I looked back again, taking in the yard and the flowers and the creek.

I could leave at any time—whenever I wanted—but I didn't think I'd be leaving soon. At least, not until after wildflower season.

CHAPTER FIVE

I'd gone through my father's house on Silver Street with an eye to the move. The inside was orderly and not overstuffed. As to the outside, he'd never used the yard much in either of our homes. I remembered our first home, the one with Mom. We'd had a birdhouse. Dad hadn't chosen to hang anything like that in this yard or on his deck. Dad was always at work anyway—had been all my life, it seemed to me.

Out at the wildflower house, I'd felt like a new person. I knew it sounded crazy, but I couldn't seem to express it better. For my dad? Oh my goodness. The way he talked about his plans for that house, he seemed almost like a stranger—a happy, newly energized stranger.

It was almost eerie the way he talked about the new-old house as if it would be his last, but totally enthusiastic, hurrah. He was barely sixty, a youthful sixty. He could be around for another thirty years or more to mystify and confuse me but also to rescue me. I couldn't picture him rambling about that huge house alone, perhaps growing more alone as he grew older.

I packed many of my personal items, including clothing and such, and did the same with the linens and even my father's clothing. I labeled the boxes clearly.

"The movers will do that," Dad said. "Leave it to them."

"I could. But I like to do it my way."

Dad saw my notes here and there, like on certain closet doors, and he'd stand and stare at them for long moments. For a brilliant man—because my dad was supersmart when it came to numbers and business—he could stumble over the simplest things.

"Just instructions for the movers, Dad."

"Oh."

"What's in the closet is off limits for them. I packed an overnight bag for you, and it's in the closet too. We'll stay at a hotel tomorrow night."

He nodded. "Good thinking."

I smiled at him. "How did you manage the move the last time?" The words came out sounding a little mocking and disrespectful, but Dad didn't seem to notice.

"It worked out. Nicole helped."

"She did?" I shook my head. "Definitely a full-service real estate agent." Again, I was hearing that snarky tone in my voice and resolved to ditch it. It didn't make sense for me to dislike Nicole—she hadn't done anything wrong—and yet something about her irked me. "I'm heading out to the house again. I want to take measurements and snap a few photos for planning the furniture placement, paint colors, and other things like that. Sometimes having a picture makes a difference. I need to be out there for the floor cleaners anyway."

Dad reminded me, "Nicole said we don't need to be there."

"I feel better about being on-site. Would you like to come along?"

"No, you go ahead."

That suited me fine. I had my own set of keys now.

But instead of turning away, he kept his eyes on my face. I couldn't read his expression.

"What's wrong, Dad?"

"Nothing. I was just thinking. I get the feeling that maybe you're looking forward to the move. You like the house?"

"I can't decide whether I'm crazy or not. Maybe you and I are both crazy together. But yes, while I'm not looking forward to the work, there's something about the house or maybe the gardens . . . maybe I'm just looking forward to a change."

He nodded. "Good. If you want any advice, let Nicole know. She always has lots of good ideas. She also knows a lot of people in the area that we can hire to help with jobs, as needed."

"Like the floor cleaners."

"True."

"I'm glad you agreed to get it done before the move."

"Don't feel like you have to stay and supervise them."

"I understand. But you know I like things done a certain way. I'll feel better if I can talk to them, make sure they get it started right."

~

So on my third trip out to the country, I felt hopeful. My old confidence was returning.

I arrived before the cleaners on purpose. I wanted to walk through the house again without distractions. The electricity was connected now. I checked the lights, flipping switches as I went. Good. My cane tapped the floor at times, extra loud in the empty house, so I hung it over my arm, where it would be handy and available if needed. For now, I was good. I flushed toilets and turned on faucets. The house smelled musty, so I opened a few windows. Some opened more easily than others. This was spring in Virginia, and with it, sooner or later, came humidity. As the heat rose, that old musty smell would worsen. Thank goodness for air-conditioning.

With no curtains hung, I could appreciate the views, especially in the back. The view through the front windows showed trees and bushes but nothing special like the field of flowers. I tried to focus on first steps and ignore the amount of work ahead of us lest it discourage me.

Instead, I set my phone on the stained kitchen counter and found the music I'd downloaded—I wanted to hear Copland's strains, the music that kept popping into my head. Ridiculous, perhaps, but I wanted to stand inside the house, play that music, and hear it swell and echo—the real thing, not the thin version stored in my memory.

I stood at the window and watched the flowers as the music began. Soon I was moving back through the first-floor rooms. The vision accompanied me along with the music. The long empty foyer stretched ahead of me with the various rooms opening off it. Music filled the rooms and me. My arms moved. My feet moved. Finally, I gave in and did it: I twirled. As light as a young girl, and as easily as if my body had never been battered, I held my cane above the floor and twirled again and again, in and out of the huge empty rooms, crossing into the parlor and the sitting room and the dining room. I'd worn flat, smooth-soled leather shoes, as if this part had been planned. And I whirled across the floors with not a single splinter of the old wood planks objecting.

The dance lasted less than a minute. The music was still playing when I came to a standstill in the middle of the dining room. Was that a sound I'd heard? Something not music?

I held my breath and stood stock still, trying to identify the sound and where it was coming from. Footsteps? I tiptoed into the kitchen and carefully lowered the volume of the music. I heard more footfalls, and then a man appeared in the kitchen doorway. Phone still in hand, I edged toward the open back door.

"I'm sorry I startled you." He raised his hands, as if in surrender. "I promise I'm harmless. I'm Nicole's brother. She asked me to come by and make sure the house was unlocked for the floor cleaners."

He stopped, waiting, probably seeing the blank look on my face—as blank as it felt in my head. He was holding a large roll of brown paper hoisted over his shoulder.

"Thought I'd drop off the paper while I was here. We'll put it down after the floors are clean and dry to help protect it and to remind the movers not to do more damage, gouging or anything, than is already present."

He waited again. I couldn't find my words. Was he harmless? He was handsome, with light-brown hair and blue eyes and a friendly smile. All the better to disguise the fact he was an ax murderer?

No, I didn't believe that. He wasn't dangerous. He was Nicole's brother. He knew about the floor cleaners. He was here to unlock the house and to leave the paper, exactly as he said.

I reached up to touch my hair. I knew it covered my scar, but I couldn't stop myself from checking.

"The door was open, and I came in. I can leave and come back later if you want." He gave a one-shouldered shrug. "In fact, since you're here . . . if you were planning to supervise the floor crew, I can just move along." He patted the roll of paper. "I'll drop this off first. Thought I'd leave it here in the kitchen."

His words were penetrating my brain much too slowly. Had he seen me dancing? How long had he been here before I'd noticed him? He couldn't have missed the music. I felt heat rising up my neck and burning my face. To break it, I shook my head and spoke, determined to pretend there was no embarrassment going on and no reason for it. After all, didn't everyone twirl in empty rooms from time to time if given the opportunity?

"No, that's fine. Kitchen is fine." Abruptly, I turned away, glad to hide my face but feeling awkward. I saw another roll was already there. It hadn't been here when I'd arrived. He could've walked through the foyer and hallway while I was twirling through the dining room . . .

I wouldn't blush. I refused to. I faced him.

His expression was unreadable.

He said, "The day before the move, I'll come back and put the paper down to cover the main walkways on this level and the hallway upstairs."

"Good." *Now, go,* I told him silently. *Go, and let me recover my dignity.*

He did an awkward shuffle, then said, "Well, I'll get on with it. Are you planning to stay all day?"

I shook my head. "Not unless I need to."

"Okay." He nodded and walked away.

The mood was spoiled, and I was uncomfortable now. Of course I was. There was a strange man in the house with me.

I walked out to the back porch. My embarrassment lingered. But as I stood there, the view of flowers and water and trees worked its magic on me.

I'd been that kid back in middle school that people didn't notice. I was smart and pretty enough but didn't have a mom who could show me the ropes, how to interact with and win friends. I lacked a feminine influence that would bolster my confidence. I wasn't bullied. I kept mostly to myself. I was accustomed to not being seen. I thought of middle school and high school as my invisible years. That had changed in college. Meeting Niles, each of us falling for the other, being inseparable, had opened up a social world I'd never had a place in before. Had I regressed? Back to that lonely time as a teenager? Is that why I'd thought dancing in an empty house to classical music while waiting for the cleaning crew was a reasonable, normal pastime?

I smiled, first at the flowers, then at myself. I could almost laugh at having taken myself so seriously.

If a person couldn't laugh at herself, then what was the point? Life was grim enough on its own. If this man also wanted to laugh at me . . . well, what did I care what he thought? It just meant that he was the petty one, not me. I did like the idea of putting down protective paper. I liked it even better given that I wasn't the one having to do it. So all in all, it worked out.

I should dance right up to that man and see if his bland expression stayed impassive. As if I could do such a thing. He was Nicole Albers's brother . . . Had he mentioned his name? No. I should ask. After all, if he was willing to roll out and tape down paper, then he might be useful for other projects . . .

His footsteps echoed as he moved in and out of the kitchen and the hallway. I stood taller, pulling my dignity around me, and went toward the sound.

I guessed he was Nicole's younger brother because he didn't seem much older than me. Midthirties maybe. Nice build, not too slim, not too . . . whatever. He was in the kitchen, checking the cabinets.

He stopped and looked at me. "If you'd like me to leave, just say so."

"No, you're fine. Sorry," I said, offering an apology. "I was just surprised."

He smiled. "I understand. Don't blame you."

I offered my hand. "I'm Kara Hart, Henry Lange's daughter."

"I guessed. Nicole told me about you. I'm Seth. Seth Albers."

"Pleased to meet you." So far, so good. "I came by to do a last check, make sure the floor people could get in and make a good start, and tape up paper signs to direct the movers to the right rooms."

Seth said, "They should be here anytime now. I was checking the kitchen and bathrooms for lights and flushing and that sort of thing." He touched a dark blotch on the kitchen cabinet. "Nicole hired someone to clean, but I wanted to make sure nothing was overlooked. Honestly, these are stains. Probably can't get it much cleaner."

"It's old, so that's to be expected."

"True. If it was me, I'd tackle the kitchen first."

"I agree. Dad has this idea that he can do it all himself."

"Well, I wish him luck. The good news is there's always folks to hire when reality hits."

I laughed. I didn't mean to, but his words were so close to my own thoughts that I couldn't help it. "It all looks dusty and dirty to me. I'm sorry if that sounds awful. But the floors are in good shape. I can see that. They just need a good cleaning."

"Mary and Rob, that's why."

"Who?"

"Mary and Rob Forster. They lived here. They were proud of these floors, this house. Their life together. But the last few years were hard on them. They couldn't keep the house up. They passed within a few months of each other last year, and then the house sat empty for a while."

"No children?"

"No."

"You sound like you knew them well."

"Sure. Long time. They were married forever," Seth said. "They were devoted to each other." He nodded toward the kitchen. "Those flowers out back?"

"The flowers are amazing."

"There's a story that goes along with them."

"Really?"

"If you're interested, I'm happy to share it after the floor cleaners get here."

"I think they are overdue. Maybe they're lost?"

This time his expression was totally readable. "Lost? Why . . ." He laughed. "No offense, but they're from the area. They won't get lost. I can understand, though, why you might think that. You being a city girl and all."

"Me being a city girl has nothing to do with people getting lost . . . or just plain being late."

He laughed all the louder. I wanted to be offended, but I wasn't.

Someone knocked loudly.

"Nick of time," Seth said and headed for the front door.

They arrived in a van and a large truck with an uncovered back end. The truck bed was a jumble of cleaning tools and buckets.

After a quick look at my face, Seth said, "They're good. Don't worry."

Could he read my mind? Was I that obvious?

He introduced me and the crew to each other, told them to yell if they had any questions, and then turned to me.

"Take a walk outside with me?"

I glanced at the workers. They were setting up to work, and I was in the way. "Sure."

As we passed through the kitchen, I couldn't help looking back.

"You can trust them," Seth said.

"It's not that. All the work that needs to be done . . . it feels like a huge responsibility."

"It's a long road between livable and ideal. Once you're past livable, enjoy the journey to ideal. With a little luck, you'll take a long time to arrive."

"That sounds clever, but I enjoy modern conveniences. When I clean something, I want it to look clean. No soapy water or paint will fix this nasty linoleum or these cabinets or appliances."

"Well, it's your canvas, right?"

"Canvas? Oh, you mean as in a 'blank canvas'?"

"Sure. I don't doubt your dad will do whatever you suggest. Get new stuff. Get top of the line."

"Whose father are you talking about?" But even as I asked, I realized Seth was close to right. Dad might not pick up on hints and wishes, but I couldn't think of a time he'd denied me any outright request.

We walked out to the back porch and stood facing the railing. Seth waved his hand, gesturing as if to encompass the entirety of the backyard.

"Gorgeous, isn't it? Even after neglect." He smiled. "Honestly, perhaps more beautiful because of it. Those wildflowers have taken over." He asked, "Did you see the gazing ball grotto?"

"Gazing ball? A grotto? I didn't see any gazing balls or grottos."

"Well, it's not really a grotto, and the gazing ball vanished a while ago, but the pedestal is still there." He walked down the porch steps to the terrace. When I didn't follow, still thinking about the gazing ball that wasn't there, he asked, "You coming?" He glanced at the cane.

"Okay. Sure. What about the floor cleaners?"

"They don't need us."

I opened the back door and called in, "Is it going okay?"

Voices returned yeses.

I tucked my cane under my arm and held the railing carefully as I descended.

"You move well," he said. "Do you need the cane all the time?"

"Not too often, but that said, the injury flares up at times. All sorts of triggers. Some I know to avoid. Some are unexpected. I'd rather have the cane with me and not need it than otherwise."

"The injury is from your accident?" Before I could answer, he waved his hand. "No, wait. Apologies. Not my business. I shouldn't have asked."

"Well, it's not a secret. I don't talk about it much."

"My sister mentioned you were staying with your dad while you were recovering from a car accident. Sounded like you had a hard time of it. But again, I'm sorry for bringing it up."

The grounds had been terraced, so it wasn't a straight slope down to the creek, but rather every few yards, there was a slight dip that had probably been more like a step before erosion. Each of those dips was just awkward enough to cause me a bit of hesitation, and after the second one, Seth took my arm lightly by the elbow.

"I don't need help," I said. "Thank you, though. I appreciate the consideration. I'm fine."

"Looked like it might be a problem."

"I can manage. It just takes me an extra moment."

"Yes, ma'am."

"Now I'm sorry. I didn't mean to sound ungrateful."

"No problem."

He continued moving downslope, and I followed. Before we reached the grassy area between the wildflowers and the creek, he gestured to the left, toward the tangled greenery crowding the tree line. "Over here."

"Looks like some of these bushes were sculpted at some time in the past. Topiary?"

"Ages ago." He touched my elbow again, but lightly. "Watch your step." He pushed a low-hanging branch aside. "It's the stone steps. The leaves fall and make it slippery. You don't want to miss your footing."

The low stone steps descended in a curving pathway down to a small pool. No running water, though. The water was stagnant and full of leaves, leaves, and more leaves fallen from the overarching branches.

There was an iron bench with a single chair that had fallen over. It was half-lost in the weeds. Seth righted it and brushed it off. He sat, leaving the bench for me. I brushed at the seat, and my hand came away dirty. I held my breath and sat, subtly smoothing my hand along my pants leg. The thigh muscle was a little tight, and I tried to shift my leg subtly to ease it.

"That's the pedestal?" I pointed at the decorative pitted concrete post.

"Yes, ma'am."

"I wonder where the ball went?"

"Maybe into the brush, or maybe a family member took it. I don't know."

"Of course. That makes sense."

Seth started speaking, but I was distracted, realizing how private we were here. Yet right at the top of the steps was our yard and the wide-open view between the creek and the house; then suddenly I spied the little figures in shadowy spots of this . . . I didn't know what to call Seth's grotto. A garden nook? A meditation spot?

I'd never heard of meditation spots with trolls and elves. Not quite garden gnomes, but the same principle. One was a squat troll; another was an elf sitting on a post reading a book. They were concrete or convincingly fake concrete.

"Kara?"

"Sorry, I was thinking about how set apart this spot feels. And those creatures . . . the little figures."

"Yeah, funny how they aren't obvious until they are."

"Oh, exactly. Yes. That's on purpose, right?"

"Yes. And there are other spots just off the main area of the yard. I'll let you discover them for yourself. This is my favorite."

"I can see why. You said there were others? Who does this in their backyard?"

"A woman who loved working in the yard, with forty years to work it, especially one whose husband supported every project."

"Most people plant and then maintain. Not this one?"

"No. Not Mary. She was a builder, not a weeder."

"Mary. Tell me about the former owners."

"Mary Forster loved gardening. She arranged every grain of dirt, every blade of grass personally." He grinned and shook his head. "Okay, that might be overstating it, but if you'd known her, you could believe it was true. Her husband, Rob, was a professor over at the University of Virginia. Taught history. She was on her own most days, but she didn't complain and spent that time gardening. Rob was never a gardener himself, but he supported whatever she wanted."

"Children?"

"No. I'm sure they must've thought they'd have kids one day, though. Otherwise, why buy such a large house? They didn't talk about it, though, so just a guess."

"I can see the earthen terraces, and I've found a couple of sitting areas. Some huge crape myrtles, too, over that way." I gestured in their direction. The tops of their branches were visible about the rest of the flora that surrounded them. "Their trunks remind me of the color of rich cinnamon. They must be ancient."

"It's too bad most of Mary's efforts have gone . . . to seed, I guess you could say." He flashed a quick grin. "As she and Rob got older, she hired help for a while. I cut grass and did some work for them when I was younger. Mostly upkeep. By then, their health was failing. For the last few years, Rob would bring Mary out here to sit on the porch. Finally, one day, he got tired of hearing Mary complain about how her garden was deteriorating. He purchased a bunch of wildflower seed. Had me mow the grass practically down to the dirt and then till it. Together, we spread that seed. Mary was so angry that he'd messed up her lawn—she let loose on both of us. But the next spring when the flowers came up, she sat on the back porch and laughed."

"How sweet. Or sad."

"Both. They call that bittersweet, right? That was a year ago. It was Rob's gift to his wife. She told me it was ironic. I asked what she meant."

"And? What did she say?"

"She said that after all those years of planning and sweating over her landscaping, she'd never created as much beauty as Rob did by throwing out seed and letting Mother Nature do the rest."

"Nice of Mother Nature to oblige and provide sun and rain at the right times."

"True."

"Well, I'm glad they returned this year."

"The perennials did. The annuals didn't, of course."

"Are you sure? I'm not an expert, but I thought I saw some annuals in there."

Seth grinned. "I found some leftover seed. I tossed it out earlier in the year sort of in Mary and Rob's honor."

I wanted to say something, but I couldn't think of anything that felt appropriate. My eyes stung. I sniffled. "Allergies." After a longish pause, I asked, "Who went first?"

He frowned. "Huh?"

"Mary or Rob?"

"Mary. She passed in her sleep. Rob went two months after that. The last few years that they lived here, admittedly, the housekeeping was neglected. They stayed on the main floor. Rob used to joke that folks could move in upstairs, and they'd never know except for when the toilets flushed."

I laughed. "Well, I hope the plumbing is in good shape. Dad said those things were checked out."

"Nicole's good with that stuff."

"She seems to be."

"They actually spent their last days in a nursing home. They didn't last long after they left here."

"But they had good lives and a happy marriage."

"They did."

"Then I'd say they lasted as long as they should have, probably as long as they wanted."

We shared a silence that at first seemed companionable and then grew into an acute silence where you became too aware of the person with you. I cast about for something innocuous to say.

"But gnomes. I mean, he was an academic, and she was clearly creative. Gnomes?"

His eyebrows lifted in question. "You have something against gnomes?"

"No, of course not."

"Have you ever had a garden gnome?"

"No."

"Me either," Seth said. "But I do get a kick out of Mary Forster's."

"Me too." I smiled. "They're in other areas of the gardens?"

Another silence, and during this one, Seth's grin grew. Finally, he said, "I think I'll let you find out for yourself."

Companionable again. It was a much better feeling.

It occurred to me that on the route from livable to ideal, dingy paint and wallpaper were little more than a short detour.

"I'll check on the progress, then be on my way, if you're sure that's okay."

He said, "Yes. I promise it's okay. The crew leader, Burt? I've known him all my life. Probably related to me in some way. Lots of cousins around here. No worries. He'll do good work."

"Glad to hear it."

Seth held the door for me as I went inside, and we stood together in the kitchen doorway. I loved the smell of floor cleaner and wax and hadn't even known it. I breathed it in. It was a . . . clean smell, but it was more than that, and I couldn't find the right word.

He said, "Yeah. I feel the same. The smell takes me back to being a kid, to Mom and Dad waxing the floor and letting us kids buff it with the seats of our pants."

I smiled at him, almost wishing I had a memory like that.

Seth added, "We'd run and slide." He shook his head. "Long ago, right?" He turned to me, saying, "I'm glad you and your dad are making the move out here. I hope you'll be happy. I know it needs a lot of work, but I hope you'll give it a chance."

I nodded despite myself. "I will . . . give it a chance, I mean." It seemed important to add, "But I don't know how long I'll stay."

"A day at a time," Seth said. "Any journey worth taking is worth finding value in each step."

"Wow," I said. "Does that come naturally to you? That sort of zen speak?"

"Ha, no, it doesn't. Lessons learned, I guess. And relearned many times. But I try."

"Thank you, Seth."

"You're welcome," he said, smiling, then crinkled his face in confusion. "But for what exactly?"

"For the kind words. For not easily taking offense."

He raised his eyebrows and looked amused. "Same back at you. Give it time, Kara. You might be pleasantly surprised."

"It's possible." And yes, looking into his kind eyes, I thought it might be possible, indeed.

"We're practically neighbors, you know."

"Neighbors? I don't see any other houses around here."

He pointed toward the kitchen window and the world beyond it. "Not too far from here. Across the creek and down that way."

I'd been comfortable walking with him back up to the house and even standing here in the kitchen smelling floor wax and chatting, but neighbors? Somehow the idea of him living in convenient proximity made me uneasy again.

I'd been a widow for a year and a half. A long time, yet not very long at all.

I thanked Seth for his neighborliness, trying to hit the right note between nice and not too nice. I think I missed the mark because his smile dimmed. I found my cane and reclaimed my purse.

"I'll be on my way home now."

He offered to walk me to my car, and I declined. He didn't repeat the offer. I left via the back door and walked the long way around.

Of course, I relived the whole encounter all the way home, second-guessing my actions and his motives. Thinking about the things I might have said. What he'd thought about what I had said.

Maybe the journey on the way to ideal came with potholes, too, and I was stumbling into a few of them. So be it. Regardless, I was looking forward to our next meeting.

~

I might've expected anxiety-induced dreams the night before the move. Even in my sleep, I knew I was dreaming as I walked through the wildflower house. Dim light, empty rooms—much as it had been when I'd played the music and met Seth. But these floors were gleaming. Not just clean but luminescent—a rich, earthy shade of brown that reached into forever. The rolled-out paper walkways had presence, too, almost like fine carpeting. I was wearing a dress. Full skirted. I didn't see myself in the dream, but I saw that white skirt. I lifted the gathered folds and let them fall. The fabric floated gracefully downward, in slow motion, until the hem brushed the floor. I looked around. I was standing in the parlor. I was waiting.

Seth appeared.

Even in my dream, I was struck by the presence of Seth. Not Niles. It was as if Niles didn't belong in this dreamscape.

Seth moved toward me, still wearing jeans—but jeans that somehow looked as sleek as a tux. His cotton shirt was of such glowing whiteness that it was almost blinding. He moved toward me, holding out his hand in invitation. And paused.

I reached out my own hand. My hand seemed willing, but my arm couldn't quite extend itself far enough. There were reservations. I made another effort. My arm seemed to have a will of its own and refused. In frustration and alarm, I watched Seth pull his hand away. His face changed expression, and I read his disappointment. I tried again, reaching both hands out, and saw another man beyond him, standing in shadow in the next room.

I woke. Abruptly. It was dark. I was awake enough to know I was thirsty. And feeling vaguely guilty.

Never mind symbolic dreams. Mine had been laid out like a guilty road map with big, bold signage.

But guilty over what? Seth? No one could control a dream. Or who was in it.

The dream wasn't my fault, Niles.

I rejected the guilt. I lay in bed and reran the dream in my head like scenes from a movie. Was it more than it seemed? I wanted to give it a chance to explain its message. But no one could hold on to a dream. So I chose one word—the foremost message in the dream, as it seemed to me on reflection: *invitation.*

An invitation.

I sat on the edge of the bed. It was early morning and pitch dark. Three a.m. Out of long habit, before standing, I flexed my ankles and stretched my toes as I massaged my thigh. Never good to surprise temperamental body parts.

Had it been an invitation to dance? To be happy at the wildflower house with its nice, convenient neighbor?

Or was it something more . . . something about being lonely and enjoying the company of a pleasant, good-looking man?

Again, that twinge of guilt hit me. I refused to dwell on it. Not now.

I headed down to the kitchen, being careful not to disturb my father. I'd heard him come in late and knew he'd be sound asleep at this hour.

The kitchen door was closed, but a thin light shone around the edges. I might have left a light on accidentally, but I wouldn't have closed the door.

I approached it quietly and opened it, asking softly, "Dad?"

"Did I disturb you, Kara? I'm sorry."

"No, I woke and was thirsty."

He put his eyeglasses on the table. He didn't wear them often, usually sticking with his contacts unless his eyes were especially tired. I noted this as I went to the fridge to get my pitcher of fruit water.

"Want some?"

"No, thanks. I'm finishing up and heading to bed."

"Problems?"

He shook his head. "No. Just trying to compose a letter. After all these years . . . I know the business will continue without me. I've done everything I can to ensure that as part of the sale. There are things I'd like to say to my employees. I don't know . . ."

"I'd be happy to help you write something."

Dad sighed and rubbed his eyes. "No, thank you. It should come from me."

"That's a good idea, Dad."

"I'm taking some of the office staff out to lunch. Olive scheduled it for tomorrow, so I'll be gone for part of the day. She didn't know about the movers. Do you need me here?"

"Nope. I've got this. I think it's a good idea if you're here when they arrive and hopefully be here before they finish. I can handle the middle just fine."

"Thank you, Kara. I hope you know how much I appreciate the help."

"My pleasure."

I went back to bed wondering if the dream might return. I wouldn't mind if it did. It didn't. Come morning, all the craziness of moving-out day banished it from my mind completely.

CHAPTER SIX

The movers carried cardboard boxes down from the attic and out to the truck. I tried to keep up with their progress, sweeping and cleaning as they emptied the house. Today was the move-out and tomorrow was delivery day. So fast. Too fast. But that was what a cash deal got you—a quick closing.

I wished Dad a good last day on the job as he was leaving, then added, "You have to be on hand when they deliver tomorrow, so whatever is left to be done, get it done today."

"Will do."

"Promise?"

"Yes, ma'am. After today, I'll have no reason to go into the office."

It was a bit of a breath-stealing moment to hear him state that—to acknowledge it. I tried to gauge the feelings he might be hiding behind those words, but what I saw was eagerness and energy. As if he'd been freed.

"I still think you should've gotten some of the renovation work done before we moved in."

"But that's the point, Kara. I want to be hands on." He spread his hands wide as if to illustrate. "I want to get into those projects, and it's no good trying to do it while living an hour away. I need to be there, on-site, to really dig into the renovation."

Dad was in good shape for a sixty-year-old business guy. But he was talking about "digging into" work—physical labor—that he was in no way prepared for. But since when had he needed me to protect him? Never. Maybe that was changing. These seemed to be different times.

"Besides," he said, "I don't want to live in this house while it's for sale. No one wants to do that. We'll move and then put this house on the market."

"Okay, Dad, I agree about not wanting to live with strangers coming and going, but as for the rest, the work may involve more than we can handle. Old houses are different. They're old, for one thing. They need specialists who know all the ins and outs of what can go wrong."

"Kara, trust me on this. I'm smart enough to know that if I get in over my head, I'll bring in those old-house specialists." He smiled. "I took your advice on cleaning the floors, didn't I?"

"They are beautiful, aren't they?"

"They are."

He left for work, one last time. I worried. His business had always been his life, to the exclusion of almost everything else. Was this new-old house my father's flavor of midlife crisis? If so, I hoped he wouldn't wake up in a few weeks with regrets enough to fill it.

~

Indeed, in the same way that the flowers had received the sun, both soaking it into their petals and leaves and reflecting it outwardly to every other living thing, this floor gleamed with rich wood tones, soaking up the light from the windows and taking it in along with the patterns and textures of the walls and ceilings. There seemed to be worlds reflected in the deep, glowing grain of the wood.

If I'd wanted to dance before—and I had, no matter how silly that sounded even to me—I saw those cleaned, waxed, and buffed floors, and the strings inside me wound up and spun me like a top—almost.

Outwardly, I was slightly more discreet than before. I executed a quick twirl with my cane under my arm like a Fred Astaire prop and then stopped.

Good neighbor Seth had done as he'd said he would. The heavy brown paper was in place in the most likely walkways, and I intended to be the sheriff today and make sure those movers watched where they were putting their feet.

I had arrived super early this morning. The movers were an hour late. They called to say they were on their way but had missed their turn and not realized it until they'd passed through Mineral. Now they were working on turning around and coming back.

Dad walked in the front door. "Any sign of them?"

"Nope. Have they called?"

"Not yet," he said.

"Not locals," I said, thinking of what Seth had said about the floor-cleaning crew when he was teasing me.

"Probably not, Kara." Dad nodded upstairs. "Are you sure you're happy with your room? It's not too late to switch those instruction papers you taped up."

With my encouragement, Dad had chosen the master bedroom. It was large, and if you looked beyond the old paint and paper, it was lovely with its turret sitting area and wainscoting. It overlooked the front of the house. The room I'd chosen was plenty big and overlooked the back. There were three empty bedrooms besides, so I could use any of those for overflow boxes.

"I prefer the backyard view."

"The flowers?"

"That and the rest. I enjoy the gardens and the creek."

He nodded. "Then I'm glad we have a back-facing window." He looked at his watch. "Maybe I'll walk up the drive. Be there to wave the truck down."

Eventually, the moving van arrived. The moving crew from the day before was there to unload the contents. What had filled up the rooms in my father's old house didn't impress this house one iota. The house might be shabby, but the modern furniture looked sparse and very short on style.

"Is something wrong, Kara?"

I shook my head. "Not exactly wrong, but not right. The furniture looked great in your other house, but here . . . well, it looks rather sad."

"It will look more compatible when the old wallpaper is down and the walls are painted."

I forced a smile. "Compatible? Maybe so. I brought a bunch of paint chips with me." In fact, I had a case of folders with photos, paint chips, and assorted decorating ideas.

He patted my shoulder. "It will work out. We'll manage."

"We always do, don't we?" I threw those words out, half-muttered.

He looked surprised. By my words or by my tone?

"That sounded harsh, Dad. I didn't mean it that way. This is what you wanted—a place to fix up and renovate, right? We'll get it done."

"You wouldn't know this, Kara, but some of the greatest joy I ever took in my business was the building of it—literally. Planning the lay-outs, moving the merchandise. Choosing and planning the satellite locations." He shrugged. "It was for tires, I know, but . . ."

"Well, you're right. I wouldn't know. In fact, I rarely saw you doing business at all. Or home activities, for that matter. You never mixed business and personal."

"Business and family don't mix well. You're right about that."

After he left, I sat in the kitchen and sipped my coffee. Only a few days ago, I'd danced across the floor and met Seth. Then the dream.

Meeting him alone, at that moment, I'd been vulnerable. I was missing Niles, whether I wanted to admit it or not, but unable to for-give him. I was grateful to my father. How often were our biggest flaws also our greatest strengths? I'd learned from him to compartmentalize events and focus on real life. Sometimes it was hard. But focus was often the lifeline that got a person, me, through difficult times and on to the tasks at hand.

I understood why I had reacted as I had to Seth. Now it was time to tackle putting our belongings away. A place for everything and everything in its place.

I set my cup in the kitchen sink and went to work.

~

"Hello? Anyone home? Kara?"

I froze on the stool, holding the casserole dishes that were destined for the top shelf.

"Seth? Is that you?"

"It's me."

I heard the beat of his shoes on the wooden floor. There was still more than enough emptiness in the house to create an echo.

"Just came by to see if you need any help?"

He was dressed as before in jeans and a T-shirt. Not glowing white like in my dream. The jeans were ordinary. He looked good.

I said, "Well, we're in."

"Congratulations."

"Are you bringing a housewarming gift? Maybe a casserole?"

He looked briefly blank; then his eyes hit on the dishes I was holding.

He laughed. "Sorry, no. I wouldn't do that to a friend. Clearly, you've never tasted my cooking."

I smiled and finished stowing the dishes up top. As I stepped down from the stool, Seth reached out, perhaps to offer a hand. I didn't take it because I didn't need it, but still, it was a thoughtful gesture.

"It seems kind of foolish to be putting all the dishes away when I know we're going to pull it all down again when we redo the kitchen, but we need to live in the meantime."

"Makes sense," he said. "Nicole called. Your dad mentioned a problem in the bathroom. Something about the toilet not flushing right."

"You're here for that? You're a plumber?"

"No, sorry again. Not a plumber. More of a guy-of-all-trades."

"A guy . . ."

"Jack-of-all-trades. You've heard of that?"

"Of course."

"I say 'guy,' or otherwise people start calling me Jack. Not my name."

I found Seth interesting. He had humor and a touch of mystery. Everyone needed a little mystery.

"Why not Seth-of-all-trades?"

"Because Seth has other skills that, one day, he hopes to return to."

For a moment, I wasn't sure how to respond. Did he want me to ask? I rather thought he did, so I obliged. "What skills are those? Other than being handy and useful?" I caught my breath, suddenly embarrassed. Had that sounded flirty? Suggestive?

But Seth, apparently not interpreting my words or tone in that way, answered, "I wrote columns for the newspaper and some freelance gigs, including marketing copy. I earned enough, for a while, but the newspaper cut back, the marketing copy went in house, and suddenly I wasn't making a living. Not sure what I'll do next."

"Oh."

"Oh, what?"

"Not what I was expecting." I added, "Not sure *what* I was expecting, but a newspaper reporter, a journalist . . . that wasn't it."

"Hey, that's okay. My columns were more in the human-interest vein as opposed to cutting-edge reporting. That said, I don't think reporters or journalists have any particular look. When you figure out what you were expecting, I'd like to know."

There was something in his expression—the lack of a grin but a glint in his eyes—that made me uneasy but interested. Maybe he *had* taken my words as meaning something more.

I had that vision of bobbing heads again—not of my dad and me talking past each other but of Seth and me with foolish, grinning faces uttering polite words and totally failing to make a connection. I put my hand in my pocket to prevent myself from reaching up to my scar. Thankfully, I was spared the need to respond by a slamming door—the front screen door—and light footsteps skipping along the corridor.

A child with corn silk hair appeared in the doorway. She was wearing purple sneakers and a pink-and-purple shorts-and-shirt outfit. Very cute. In one motion, Seth leaned toward her, stretched out an arm, and swung her up. She had to be about four, maybe five. Her eyes were the bluest I'd ever seen, and her joy was evident. She started to speak but then caught sight of me, and the words stopped. Her smile dimmed.

I hadn't known he had a child. A wife, too, presumably. That hadn't occurred to me.

Why should it? What would it matter anyway? Still, I was glad we hadn't gone past the bobbing-heads stage.

Seth Albers was our "guy-of-all-trades." That was all.

"Maddie, this is Mrs. Hart. I told you about her. She and her dad live here now."

Maddie nodded. Her long lashes brushed her cheeks. She was as perfect in appearance as a china doll.

Seth looked at me, saying, "She's a little shy at first. When she gets to know you, that will change." He ruffled the child's bangs and set her back on her feet. "Mrs. Hart, this is Maddie Lyn. My niece. She'll be hanging with me today."

His niece. "Oh?"

"I hope you don't mind. She won't be a problem."

"Of course. Is she Nicole's child?"

"No, but it's a story for another time?"

"Certainly."

"Mom dropped her off here. Grandma, that is. Right, Maddie?" He looked back at me. "Grammy has a doctor's appointment, so Maddie Lyn is my assistant this afternoon. We'd better get on with our work, right?"

He was asking Maddie, but I nodded. I felt foolish.

"We'll get on with it, then, if that's okay?" He paused. "Nicole asked me to check some of the windows too. Said they were sticking. Thought I had all of them working, but weather and temps can play havoc with them."

"Certainly." I gestured at the kitchen. "I've got work to do too. If you need anything, have questions or whatever, give me a yell."

"Sure."

Seth and Maddie Lyn disappeared. As soon as they were out of sight, Maddie resumed her chatter. The threads of her words wound throughout the house along with her laughter. She was saying something about her day and her Grammy. For a moment, I waited, almost lost in time; then I turned away and went back to work.

After a while, I realized everything was quiet. If not for Maddie's occasional noise or the squeak of a grown man walking on the old floor planking—which, however good it looked, was still quite old—I might have believed I was alone in the house.

I stood at the foot of the stairs. There were so many jobs, inside and out, that needed doing. Some needed it sooner than others. For instance, I needed to make the beds. We'd be staying here tonight. We were home now.

We were home. Those were sobering words.

Seth was working on one of the windows in Dad's bedroom. When I paused in the open doorway, Maddie looked up with a swift glance. She was sitting quietly on a chair near her uncle, looking downcast.

Perhaps the assistant role hadn't gone smoothly? I moved on to the overflow room and pulled clean sheets out of the box marked "Linens." I carried one set into my bedroom.

I was putting the mattress pad and topper on the bed and then the fitted sheet when a small hand grabbed the other side. Maddie focused her baby blues on me and said, "I can help. I know how."

I'd never made a bed with anyone's help, much less a child's. But what could I say?

"Thank you, Maddie."

And we did. I'd have to retuck that corner later, but it was good enough for now. I found my cotton bedspread in a box and shook it out to smooth it across the bed. Maddie took her side and pulled and patted it with her little hands. Then she looked up at me with expectation on her face. I refrained from reaching out to tug her side of the spread into proper position. Instead, I smiled and thanked her for her help. She seemed to expect more, but I had no idea what that could be, so I reached for the pillowcases. Maddie and I were each working on stuffing a pillow into a case when Seth joined us.

"Everyone doing okay?"

I turned and saw the question on his face. Lots of questions, spoken and unspoken, on these faces. But I understood his.

"Maddie Lyn is a big help."

He nodded. "Great." He flashed a quick smile. "How are your windows? Any issues with the plumbing in this bathroom?"

There was a bathroom not directly connected to my room but next to it.

"As far as I know, it's all fine. Windows *and* pipes."

"Given their age, that's a condition that could change whenever. Just let me know if it does or if anything else comes up."

Maddie placed her now-covered pillow on the bed and moved her hands across the case, trying to make it perfect.

"Ready to go?"

She nodded.

"Thank you for your help." I smiled at Maddie and turned to Seth. "Both of you."

I led the way downstairs. "Thank you for putting that paper down for the movers. It did its job well. I almost pulled it up last night but ran out of energy."

Seth said, "Leave it until the rest of the furniture arrives."

It was an odd, offhand remark. Was it a criticism? I paused at the base of the stairs, in the foyer, bristling a little. The almost empty sitting room, now our living room, was on one side. The dining room behind it was empty, as was the parlor on the other side of the foyer.

"We don't have much in the way of furnishings—it's true. We'll get more furniture as we decide what we want. For now, I'd rather not be tripping over the paper."

He gave me a sharp look before his expression relaxed, and he smiled. "Nicole suggested bringing some of the original furniture back. Not the junk, of course. Your father seemed happy with the idea."

"What?"

Seth's smile became a grin. "Sorry. I know your dad isn't much for small talk, but I assumed he'd told you. I think they're over at the Deales' house checking it out now. He should be back soon. I'm sure he'll tell you about it then."

"Wait. Furniture that was here?"

"A cousin took it all. Rob's second cousin once removed, or some such thing, was the heir. Name's Sue Deale. My guess is she didn't think it through. She can't use it all and didn't want to dump it in a thrift shop, so she suggested sending some of it back."

I didn't know what to say. I shrugged. "Well, this is Dad's thing. His home. His choices."

Seth nodded. "Maddie Lyn and I will run on home."

He opened the front door. The child gifted me with a shy smile and raised her hand in farewell. I closed the door and locked it, suddenly overwhelmed with the need to run my fingers through my embroidery threads, to feel the canvas in the hoop, properly taut like a drum—in short, to find comfort in my quiet place.

The walnut cabinet with my embroidery supplies was next to my favorite chair. I sat but didn't open the cabinet. My mood wasn't right for needlework. Too many distractions.

Like my father being off somewhere with Nicole looking at old furniture.

I craved fresh air. I stood and walked down the hallway and into the kitchen and out the back door.

The view was beautiful. I stared across the backyard, then closed my eyes and breathed in deeply before exhaling slowly.

So here we were. I'd been brought here, drawn along with my father, in part to help him, partly because I had nowhere else to go, but also because of these wildflowers. Flowers that were doomed to die at the end of their season.

I'd be gone by then. When the flowers were done, I would leave. It was an artificial, arbitrary date set for finding a job and my own apartment in the city, but I needed a date. A goal.

This was my father's dream. I needed my own.

Furniture. *Bah.* Was Nicole simply the best, most full-service real estate agent ever? Were they truly no more than friends? My intuition was twitching big-time now. Had Dad moved out here to pursue her?

She didn't seem averse, but then what did I know? Maybe she really was just a thorough, make-the-client-happy agent, even offering her brother and niece for extra services.

Maddie Lyn was a sweet child. I wondered about her mother and father. Seth hadn't wanted to share details in front of his young niece, so clearly there was a story there.

A swift memory of my own lost pregnancy touched me. So much had happened since then.

Fathers and daughters. Niece or not, Seth and Maddie were close. He was filling the role of father for her. I would've loved more communication and warmth from my own dad. I might've learned the techniques of being close and enjoying it. Maybe my relationships, including my marriage, would've been more successful.

~

Dad didn't return until shortly before supper. I waited for him to mention the furniture. When we sat down in the kitchen to eat supper, and he still hadn't, I said to him, "I heard your news."

He stopped moving. His fork was suspended above his salad, and he stared down at the plate for a few heartbeats before saying, "Heard my news?"

There was a staggered, almost breathless quality to the words.

"Yes. Seth came over to take care of some stuck windows and plumbing, and he let it slip."

He dropped his fork and reached for his napkin. He was pale.

"Are you okay, Dad?"

"I'm okay. I'm fine." He paused. "But you? What about you?"

"Dad. Really. It's not a big deal."

He frowned in a confused way.

"Seriously, it's just furniture." I started to say, *Besides, it's your house and your choice*, but that might've sounded like I was truly angry, so I didn't. "Just furniture."

"Furniture," he whispered without inflection. He coughed; then in a more normal voice, he added, "Seth told you about the furniture? Are you sure you're okay about it?"

He still didn't sound right. For the first time in perhaps forever, I considered his age and the fact that he wasn't indestructible.

I put a smile on my face and infused my words with an upbeat tone. "So tell me about it."

"About . . ."

"The furniture, Dad."

He shrugged, but carefully. He exhaled a long breath, and his shoulders seemed to relax. He nodded, saying, "It's furniture. If you don't like it, we'll send it to one of those thrift shops or antique stores in Louisa and Charlottesville. Plenty of those around." He added, "The lady who has it can't bring herself to get rid of it, so Nicole says we're doing her a favor by taking it for her, one way or the other."

I was relieved he was himself again. "Still sounds odd to me."

He offered a sheepish smile. "I didn't think you'd care, but in retrospect, I should've asked your opinion. You seemed dissatisfied with what we already had. Not that I blame you. When Nicole mentioned Mrs. Deale wanted to return some things, it sounded like an opportunity."

"No worries." I shrugged. "Besides—and I mean this—it's your house to do with as you please. I'll be moving on soon; you know that. For now, I'm happy to help."

I meant it. I did.

He nodded.

I said, "You should get some rest. I made your bed but left your clothing and personal items for you to put away. Do you want help with that?"

"No, I've got it. But you're right. Long day."

I felt the sag myself, in my posture and in my shoulders, and then I realized, marveling, at how my aches and injuries had stayed quiet for most of the day. That was a good sign, but I suspected I'd be feeling it tomorrow. To that end, I intended to make good use tonight of the claw-foot tub in my new-old bathroom for a long soak.

Dad paused as we went through the foyer toward the stairs. He stood surrounded by dark rooms—I'd left night-lights burning in the kitchen and on the stair landing, but the light was weak. He surveyed the landscape of the house.

"Was this a good idea?"

I was startled. "Is it?" I said. "I think so, Dad. You wanted this for a long time. You were quite clear about it—when you finally told me. Now, at the end of a long day and after such a huge change, second thoughts, doubts, are normal. Don't even think about it tonight. Tomorrow, in the morning and rested, if you still have any question about it—that's the time to ask. In the light of day, I suspect you won't give it another thought."

~

It wasn't so very late for a normal day. Only about eight p.m., and I intended to let everything go and take the advice I'd given Dad. I focused on preparing for bed and a well-deserved night's rest. But those words that had struck me earlier came back like an echo—we were home.

The lamp from the bedroom spilled light into the hallway. I'd had the movers put the overflow boxes in an adjacent room. In my pajamas and ready for bed, I stood at that door. The moon was out, nearly full, and sharing its light through the uncovered windows, but the shadows made the boxes seem overwhelming, almost looming.

Time enough to worry over those tomorrow and the next few days.

Dad had left his bedroom door cracked open an inch, showing no light. I listened and heard nothing. He was exhausted too. I hoped he wasn't experiencing regret.

He didn't normally leave his door ajar like that. He'd done it for a while after Mom had left. After the accident when I'd come home with him to recover, he would pause outside of my door, listening. For a time, he'd even slept on the sofa since there wasn't another bedroom on the main floor. He'd wanted to be available and nearby in case he was needed. I'd been touched. There were many things my dad wasn't, but it was the small actions that often told the true story.

I wasn't familiar with the squeaky spots on these floorboards or stair treads, so I moved carefully, carrying my cane in one hand while gripping the stair rail with the other. The main stairway was wide and gracious, and the night-light was enough to show me the way. I paused in the foyer to get my bearings and assess the temper of the house; then I strolled slowly along the rows of windows in both front rooms.

We'd left an exterior light burning. It lit part of the porch but barely touched the grounds.

Everything seemed peaceful. Quiet.

The interior, with so little furniture occupying it, seemed to stretch forever. The floor was silky beneath my feet. I touched my thigh, and the muscles felt relaxed, so in honor of my little dance that first time I'd been inside the house alone, I executed a sedate pirouette as I exited the sitting room.

All was well.

In the kitchen, I drank a glass of cool water, then stepped outside to the porch. I was high enough above the landscape that I felt safe—like being on a balcony above the masses—but not so removed I couldn't appreciate the scene. An owl cried from the trees. Something rustled among the flowers.

The moon sparkled on the water, blinking and shifting, and lit the field of flowers in a way that was abstract and disturbing—and mysterious and elemental too. There were secrets here. I didn't have the answers. And that was okay. I'd learned to let go a year and a half ago. To let go of Niles. My professional life. The baby I'd wanted. I'd had to let go of them when they were taken from me, and I'd done it so well that I'd also let go of everything left that mattered. I might as well be gazing blindly into the distance as my mother had done. Just sitting and staring. What else was my life about? Aside from helping my father, who could probably have managed well enough without me? Not much.

CHAPTER SEVEN

The next morning, I leaned against the doorway of the overflow room, eyeing the waiting boxes.

What would I do with the items that needed to be stored? Some of those boxes looked older than the others. If Dad hadn't unpacked them in years, maybe he didn't need what was in them.

What about long-term storage? We had a usable attic, or so Nicole had said.

I groaned, not in the mood for sorting and deciding.

As I procrastinated, I heard noises downstairs. Must be Dad. The boxes could wait.

My father wasn't suffering from the lack of energy that plagued me. He was busy unloading ladders and buckets and all sorts of tools, creating a trail of paraphernalia from the front door to the parlor.

"Dad, we're hardly in the house. We need to finish unpacking."

As he passed, carrying a step stool with the manufacturer's tags still attached, he said, "Tell me what you need me to unpack, and I'll take care of it."

I followed him into the parlor.

He said, "Figured I'd start here. It's a little more set off from public view, so less disruptive, don't you think? Plus, this paper is . . . well, it just needs to come down."

He spoke the truth. I found the cabbage roses disquieting. Also, and perhaps because of the enclosed nature of the room, the paper had absorbed stains and odors, including tobacco, which contributed to the mustiness.

I opened a window. "As much as I agree about this paper, I worry that its removal is too much for us to undertake."

"I can handle it."

"There's no way we can take all of this paper down. So many walls, including the foyer and stairwell, which we can't do unless you're willing to set up and climb scaffolding . . . or maybe you think we can do it on stilts? If we must hire people for the harder parts, then it makes more sense to hire them for the whole job."

He frowned. "No. This is what I want to do. This is part of my plan."

I shook my head. "I think you need to consider this from a business perspective. This is about practicality, reality, and skills."

He gave me a long, serious look before standing taller and pulling out a tape measure.

"I'm about to measure for blinds. You can help me. I need to special order them, so no point in waiting."

"Blinds? Blinds," I repeated. "They won't work in here at all. No blinds. Shades, maybe. Or spruce up the woodwork and clean the glass and leave the view open."

"No blinds?"

"Look at that view!" I swept my hand toward the window, then pulled it back. "Well, the view isn't so great now, but it will be when you get it cleaned up. We're so far from the road—why do we need anything covering these windows?"

He shrugged. "You make a good point."

"Of course I do. I'm your daughter." I earned a slight smile with that remark.

"Okay, then, Kara, you tell me where to start." He gestured toward the wallpaper. "I'm going to do this job. I'm going to remove the paper, then paint the room. The only question is, Where should I start?"

I sighed. "If you are determined to start on the wallpaper, then start in that corner. Then when you run into trouble—*if*, I mean—the fix will be easier."

"Minimizing risk? Is that your goal?"

I smiled. "Maybe."

"Well, my goal is to have fun. Isn't there a song about that?"

"The one that says girls just want to have fun?"

"That's it. Guys just want to have fun too."

"Go for it, Dad. But don't overdo. Be careful."

"I've got this, Kara. You'll see."

"Make sure you put plastic down to protect these floors."

"I've got it covered." He laughed again at his own wit. He added, "Don't forget the other furniture is coming this afternoon."

I shook my head.

"It's all good, Kara. The price is right, and it might work out well." He turned away, not waiting for a response, and went back to arranging his tools.

~

Procrastination wasn't going to unpack those boxes for me. I carried a glass of iced tea upstairs and emptied a few of the quicker cartons, like towels and other linens. I knew where to store those items.

What about the harder ones?

I opened the second-floor door to the back stairwell. These stairs were very different from the main staircase. The steps were narrow, but the handrail seemed sturdy. I made sure the door would stay open, and then I held the handrail and made my way up carefully to the attic. I'd left my cane behind. With this handrail, I thought I'd be okay.

When I opened the attic door, I was struck by the scene. There were walls, rooms presumably, and a hallway that was bright with daylight. The smell was slightly musty but not badly so.

I listened and was reassured. As with the stairwell door, I left this one open. I didn't want to get locked in.

The light was coming from the turret at the right front corner of the house. It was the same turret that provided a sitting area in my father's room and an interesting nook in our sitting room. The windows were dirty but still allowed in lots of natural light.

The rooms along the hallway were small and dark.

Who had stayed up here? Servants? Teachers for the school?

This wasn't like any attic I'd ever known.

In a house this large, we'd never do anything with this space, except use it for storage. There was plenty of room for our boxes. In fact, this vastness would dwarf them into nothing.

I felt the change in the air—a slight vacuum feel—more than heard the door close. The door wouldn't likely have closed on its own except for the air currents. Old houses, many doors—open one door, and it could start a current of air that would move throughout the house.

My imagination was freaking out a little, and I stepped quickly back to the door. It opened easily. I stuck my head out to see if anyone—maybe Dad—was there. Someone screamed.

It was a high, young scream that echoed up the stairs. Because of the closeted design of the stairwell, I couldn't see beyond the next flight of stairs and caught only a glimpse of corn silk hair before the sound of running footfalls—small, light feet—rebounded back up to where I stood.

"Maddie? Maddie Lyn?" I hurried down the steps to the second floor, afraid Maddie would take a header down the last flight of stairs in her haste, but I had to move carefully in case my thigh chose to freeze up.

What had frightened her? Was it Maddie who'd shut the door? Why?

As I turned at the second-floor level and started down the next set of stairs, I saw Seth standing at the bottom—the main-floor landing—halfway in the open doorway and already holding Maddie. She was clutching him in fright, her face buried in his neck. He was looking up the stairs.

"Kara?" he said, clearly as surprised to see me as I was to see him.

"Is she okay?" I asked, stopping midway down the flight, taking a moment to discreetly flex my leg.

He frowned and unhooked Maddie's arms from around his neck. "Maddie? Did you go upstairs?"

She didn't answer.

I said, "I was in the attic. I believe she shut the door not realizing I was in there."

Maddie's head moved as she whispered in Seth's ear.

"I understand." He put Maddie down, and when she was steady, he stepped away.

"Maddie Lyn, you owe Mrs. Hart an apology for going where you weren't supposed to go. This is her home, and we are guests. When you shut that door, you might have scared her. And you owe me an apology for not staying where you were supposed to."

"Oh, no, it's okay," I rushed to say.

"No, it's not." Seth shook his head. "This is a big house, Maddie. It's not your house. If you want to come with me when I go places, then you have to promise to do as you're told."

She nodded. "Sorry."

Seth said, "She closed the door. She said that when it came open again, she thought . . . she thought she'd made the ghost angry."

"The ghost?" I descended the last steps and, ignoring Seth, touched Maddie's chin and lifted it slightly so that our eyes met. "There's no ghost here, sweetie. And no harm done. But I agree with your Uncle Seth that it's not safe for you to wander on your own."

Maddie nodded, her eyes a little teary.

Seth said, "Go downstairs and play with your dolls. You made me bring all of them with us, so please go keep them company. The furniture will be here very soon."

Maddie went down the hall. I heard her footsteps pause, and then there were shuffling noises.

Seth was blocking the stairwell exit. Unintentionally, I was sure. I made a small movement to go around him, but he countered my move.

"I owe you an apology too. I'm sorry we barged in and surprised you like that."

"How were you to know I was in the attic? No harm done. I guess Dad let you in? He's probably wondering what all the noise is about."

"He *was* here, but now he's gone with Nicole. She dropped us off. They're going over to Sue Deale's place. They'll meet the guys with a truck over there to bring the furniture back."

I stopped short of saying something rude and crossed my arms instead.

"What's wrong?" he asked.

"Nothing. Or maybe I just don't understand."

"Understand what?"

"That furniture. Why is it coming back here? What's wrong with it, exactly?"

"It's just old. Her husband convinced her that if she didn't get rid of some of it, he'd leave."

"That's mean."

Seth shook his head with a small grin trying to grow on his face. "You'd have to see the situation with your own eyes to understand. When Sue inherited everything, she took every stick and scrap. Her house isn't all that big. Stuff is piled everywhere, including in her husband's shed, workshop, and garage. They can hardly walk in the house or any of the outbuildings. Her husband, Johnny, convinced her that letting some of it go back to the house was like creating good karma. Restoring the earth's balance. Almost poetic, really. I heard him go on about it. It was crazy, but Sue looked so relieved, like being let off the guilt hook. Restoring the earth's balance versus selling or junking the furniture seemed to release her from whatever was holding on to her. That's how it came to be that they contacted Nicole . . . and, well, the rest is history." He laughed.

So Sue Deale's problem was now mine.

Mentally, I kicked myself. Not my problem. Dad's. And he could handle it in any way he saw fit. Why did it annoy me so much? Did I have to control everything? An unhappy memory of that last evening with Niles ran through my mind.

Seth said, "I'll wait out front. They should be here soon." He added, "I'm sorry about Maddie. She saw the door open. It's not usually. She's always being told to close doors."

"What was that about a ghost?"

"I'm glad you told her there wasn't one. She's at that age. She's always imagining and making up things. She's very bright. She probably saw a show with a ghost on TV. Attics and basements are prime territory." He looked at me. "Which reminds me—you own a basement. Have you checked out the one here? You have, right?"

"I took a quick look."

"Basements—old basements, especially—can give people the creeps. I'll give you a tour of yours, if you like? It's good to know where the electrical panel is and how to handle the heating and AC system."

"That's kind of you, but I promise you if anything goes wrong that requires a trip into the basement, that will be Dad's responsibility."

"Chicken?"

"Me? Not hardly."

"Hey, even I get that watched feeling sometimes in basements and attics."

A loud banging noise came from the front of the house.

I pushed past Seth, calling out, "Dad? Are you okay?"

Seth was there beside me as I rushed up the hallway. The front door was open, and I saw Dad outside. He was standing beside a white panel truck. I stopped.

Seth put his hand on my arm. "He's fine. That was the back of the truck you heard. It bangs when they open the roll-up door." He took my hand. "Hey, are you okay? You're shaking."

"Shaking? I'm fine." And I shook off his hand, but not too roughly. "Sound travels funny on the breeze and through this house, I guess." I nodded. "Yes, I'm fine. Dad's fine." I looked down, then up at Seth. "Thank you."

"I'm going to check on Maddie Lyn and then go help with the furniture."

"Why don't I check on her?"

He seemed to consider. "That would be great. Give her a chance to know you better. I'd like to see her easier with people."

Maddie Lyn was in the corner of the sitting room, in that area of the turret. Seth or someone had placed a scatter rug over the hard floor. Maddie had a doll suitcase opened wide.

I walked over, then knelt on the floor beside her. I looked at Seth, smiled, and said softly, "I'll hang with Maddie for a little while."

He nodded and bowed out.

"Are you okay now?"

Maddie Lyn stared at her dolls. She wouldn't look at me or speak. I picked up a gown, full skirted and gauzy.

"This is fancy."

"It's a ball gown. For dancing."

"I see. Yes, it would be perfect for dancing."

She dug her little fingers into a small drawer in the case. When she opened her hand, she said, "Shoes."

"These pink shoes would look nice."

Maddie giggled and shook her head. "No." Her small shoulders moved with her giggle. She flashed me a shy smile. "The gold shoes."

"Of course. The gold shoes would be perfect."

"Kara, come see. I think you're going to like this."

It was Dad. He was standing in the opening between the foyer and the sitting room. He sounded so cheery I couldn't help smiling. Seth walked in behind him and picked up my smile and returned it.

He said to Dad, "They're coming through."

Both men stepped aside.

"I'll be right there, Dad. Excuse me, Maddie Lyn."

I pushed to my feet. It seemed a long way up, and my knees and shins weren't happy, but it wasn't due to the injury. It was the hard floor with an inadequate covering. Rugs, nice thick ones, moved up on my priority list.

Dad was in the foyer. He was running his hand along the top of a large piece of furniture, grinning at me as another man joined us.

This furniture looked old. Antique, yes, but not in a way that begged to be bought and displayed. More tired than vintage.

Nicole walked in. "Hi, Kara."

There was a china cabinet, and a sideboard stood next to it. Both pieces of furniture looked beyond ready to be retired, especially in contrast with our lovely floors. The walls, however, looked worse than the furniture. Small consolation.

Why were we moving furniture in before we'd dealt with the walls?

Because that was what Dad wanted.

An idea nibbled at the back of my brain. Did Dad want this because Nicole wanted it?

I said, "I think the china cabinet must go here, because it's the only place that huge piece will fit."

"I can tell you're thrilled," Seth said.

I shrugged.

At that point, one of the other men walked in. He was carrying the headboard of an old iron bedstead.

"Ma'am. Where do you want this?"

I shot Seth a quick look. "Really?" I told the man, "Upstairs. There's a bedroom near the top of the stairs . . . overlooks the front of the house. It's the empty room with the gray-striped wallpaper."

"Yes, ma'am. I'll find it."

As the headboard went past, I saw the bedstead and mattress and box spring following.

"Wait," I said. "Dad? Are we taking used mattresses too?"

"No worries. It's new. Nicole had a new set that she decided she didn't want. They're only a full size. She needed a softer, larger set."

"Lovely." I didn't even want to think about that revelation and what it might mean.

The parade of old used furniture depressed me. I didn't know why. It could've been worse. Maybe I preferred the potential of empty space. Unfulfilled potential, that was true. It was also true that this furniture was someone else's castoffs.

Nicole said, "It will look much better with some polish. A little care and cleaning will spruce it up and give it new life."

I looked at her.

"I have someone reliable who'll be happy to drop over and clean it up. It'll make all the difference in the world. You'll see!"

Dad included me in his grin as he walked out with Nicole. They stopped in the sitting room and chatted quietly.

I left Dad and Nicole and Seth. They seemed like a unit anyway. No one would even notice I was gone. I needed light and air. I fled down the grass path to the bench by the creek. This and the grotto were fast becoming my favorite spots. I savored the air, the scents, and the sounds. I leaned back against the bench and closed my eyes, raising my face to catch the air and feel it on my throat. Peace descended until a voice startled me. I jumped, nearly falling off the bench.

Seth grabbed my arm. "I'm sorry. I thought you were just sitting quietly. Didn't realize you were dozing."

I shook my head. "No need to apologize. I wasn't dozing. Not really."

"Are you okay?"

"I'm fine. I wanted fresh air."

"I think we, the Albers family, are overwhelming you. We're all new to you, so no wonder."

"You're my father's friends." To soften that, I added, "Mine, too, I hope."

"We are."

"I'm glad you and Nicole are here to help him . . . have been for a while, I guess? If he's content, that's what's important."

Seth looked doubtful. My sincerity score hadn't registered as high as I'd hoped.

He asked, "Do you seriously dislike the furniture? If you do, I can talk to Nicole. We'll haul it back out of here."

"It's not really my choice. This is my father's house."

"What about you?"

"Me? I don't know how long I'll be here."

There was a long moment of silence. Seth moved to the single chair. It was too small for him. He sat on the edge and leaned forward, his forearms on his thighs, his hands clasped. "Any idea how long you'll stay?"

I shrugged. "For a while. I'll help Dad settle in, and then we'll see." I tried to keep the tone light. Casual. My business was no one's but my own.

"Maddie's getting comfortable with you."

"Oh?" I was surprised by the change in subject but not unhappy. In fact, I was relieved. "She's very sweet. She was so serious about helping me to make the bed when we moved in but hardly spoke at all. Same with today. So quiet."

"Were you afraid when that door shut? You weren't, right? You don't strike me as someone who gets hysterical."

"Oh, well, sorry to disappoint. I've been known to lose my cool from time to time. As for today, no. I had a moment . . . but actually the attic is pretty interesting."

"Nicole had me sweep it out and knock down the cobwebs. Not that it was nasty or anything."

"Thank you for that." I wanted to change the subject. "About Maddie. How old is she?"

"She's almost five, but she's always around adults. She needs to spend more time with kids her age. She's shy until she isn't. Then she can talk your ears off."

"She's been raised well. It's easy to see she's loved and feels loved."

"It's a group effort."

"You indicated it's something you don't talk about—at least, not in front of Maddie."

"Patricia was the middle child. My sister. She died." He paused and looked away. "Sorry. Sometimes I remember how fast it happened, and it gets to me all over again. She had an aneurysm. No one knew until it went."

"I'm so sorry."

"Tragedy happens in lots of families. We're lucky we have each other for support and to care for Maddie."

"You're right about that. A close family can make a big difference."

"Maddie knows her mom is deceased, in here." He pointed to his head, then put his hand to his heart. "But not in here. She'll understand better when she gets older."

I wanted to look away. To object. To tell him some things didn't get easier to understand with age. Instead, I changed the subject. "You and I have something in common."

Sean gave me a short stare. "How so?"

"We both got interrupted. You with your career and me with mine."

He shrugged. "True enough. You're going back to yours eventually?"

"Aren't you?"

"I'm needed here."

"That won't last, though. At some point, you'll be wondering where the time went. You should keep your toes in the water, so to speak." I waved my hands. "I'm sorry. It's not my business. You know how to manage your life and your future."

"No worries. I get it. The world changes around us. One day, we open our eyes and . . ." He paused, then said, "It's good advice for us both."

"It's also easier to see when looking at someone else's life than one's own. Again, I'm sorry for butting in." I added, "I'd better get back to the house in case Dad needs me."

Seth nodded. Neither of us made a move to stand.

I sighed. "The furniture doesn't matter, really. As I understand it, it's our choice whether to keep it or get rid of it. That relative doesn't want it back, right?"

He shook his head no.

"So we'll see how it works out. If it doesn't work out, then we're free to find something else. Or not. Whatever." I waved a hand to show I didn't care. "As I said, it's Dad's decision anyway." Impulsively, I added, "Nice of Nicole to work it out for him. She's very dedicated to her job and clients." I said it with a twist and a wry smile as if to indicate there might be more to it than business and that I was no one's fool.

"They've known each other for a long time now."

"So he said." I forced that smile back on my face. Such good friends, yet Dad had never mentioned any of the Alberses to me. Or his dream of moving to the country. What else might he not have bothered to tell me? How had he had time to lead this secret life while so absorbed in his work?

Then it came to me. Perhaps all those days and late nights at work . . . maybe he wasn't only working.

No. I rejected that.

"Where do you live? The Albers clan, I mean? You said close by?"

"I don't think there's enough of us to qualify as a clan. But we're pretty easy to find." He pointed at the trees on the far side. "There's a path over that way, and it leads to the creek. You'll see a small bridge. We're on the far side of that bridge. Not much of a walk. Much farther to drive because you have to go back up to the main road and come back this way from that side."

A short walk through the woods and over the creek. Very handy, indeed. Finally, I stood. "I'd better get back."

"I'll walk with you, if you don't mind."

"Not at all."

As we approached the terrace, I saw that a modern cushioned settee and chair, along with end tables and a coffee table, were arranged there.

"Did you bring this outdoor furniture too?"

"Yes. But not from Sue's house. These are new. Your father asked me to pick them up and deliver them along with the rest."

"Thank you."

"Your father is talking about covering the pergola with either a true roof or an awning. He thinks you'll want to spend time out here."

The question hung there. I heard it in Seth's voice.

"I think it's better to sand and paint the frame and the arbor top. Maybe encourage something flowering to grow up there. At the least, hang a few potted flowering plants." I shook my head. "That's just my opinion."

I saw in Seth's eyes that he approved. He said, "He's ordered a grill. A big fancy one."

A grill? "To my knowledge, he has never cooked outside."

Seth laughed. "Then it's about time he did."

I matched his laugh, saying, "Maybe you're right."

I stopped and ran my hands along the top of the settee. I knew Dad intended this as a spot for me to do my needlework in. With a canopy of some sort, the filtered light would be just right. But not at the expense of obscuring the beauty of the pergola.

My needlework . . . not that I hadn't been busy otherwise with the move, and I still had work to do, but that was too easy to blame. Truth was since I'd been involved in Dad's move, I hadn't felt the least desire to pick up the hoop and needle. My half-finished canvas of daisies was languishing in the walnut cabinet.

It was a hobby. A hobby was an activity to be enjoyed when it was enjoyable. It wasn't a commitment.

"Give yourself a break," I muttered aloud. Great. Now I was talking to myself. I sighed.

"You okay?"

I'd forgotten Seth. How on earth had I managed that?

"I'm fine. Truly. Just thinking of things unfinished."

"And things interrupted?" He turned a bit serious. "If you don't mind me saying, better to think of things you'd like to do. Set your sights on the future. Like on a cookout. The rest will get taken care of . . . or not."

"Are you a philosopher in hiding, Seth?"

"No, ma'am. No philosophy. Just common sense."

CHAPTER EIGHT

The woman who showed up to clean the furniture arrived with a plastic laundry basket filled with cleaning cloths and polishes and who knew what else. I heard her truck pull up to the house and then saw her lifting the basket out of the back. The basket probably outweighed her. She was a tiny woman—petite and thin. But she gave me a smile and thanked me as I took the basket from her hands and carried it up the steps to the porch.

I reached the door and stopped to open it, silently giving myself a congratulatory mental pat on the back that I'd helped without even considering whether I might need my cane.

"Name's Mel," the woman said. "Did you know that already?"

"No, ma'am. I'm Kara. Pleased to meet you."

She looked old, but her appearance might have been misleading because there was no fat beneath the skin to plump it out. She moved with energy. She had short red-brown curls with a lot of gray threaded through them.

How could I stand by and allow this older woman to do the work I hadn't wanted to do? I controlled my guilt and said, "Please come in. I'll set the basket in here."

I led her to the dining room. I felt selfish and whiny. Why should this woman be tasked with doing what I could've—should've—done myself, except I was put out because I hadn't been consulted? Yeah, selfish and self-centered: that was me.

"I'm sorry. I should've done this work myself."

"You don't want me to do it? I can do the job well. I know how to clean and polish up old furniture."

"Oh, I'm sure you do. I'm not lazy, truly."

"Have you got a ladder?" She squinted at me. "Name's Kara, right? You spell that with a *K* or a *C*?"

"*K*."

"You have a low ladder or a step stool, Kara?"

"A step stool. Are you sure you want to do this?"

She frowned. "Happy to, so long as I'm paid to do it."

I had a moment of thinking I should fetch my wallet and give her money and send her home to . . . rest? I controlled myself.

"I'm sorry. You said Mel?"

"Short for Melanie." She ended on a short burst of laughter. "The step stool?"

"Be right back." I rushed to the kitchen and carried the step stool back to her.

"You walk okay as far as I can see."

"Pardon?"

"I heard you had a limp. An injury from that accident."

"It comes and goes." My face was growing warm. I gripped my hand to keep it from creeping up to that scar.

"Uh-huh. I got arthritis. Comes and goes too. Never quite goes all the way away. You reckon yours will?"

"Hard to know." I shrugged.

"Well, you're young yet. Likely it will."

I moved the step stool over to the china cabinet.

"I'm not complaining. It's better than it was, and it was a very serious accident, so a limp isn't such a bad thing." I saw no need to go into my other issues.

"You're right about that." Mel set her cleaner and rag on the top step of the three-step ladder and held tight to the top rail as she climbed up to the second step. "Hand me that polish, will you?"

"Certainly. Do you live around here?"

"Oh, yes."

"I thought you must. Nicole Albers assured me you do good work."

"She did, huh? Well, that's good—otherwise I might have to give her a talking-to."

I stopped for a moment, thinking. Not exactly the remark of someone who picked up piecework from someone else. A talking-to?

"I can tell by that look on your face you don't know she's my daughter."

I was still holding the bottle of polish. It smelled like lemon. "No, she didn't mention that. Just said she knew someone who'd take the job."

"Uh-huh."

"I'm sorry, Ms. Albers."

"Call me Mel, honey." She was looking away from me, applying the rag and the cleaner with elbow grease. "It's all good. The exercise is good for me, and I like having pocket money I'm not answerable to anyone for." She glanced at my face. "Don't be thinking my kids don't take care of their mama. It's not true. They would do entirely too much. I like feeling independent. I don't fool myself that I really am, or even could be at this point in my life, but I hold up my head and pretend."

"Then I'm delighted to support that."

"Let me know if you have any other jobs that need doing."

"Will do." I smiled. "I think we'll stay away from chopping logs and such."

"Oh, don't underestimate me. I'm small but tough." She stepped down to move the cleaning materials and stool to the other end of the china cabinet.

I moved to intervene and do the lifting for her, but she waved me away. "I've got this," she said.

"Yes, ma'am." I stepped back and clasped my hands politely together.

She gave me a sharp look. "Are you putting me on?"

"What do you mean?"

"The way you talk. You don't talk like any other woman your age that I know."

I shook my head. "I don't understand."

"Not sure I can explain it. Word for word . . . it's fine. They're good words. But you put them together like . . . not prissy, but more like a put-on air. I'm not criticizing. It sounds good, just different."

Loud laughter sounded behind me. A woman said, "Oh, Kara's talked that way for as long as I've known her."

Mel looked up at the newcomer, and I spun around.

"Victoria! What a surprise. How'd you find me out here?"

She crossed the floor, tossing her dark, curly hair back over her shoulder, removing her sunglasses with a certain flair, and taking in everything around us in a sweeping glance. As she closed for a hug, I noted her black knit slacks and heels, topped with a crisp white blouse. She pressed her cheek to mine for a quick second, still talking. "Sorry for inviting myself in. The door was open, and I heard your voice. Decided to surprise you! First by coming and then by sneaking up on you."

I turned back to Mel. "This is an old friend of mine. Here to surprise me."

"Yeah, so I heard." She refolded the now-dirty cloth. "I'd better get back to work."

"Mel, can I get you some water or tea?"

"I'll help myself in a little while, if that's okay?"

"That's perfect. Excuse me while I visit with Victoria?"

She grunted and resumed working the wood cleaner into the surface of the cabinet.

I took my friend's arm. "This way," I said.

We made it as far as the foyer before Victoria blurted out, "What is this mausoleum? I can't decide whether it's amazing or just amazingly old."

I cringed at her words, her voice, and the way they seemed to travel through the house, dispelling any harmony along the way. Would her words bother me so much if Mel weren't here? Was Mel offended? Maybe it was the house I felt protective of.

In a deliberately low, calm voice, I said, "I've had doubts of my own, but I'm becoming a convert. I'll show you around while you tell me how you happened to show up here."

"Oh, no secret there. I called your father. He gave me directions."

"He didn't say a word."

"It was earlier today, so he probably isn't even back home yet. He was out somewhere having lunch with someone."

"I think he's just running errands."

"He was speaking to someone named Nicole while we were on the phone."

"Oh, well, she's the real estate agent he was working with. And a friend," I added.

I was glad we were upstairs at that point. Mel probably hadn't overheard Victoria, I reassured myself, but what if she had? Likely, she already knew my father and her daughter were having lunch together. No one bothered telling me anything—that was for sure.

"So anyway, I'd planned to visit you soon, and it's a gorgeous day for a drive, so I decided to come on along." She peeked into the rooms as we walked along the hallway. "You've got lots of room here. I can't imagine what you're going to do with it."

"Do with it? Me? Nothing. I'll help Dad settle in, but I'm not staying. It's time for me to go back to work and find my own place."

There was a long moment of silence, uncharacteristic of Victoria. Was she thinking of Niles? We three had been good friends in college and continued that into our adult lives in the DC beltway. She was the only friend I could claim, really. But I hadn't told her I was moving. What did that say about me?

"I'm sorry I didn't think to tell you about the move. It happened so fast. Dad surprised me."

Victoria walked into my room. There wasn't much to see, so she went to the window.

"That's a gorgeous view. Very rustic."

"The flowers," I said.

"The flowers, the trees, the river . . ."

"Not a river. That's a creek. Cub Creek. It's just wider here."

"Whatever. There must be something you can do with a place like this. After you get it fixed up, you can probably rent it out for weddings and such. People do that a lot with these big old monsters."

Hearing her say the word *monsters* threw me. I objected, "It's a nice house with lots of old-fashioned charm and modern amenities."

"In the middle of nowhere." She shook her head and turned away from the window. "That's the worst part."

Middle of nowhere. I'd had that same thought. I said, "That's also a virtue. Out of the city . . . peace and quiet . . . beautiful landscape. Or will be. We do have work to do."

"But you won't be here. You said you're leaving."

"Not until Dad is settled. Besides, he can hire people to do that work for him. I'm not of much use when it comes to labor of that sort."

"Not with your injuries, certainly. How are you feeling these days? Better? I see you're still carrying that cane around."

Yes, I was clutching my cane, suddenly feeling the need of it. Perhaps I shouldn't have been so quick to carry Mel's basket up those steps. I'd overdone it.

"Getting better all the time. Actually, I haven't been using my cane all that much lately."

"Who is this Nicole person?" Victoria snagged my sleeve between her thumb and forefinger. She leaned closer to me. "Not so fast. I saw your face. You forget how well I know you."

"I told you. Nicole is our real estate agent. She also helped Dad find his last house, so they've known each other awhile. She's been very helpful." I stopped short of mentioning Seth and Maddie. Victoria didn't need to know every detail.

She led the way down the steps and out to the terrace. She sat on the lounge cushions, testing them, then leaned back. "What a view. I think the flowers are past their prime, though. Are they wild?"

"Yes, I'm not an expert, but I recognize a few."

"Uh-huh," Victoria said, apparently satisfied. "I'll bet you get deer through here. Maybe even bear or other wildlife?"

"Deer. I've only seen deer. I've heard coyotes a few times at night, though."

Victoria bounced up from the lounge, and we struck off down the grassy side path. As she walked along, she ran her hand in the flowers, like one might through water in a canoe, and even swept her hand through them roughly a few times.

"They aren't dead yet. Take it easy on them, would you?"

She stopped and pivoted to face me. "You like these flowers, right? I do too. I'm just less sentimental." She smiled and hooked her arm through mine and drew me along with her.

I asked, "What about your job? Are you taking vacation days? How's your mom?"

Victoria was from Richmond, though I hadn't known her before college because we came from different areas of town and attended different elementary and high schools. When Victoria came to Richmond, it was to visit her mom.

"She's fine. Always good. She's after me to move back to town. Says she never gets to see me."

"That's true enough, right?"

"Yes, and the job is great. They love me. Always going on about what a star I am. But it gets old, you know? And frankly—I don't say this to make you feel sad—it just isn't the same up there without you and Niles."

I cast about for something reasonable to say and came up empty.

"So anyway, I decided to take a few days off. See you, spend time with Mom. Though you almost gave me the slip. Good thing I had your dad's cell number."

"You could've called mine."

"I did call you. You didn't answer. You've never been reliable about catching calls or checking voice mail. Guess that hasn't changed. In fact, I bet you don't have your phone with you now, do you?"

I slapped my empty pockets. "Right you are."

"More often than you'd like to admit," she said with a big Victoria grin and a loud laugh.

I joined her in laughter and hugged her, saying, "I'm glad you drove over here."

We'd passed the end of the flowers and reached the grassy area that went to the creek and stretched from tree line to tree line. Victoria turned and looked back up toward the house. She gave a low whistle.

"Nice. Very nice. I see potential. And these grounds . . . they were terraced. The flowers . . . they're beautiful, but why would anyone grow them in a big patch like this? What about an in-ground pool or a tennis court? What will you do when the flowers have finished blooming?"

"Plant more."

"Will you be here?" She gave me a surprised look.

"Oh. Well, no, not indefinitely."

"What will your dad do, do you think?"

"Why do you care, Victoria? What do you have against flowers anyway?"

"Nothing. But these aren't real flowers. These are *wild*flowers. Weeds."

I stepped away involuntarily. I looked at her face, examining her expression. "Are you serious?"

"Absolutely. Wildflowers and weeds. Sure, they're pretty in their way, but they're unreliable. Grow roses or tulips. Real flowers. You can even batch them and sell the bouquets."

I put my hand on the back of the bench. I needed to do something with my hands. I found Victoria's manner exhausting. Her attitude could be overwhelming. She was such an "absolutely" kind of person. Her heart, though, was in a good place. She'd been a good friend to me and Niles. I pushed away from the bench and pressed my hands together. I could've shown her the nooks and crannies—the special spots in the yard that Mary had arranged—but I didn't want to. Not today. Not with Victoria in this especially "absolutely" mood. The light was glinting off the surface of the creek. I closed my eyes and turned away from the water. The last thing I needed right now was one of those headaches.

"I should get back to the house in case Mel needs me."

"Mel? The lady who's polishing the furniture?"

"Yes."

"You don't have much furniture."

"We have what we need, and there's no rush to fill up the house." As we neared the house, I asked, "How long are you in town?"

"A few days."

"Can I offer you something to drink? Tea? Or a sandwich?"

"Nah. I'd better head back to town. Mom's expecting me for supper."

"Oh, sorry. Come back if you can."

"Oh, I will. No worries there. This place is fascinating."

I knew she wanted a dinner invite—if not for today, then for tomorrow or the next day. I could feel the expectation emanating from her. I grabbed my lower lip between my teeth and refused to let the words out.

With a slight frown, Victoria walked up the steps ahead of me and into the house. "This kitchen is awful."

I nodded. "Yes, it is."

"Well, pull out a bucket and fill it with suds, and I'll get to work. I don't mind scrubbing at all. It's helpful to you and cheaper than the gym." She laughed. "Mom will understand."

"Thanks, but no need. We'll hire people to handle it. I'm still trying to decide what I want done in here, anyway."

"Does it matter?"

"What?"

"You're leaving. You said so. I think you're conflicted. Are you coming back to the DC area? Maybe back to your old job?"

"No." I shook my head, perhaps with too much emphasis. "I'll probably stay in the Richmond area or maybe Virginia Beach or even Charlottesville. I'll look for something in project management since that's where my experience and expertise lie. But I'm not done here yet." I walked away from Victoria and stopped in the center of the room. "It's not just the dirty paint or a century of grease stains . . . the whole balance is off in here. It's hard to come in this room and focus on cooking." I turned back to her. "So it needs to be done right."

Victoria gave me a funny look, and I ignored her. I walked past her and into the dining room through the kitchen entrance. I'd kept that door closed, so I'd thought our conversation was relatively private, but someone had opened it. Probably Mel.

The chairs were all moved away from the dining room table, and Mel was on her knees working on the table legs.

"How's it going?" I asked.

"Oh, fine." She straightened up and asked, "What do you think?"

Victoria walked past me to the china cabinet. "Looks good. Wood has a nice glow now. The patina shows." She put her hands on her hips. "Of course, it's not high-end furniture, and no amount of elbow grease will make it that. Still, it's usable."

There was a watchful expression on Mel's face and in her posture.

I said to Victoria, "The furniture came with the house belatedly. It belonged to the former owners. They lived here for a long time. Also, we have them to thank for the flowers in the backyard."

"Really? Nice that the furniture has a story to go with it." Victoria threw the words out quickly, then shrugged, saying, "I've got to run. When should I return for a longer visit?"

"Why don't I come into town? We can meet for lunch. Maybe take your mom out with us."

She really looked at me this time. She cocked her head like a bird listening to a strange call while trying to identify and decipher it. She said, "I'd rather come here. I'd love to see your father too. He's such a nice man."

Typical Victoria. Wanting it her way and no doubt with something on her mind.

"I'll check his schedule with him and be back in touch."

I walked her out to the porch and the driveway, where she'd parked her car. As she drove away, I felt odd. I stood quietly trying to identify my problem but couldn't. Was it even unusual? Not really. There had always been something abrasive about Victoria. And yet her very openness, her brashness, often made me laugh. Sometimes it cleared the air like a thunderstorm on a sultry day.

I sat on the porch in the rocker and wondered how many other butts had parked themselves here over the years.

Mel came outside carrying her basket. She set it down on the porch. "I figured it out," she said.

"Figured out what?"

"The way you talk. You sound like a teacher, like some professor or maybe a diplomat, if you know what I mean."

"You mean polite?"

"No." She shook her head. "I wouldn't say you sound all that polite."

I stood. "I don't have a clue what you mean."

"Like how you choose your words precisely. No messy blabbing. You speak each syllable like it's important all on its own."

"Is that a bad thing?"

"Not if it works for you."

I gave her a long look. "My friend—Victoria—is more . . . she's livelier than I am."

"Not for me to say, but I will anyway because I'm a mother who's raised kids—now grown kids, though that doesn't seem to make much difference—and I've seen how they act and how their friends act. She's a lot more than most, in a number of ways. At least that's my take on it after being around her for a short time. She might be hard of hearing, too, because she sure does talk loud."

I picked up Mel's basket.

"Should you be toting that around? I saw you with that cane."

"It's feeling better now." I shook my leg as if to demonstrate. "Sometimes it just stiffens up."

"That so?"

"That's so." I carried Mel's basket down the steps to her car. As we were loading her supplies into the hatchback, I heard another car.

"What do you mean, 'more than most'?"

"Just more. Big personality, maybe. I'll think on it and let you know." She added, "Check out my work when it's convenient. That furniture looks as good as anyone can make it. But if you aren't satisfied, let my boss know."

I laughed. "You mean your daughter?"

She answered with her own laugh.

"It wouldn't have been my choice in furniture, but I'm sure you did a fine job."

"See, there you go. Most would say, 'I don't like it,' or 'It'll do.' You used sixteen words when four or less would serve."

I frowned, counting on my fingers. "Eighteen words if you count the contractions as two."

Mel laughed. That tiny woman laughed like a drunken lumberjack. My mouth gaped, and she laughed louder. Finally, I laughed too. It was funny. I'd meant the counting as a joke, but the last, and biggest, laugh was hers.

"I know now. I know exactly where you get it from. Henry."

"Get what?"

"The way you talk. Like he talks. He's your dad. Makes sense, doesn't it?"

She left me in the dust, literally, as she drove away. There wasn't much dust, actually, and I wasn't bothered about being the source of her humor. It amused me, though I wasn't quite sure why, so when Dad pulled up in front of the house, I waited. As he climbed out of the truck, I said, "We need to enlarge our parking area. Maybe even hire someone to direct traffic."

He took some paper grocery bags from the truck bed. "Was that Mel Albers leaving? How does the furniture look?"

"Yes, as to Mel. I haven't seen the results, but it was looking good last I saw it. Victoria left about thirty minutes ago."

He raised his eyebrows. "Yes, she called. Wanted to know where you'd moved to. You don't sound pleased. I thought you liked her."

"She's fine. Just unexpected."

"I didn't know she was coming here today."

We walked up the steps together, and I held the door open for him.

He said, "You don't look pleased. Is something wrong?"

"Nothing's wrong. Maybe it isn't even her. Maybe it's the associations I have with her. The memories." I rubbed my forehead. "Maybe the problem is me. Not her at all."

Dad walked straight through to the kitchen, apparently ignoring my maybes. "I brought those cabinet brochures you asked for. Let me know when you decide what you want. Takes a while to get special orders."

I let it go too. "Is there a budget?"

"No budget. You're a reasonable person. Make us a nice kitchen."

It warmed my heart. He trusted me in terms of both taste and money. "Will do, Dad."

CHAPTER NINE

I was unpacking the boxes of sheets and assorted linens in the overflow bedroom when I realized two nearby boxes, the ones I'd noticed earlier that looked older, had something written on their sides in faded blue marker. A name.

With a stack of folded towels in my arms, I moved closer. The name was Susan.

The towels fell to the floor, forgotten.

These boxes must've been in Dad's attic. For how long? Who had packed these? It must've been Dad.

I cast a quick look back at the door, my mouth open, ready to call his name, to ask him. But he was off running errands, and what was there to ask? Other than why hadn't he said anything about these? I knew the answer to that question.

I took a quick look at the other boxes. There were only two with my mother's name on them.

Two boxes with my mother's name. Susan. How remarkable and unexpected was that?

Excited yet apprehensive, I knelt on the floor and placed my hands on the cardboard. It was surprisingly warm.

What would a man choose to save of his wife's life? She'd left behind almost everything from her married life. To Dad, what would seem worthy of boxing up and keeping? There might be items from her before-married life too.

Mom's long heavy hair swirled before my closed eyes. I remembered her scent and heard her laughter, distant but happy sounding, and then, in a later memory, I saw her face more clearly but heard her silence. The silence wasn't truly silent. It was the sound of my mother sitting in the kitchen and staring into nothingness.

I leaned forward, my arms on the top of the box, and I bent my head toward them, pressing my forehead against my forearms, feeling the warmth of my flesh on flesh instead of cardboard.

A woman's life. A mother's life. At least, what would fit into two boxes. A person's life should defy containment. And two boxes were nothing . . . but more than I'd had and maybe more than I'd ever get of her.

Steeling myself for disappointment, I pulled the tape from the box flaps. I pushed aside the flaps, almost expecting to smell her scent, the memory of how it smelled to be held in her arms and consoled or celebrated. Those were early memories. My earliest. I held my breath and touched a sweater. It was carefully folded in the top of the box and somewhat smooshed. I didn't recognize it, but when I lifted it from the box, I saw a small photo book below it. The kind with clear plastic page sleeves. And there were photos.

I sank back to the floor again, away from the box. I opened the album cover and saw my mother holding a baby. It could only be me. A newborn. Mom was so young. Her hair was lank, but she was smiling, and she looked like she'd made a herculean effort to produce an infant. My life was her triumph and my prize. She had gone through labor to gift me with life.

She looked victorious.

And proud. At least for a while, I supposed.

I held that small album to my chest and closed the box flaps. The rest could wait a moment longer. My heart hurt. I stood, moving like an old woman, my thigh protesting and the scar on my face twinging as if the nerve endings were still exposed. I moved toward the window, following the path between the boxes, and stood in the warmth of the sunlight.

My fingers hurt where the plastic edges of the album bit into them. I loosened my grip.

Where had Mom's life taken her before death had caught her in Ohio? Had she found what she'd been lacking at our house, our home, out there somewhere?

Yes, Dad and I had managed well enough, but it hadn't been the same without her.

Like a game of pretend, over the years I had enjoyed thinking of her out there somewhere, laughing and happy. Even if it couldn't be with me, her daughter, I wanted her to have found happiness. She'd had two years. What had she done with them? What had she accomplished?

The boxes drew me back like magnets. I went through the rest of the opened box. It was mostly clothing. A few items of jewelry were wrapped in a scarf and tucked between a sweater and a dress. I laid the jewelry aside carefully. It didn't look unusual or expensive, but its stay in the attic might have loosened the glue on the brooch or pins or dry-rotted the string holding the necklace beads together.

As with the first box, the second box held an assortment of clothing, an old tin of scented powder, a pair of heels, and such. I thought I might remember her wearing that blouse. I wasn't sure. The shawl was a dressy one that had probably been worn on a special occasion. Below the clothing was a large, fat manila envelope. I lifted the flap and looked inside. It was filled with sheets of rumpled wax paper. I slid them out and, surprised, lost my grip. The pages scattered on the floor.

Flowers. Pressed flowers. Wildflowers. Cultivated flowers. I saw a daisy. One page was a series of rose petals. Even autumn leaves.

I picked up the page that had fallen closest to me.

My mom had pressed all these flowers and leaves? She must've done it when I was very young—or maybe even before I'd arrived. Perhaps before Dad had come along. Because otherwise, I would've remembered her doing this.

What about my needlework? Was there a connection? Had I been recreating these? Not fully remembering but having a subconscious recollection?

I set the pressed flowers aside for now, tidied the piles of clothing, and then stood, again holding the small photograph album. I'd finish the second box later. I needed air now. Fresh air. I went straight to the grotto, for privacy and for peace.

Seth had introduced me to this spot. Where the gazing ball once had been and was no longer. A place of things gone. Of things lost. There were straggly rosebushes in the sunnier fringe and rhododendrons deeper in. Between them, I thought I recognized azaleas and hostas. Azaleas reminded me of my mother, and the nearby creek made gentle music.

The cover of this album, like its pages, was plastic. The plastic tried to look like fake embossed leather and failed, but it was durable. Case in point, I was sitting here many years later with it in my hands. I held it open to that first picture again, the one I'd glimpsed of my mother holding me, her newly born daughter. I examined her face again. That woman. I'd known her, though she looked different here than I remembered. Her face was fresher. No makeup. Her hair was disheveled. I guessed she'd never looked nor felt more beautiful in her life. I thought my father must be behind the camera because there was a look in Mom's eyes of shared triumph as she smiled at the camera and held me close.

I bit my lip and turned the page.

The next photo was of a baby in a hospital bassinet. It was the clear molded-plastic kind, and a piece of white cardboard with my statistics was attached to the end. I was swaddled in a blanket and sleeping. A hand was touching the side of the bassinet. My mother's hand? I didn't know. Perhaps a nurse. Someone who'd paused long enough for another proud-parent photo to be snapped.

I looked away. One of the grotto azaleas had purple blossoms. It had been neglected. Other growth had edged in. I wasn't a horticulturist, but I could guess that things like fertilizer and bug spray had been withheld, yet the blooms were still beautiful. How much more beautiful might the blooms have been if cared for? Too much care, however well meant, could also be harmful.

The next picture was of me in a small crib, homey and cozy, and surrounded by a small stuffed bear, a pacifier, a rumpled baby blanket. It could've been any baby anywhere, but it was me, and there was only love in this picture, nothing more exceptional than that. Nothing that warned of unhappiness to come.

I heard footsteps. They crunched on a stick or some other earthy debris on the stone steps, and I looked up.

"Kara. There you are. Are you okay?"

I nodded. "I'm fine." I held out the book. "Look what I found."

"Oh," Dad said. "The boxes."

"I found them in the overflow bedroom."

"I told the movers to put them there for you."

"But you never mentioned them to me."

He shrugged and massaged his hands. "No. I intended to. Didn't want to get your hopes up, maybe, and disappoint you. There are only a few things. I made sure to keep those photos for you."

Thank you hovered on my lips but didn't seem to fit the moment. "You should've told me, Dad."

"Maybe."

I grunted in disagreement. "How can you say that?"

"Because sometimes the unknown is better than the known. Sometimes it's good not to have a question answered. One thing I do know: it's hard to be the person making decisions like that for someone else."

I shook my head. "It's always better to face the truth."

Dad looked at me with doubt all over his face. "Are you sure about that?"

"I am." Yes, those were brave words. They should be true. Should.

"Then I apologize for not telling you about them sooner."

I sighed. Dad went silent. He looked away, and there was something very sad about the sudden slope of his shoulders.

I reached out to touch a nearby branch of a flowering bush. I pulled it toward me and sniffed the scent of a waxy white bud, trying to stay calm, to allow the tension to ease out of this moment we were in. I released the branch gently and said, "I remember when her belongings started to disappear. She'd been gone awhile already, and I guess we'd both accepted she wasn't coming back. I snooped around and found you'd put some of them in the spare closets and up in the attic, so . . . so anyway, I was relieved because I still hoped . . ." I shrugged. "Well, you know . . . that she'd return. Funny how I forgot those things were up in the attic. I probably assumed you'd gotten rid of them when you moved to the new house. Until I saw the boxes with her name on them."

"After you left for college, I started going through, trimming it down, trying to decide what to keep for you. I didn't know how to make those judgments." After a long pause, he added, "I hope I made some good choices."

"I'm surprised you didn't tell me about them before."

"Are you?"

"No, not really. It was always difficult for us to discuss her and what went wrong." I patted the album. "I would like to know the truth, though, at least as much of the truth as we can understand without her here to fill in the blanks."

"I suspect you'll be disappointed, Kara, in what I can tell you. Disappointed even in my actions back then. I hope you'll remember that we are all human. That includes me. Looking back, I can see where I might have done things better. Maybe it would've made a difference.

I don't know." He glanced again at the album in my hands. "Baby pictures. You were a beautiful baby. Your mother was so proud."

"What went wrong?"

"Wrong? Nothing." He shrugged. "The doctors called it postpartum depression. Said it wasn't uncommon and would pass soon. It felt uncommon to us. Susan would look at me, hopeless and scared, and I didn't know how to fix it. It did pass. I was glad. But it didn't stay gone. Seemed like that first time opened a door. Or maybe she'd been that way before, and I just hadn't known."

He shook his head. "Business is easy. It's like a puzzle or math. You move the pieces and make decisions, and it either works or doesn't. If it doesn't, then you back up or try something else. Life is different. It's messy." He squeezed his hands together. "Are you okay, Kara?"

Dad was staring at me, and I realized I was rubbing the scar with my free hand. There was pressure but no pain. I dropped my hand to my lap.

"You looked . . . tired." He met my eyes. "Has this move been too much on you?"

"No." I wouldn't try further to explain how battered I felt. He was trying. He'd packed those boxes and kept them for me. That was something. It was important. "How did you know I was out here?"

"I saw you through the back window. You weren't . . . you weren't moving like yourself. Seemed like you vanished into the greenery."

I touched his hand. "I'm fine, Dad."

Dad waved toward the yard. "Have you checked out the other sitting areas?"

"Some. But all of this is like one huge garden in need of attention. Do we have the right tools for that? Pruning shears and such?"

Dad smiled. "I have larger shears and a shovel and rake, but you're right. We need smaller ones for finer work. Fertilizer, too, probably. I've got a list I'm keeping."

"I think I'm going to lie down for a while."

"Sure. I'll walk you back to the house."

About halfway to the house, he put his hand on my arm, and I stopped with him. He held up one hand and asked, "Hear that?"

I listened, and sure enough, I did hear. It wasn't just the butterflies who enjoyed the wildflowers. The bees had arrived. Had they been here since that first day, and I hadn't noticed? Not likely. They'd been here but not in these numbers. As I listened, their buzzing seemed to grow louder.

"I hear them."

We resumed walking up the slope. Dad spoke, but in a more hushed tone. "I think this place is missing a fountain." He cupped his hands together as if demonstrating. "A small one, but one that the birds will enjoy. Also, did you know that bees get thirsty? I read something the other day about fixing little water dishes, shallow, with smooth, rounded rocks in the bottom. You place the water dishes near the plants that bees like."

I looked at him. "Who are you, and what have you done with my father?"

Dad laughed. The hushed tone was gone, and his unabashed laughter undid me.

I tried to laugh with him but failed. Instead, I turned my face away. I went directly upstairs, intent on reaching my room so I could close the door and breathe again.

My earth felt like it was quaking. A mild tremor. But enough to rattle me.

Dad knew about bees. Dad had spoken about water dishes for thirsty bees as if it were a real thing. Something noteworthy. But he couldn't discuss my mother.

I stood with my back against the door for a long minute until something pinched my finger. It was the sharp edge of the photo album. I was still holding it.

He'd violated something. What? A tremor hit me. I squeezed my eyes shut.

We'd always had an unspoken, unacknowledged bargain. Had we adopted it instinctively, or had it developed over time? Until this moment, I hadn't even realized it existed. The bargain was that I didn't ask him awkward questions that he didn't want to hear or deal with, and he rarely said no to me and never criticized me.

Today, that bargain, that treaty, had cracked a bit, and I'd gotten a glimpse of my mother. Only a little and many years later than it should've happened. But it *had* happened. And while I was stepping so carefully, dancing around our tender feelings, Dad had grown soft-hearted over thirsty bees.

Were we truly that fragile? Maybe. And maybe that was why we wore such thick protection. We'd moved the bar a little today. We'd both survived. Suppose I had pushed it sooner?

Who was protecting whom? Was I protecting Dad? Or my own psyche?

It was progress. Next time, and there would be a next time, I would push harder. For both our sakes.

I crossed to the bed and sank onto the mattress.

I flipped through the first photos, the ones I'd already seen, and then saw the next. Mom. Smiling. But her eyes looked sad. Postpartum depression? Maybe. I felt sympathy for her. If that was the case, I could imagine that my father would not have understood why she was sad and confused in what should've been a joyful time. It would not have fit with his logic.

The next photo showed flowers. Lots of flowers. The fence looked like the one in our old backyard, the one from my childhood. I didn't remember flowers being there. Mom must not have kept them up. By the time I'd been old enough to retain the memory, the flowers had been gone.

I dropped the album on the bed and went to the windows. I opened them as wide as possible, then also opened the windows in the two rooms nearest mine. I left those doors open to encourage a breeze and set boxes in front of them like huge doorstops. The views were amazing. The air flowing through was invigorating. Soon I was feeling restored again. Restored to goodwill, restored to optimism. I returned to the overflow room and dropped to my knees beside the second box.

There was a layer of clothing that might've meant something to my dad, but not to me. I pressed my face into a blouse but couldn't detect any scent. But under that layer of clothing were baby garments. A delicate yellow dress. Small soft white shoes. A silver rattle, the gift kind not really meant for play. The engraving spelled out my name and birth date. I set these items aside. Near the bottom of the box was a large heavy-duty plastic zipper bag. Within it a dress had been folded and secured. White satin.

I pressed my hands against the clear plastic, acknowledging the seed pearls and the lace and what this must have represented on my parents' wedding day. Joy? I hoped so. I could imagine my dad standing tall and proud and looking sure on that day. I lifted the gown from the box and found one more thing—a large framed photographic portrait of a bride.

I put the gown aside and carried the portrait into my bedroom. I placed it on the fireplace mantel. Next to it, I put the small framed photo of Mom and me together. On the other side, I added one from my own wedding taken with my father.

A sham family? Maybe. Maybe a little make-believe was okay. Or perhaps it was about hope and respect for what might have been.

That portrait of my mother would end up downstairs, maybe in the sitting room, maybe the parlor. But it wasn't the kind of thing I wanted to surprise Dad with. He wouldn't object—he wouldn't deny me—but regardless of whom I was trying to protect, him or me, such consideration came down to love.

CHAPTER TEN

Our family home had been a large two-story colonial. It was pretty generic and had lots of space, especially since I was the one-and-forever-only child. Our second home (the second home I shared with Dad, that is) had been newer, modern, and pleasing to the eye but wouldn't know a nook or cranny if it came labeled. The bits and pieces that we'd hung on the walls or arranged on a mantelpiece or shelving just didn't quite look right in this house. Skipping the small apartment in the DC beltway area that I'd shared with Niles, of course, this house—which by now I officially thought of as the wildflower house—was the third home I'd shared with my father.

But we had barely begun the renovation. By the time we finished updating and painting, maybe our modern bric-a-brac would fit better.

I was trying to hang a metal art piece. It was large, and we'd both liked it at the last house, but here . . . not so much.

"It's fine," Dad said.

"No, it doesn't fit with the house. Maybe it's the wallpaper."

"It's fine," he repeated. "Leave it for a few days, and see what you think. Give it a chance."

I snorted. "You're just tired of messing with it. You want me to stop and move on."

"Which is another good reason to let it hang there for a few days." He stepped into the sitting room. "Besides, I have something for you. Nicole sent it as a housewarming gift."

"For me?" I asked. "It's your house, your gift."

He handed me a fancy box with a flashy red bow on top. "She meant this for you."

The box was large enough to be awkward. I set it on the dining room table and worked the top off to find a layer of white tissue paper protecting and cushioning something. My curiosity was engaged. I pushed the paper aside to reveal a vase. A blue glazed ceramic vase. When I pressed my fingertip against it, I half expected it to sink into the shiny depths. Impossible, of course, but somehow the glaze, combined with the texture and modulated surface, gave it a liquid look—a sense of depth.

I lifted the vase, carefully freeing it from the box and paper. I looked at the base and saw a mark, like a trademark, carved along with the words **Cub Creek Pottery**.

"Cub Creek? Really?" I smiled. "This is locally crafted pottery?"

He nodded. "Nicole said the potter is a woman who lives farther down along Cub Creek." He motioned with his hand. "South of here."

I walked out of the dining room and into the front room, stopping in front of the mantel to place the large vase on it. Even as I pulled my hands away, I was tempted to touch that textured, gleaming surface again—just in case it was suddenly as ephemeral as it looked. When the light from the front window hit it, I realized there was a subtle figure shaped into the clay where the vase was widest. Only visible in the right light, it was childlike, with large, intricate wings.

"It's exquisite. I'd love to see her other work."

"I got the impression that Nicole knows her well. I'm sure she can work it out."

"Maybe after you've finished the renovation. After we understand the look you're going for in here. If I'm still here."

"Kara, we've had this conversation before. For me, it's about having a place to live. A place for projects. I have no sense of style. The only things I ever decorated were tire displays. I appreciate your help."

"My pleasure. I'm grateful for all you've done for me too."

"Done?" He frowned. "I was glad to be able to help after the accident, but I don't think I deserve any special credit."

"Dad."

He looked concerned, showing that same old discomfort when the conversation got touchy. I'd seen it so many times through the years. That bargain of ours, I thought.

"It's about Mom."

He stared at me.

I kept my voice low and warm. Kind. I didn't want him to shut up. "I've gone through both of those boxes, Dad. It's time. I want to hear about Mom. Who she was, how she was. How you two met. The stories that are shared in every other family."

"We just talked about her, Kara. I can't imagine what else there is to say."

"We've only discussed her in the briefest terms. I appreciate that you told me about her depression, but there's so much more I want to know."

He shrugged, saying, "Well . . ."

"Please, Dad. I'm not getting any younger, and neither are you. There's no better time than now."

He shook his head and waved his hands. "We have a lot of work to do."

"I'll get you a cup of coffee. I'm thirsty myself. You sit down. When I come back, we'll enjoy our sitting room, and we'll chat." I cast a last look at him. "Please, Dad."

"It's those photos, right? Those things I saved for you. Not surprising, not even unexpected, that you'd have more questions, but . . . I find it's difficult."

"I'll be right back."

I hurried, almost afraid he'd evaporate or somehow spirit himself away until my determination gave way again and I let it all go.

I set his coffee cup on the table next to his chair. Over the years, he'd stopped reading the newspaper. Sometimes I missed the rustle of the newsprint and the smell of the ink. He, like many, had moved to e-sources. I thought of Seth and the columns he said he'd written. Could I find them online? Probably.

Back to the task at hand, I reminded myself. I didn't like dissension or drama any more than my father did. I was about to say more to prod him forward when he finally broke the silence.

He stared at me, then past me, seeming drawn into the deep shadows of the room across the foyer. I couldn't help casting my own glance that way, too, just in case something was going on in there, but I quickly realized that no matter where he was directing his gaze, he wasn't seeing anything here with us now.

"I remember her laughter."

I waited, forcing myself not to speak.

He continued, "I think that's what attracted me the most. I've never been impulsive or lighthearted, not like some people. I heard her laughing and turned. She was beautiful, but more than that. Her laughter lit up her face, and her eyes sparkled. Love at first sight is a real thing. I know, because that day I fell for your mother. I fell hard."

My mouth gaped in surprise. I closed it and pressed my lips together.

"She was working at a bank. I went there seeking financing for the business, and that's how we met. Her job was opening new accounts, so she wasn't involved in the loan, but I must've opened four or five new accounts, checking, savings, whatever, over the following weeks as an excuse to sit across from her at her desk to chat with her. Through it all, it's her laughter I remember. Even when we discussed unhappy things—we both had difficult childhoods—there was grace and charm about her.

"She loved music, and she loved to dance." He smiled the saddest smile I'd ever seen. "When I asked her out, we had to work our date in between the dance classes she took in the evening. She was dedicated. She floated and twirled. They called it contemporary or modern dance or something like that. I don't know those things. But I know she was magical. I asked her if she was planning to leave the bank and become a professional dancer. She said, 'No, I'll never be good enough, but dancing helps balance my world.' When we married, she gave it up. I've thought about that more than once over the years."

He sighed. "I've heard it said that we look for what we're missing in ourselves when we seek our mates—to complement our strengths and weaknesses. That may be true." He rubbed his temples. "Or not. I don't know."

Dad went silent for a few minutes, then seemed to remember I was there. And why we were there together.

"I asked her to marry me, and she said yes." He looked at his hands. "It was good for a while." He fixed his eyes on me. "It wasn't your fault. Postpartum depression, the doctors said."

After another long silence, during which I could almost see the past playing itself out in his eyes, he said, "It seemed to me that she should be able to shake it off. We were in love; we had a beautiful baby girl, a nice home, a good income . . . anything she might want, I tried to give her, but what she needed . . . well, I never understood that. Still, I tried. As time went on, she seemed better, and I never felt you were unsafe with her, so I started staying later at work. A distance . . . the distance between who she'd been and was . . . the distance between us as a couple. It grew . . . beyond fixing, I guess."

"And then she left."

He nodded. "She did. More than once, but for short spells. At the time, I didn't understand. I thought it was me." He grimaced.

"I'm betting most guys think it's about them. But later, years later, as I watched you grow up, I wondered if she left because she didn't want to . . . infect you. No, that's the wrong word. Not infect. But maybe she thought her depression, her . . . behavior might transfer, be learned by you." He drew in a deep breath. "I told her that once when I was angry. I told her it was bad enough that you had a father who was always working and who, well, wasn't sociable outside of the work environment . . . I never learned that skill, and I guess I wasn't inclined toward it . . . to people. Your mom was. Or I thought she was. But when I realized you weren't getting that from either of us, I was worried. I thought you needed more. So maybe I said too much to her. 'Why can't you just pull yourself together? Shake it off?' That's what I said. I would've taken it back if I could've. Maybe she thought it was better for you if she left. I don't know. I'll never know. I'm sorry it worked out as it did."

My chest felt funny. Shaky inside. My heart felt like it was limping along regardless, so I said, "Do you think she was better after she left? Do you think she found happiness?" I was in my thirties, a married woman who was now a widow, a woman who'd survived dreadful injuries, but the voice I was hearing as I spoke aloud was that of a fourteen-year-old. My face grew warm. Some moments marked our lives, like rings on a tree. They betrayed our history—parts of our history that marked us permanently. Those marks might fade over time but would never go away entirely.

Dad looked one way and then the other. Everywhere except at me. The back-and-forth settled into a headshake as he stared down at his hands. "We'll never know."

I waited a long moment, but no new words came. I said, "I like to think of her that way—out there in the world in a happy place—a happy place for her. I wish it could've been different, but if she needed to leave to find happiness elsewhere, then that's what I wanted for her too."

"Kara." His troubled eyes searched my face. "She's dead. You know that."

My mouth gaped; then I recovered. "I know. Of course I know. I just meant I . . . I know it sounds stupid."

"You'd rather think of her as gone. Gone but still out there somewhere?"

I shrugged. "I know the truth, Dad. You told me that part years ago."

He said, "I should've told you all this, too, back then. I told myself I would wait until you were ready. When you asked."

"I knew you didn't want to discuss it. You and I aren't comfortable with emotional stuff."

"Like father, like daughter?"

I shrugged.

"I hope not. I've had a good life in many ways, Kara, but I've always felt the lack of close personal relationships. Like watching others from afar. It's like a missing piece in me, and it's hard when you know something's missing but can't do anything about it."

"Is that why you and Nicole aren't an official item?"

He cast a sharp glance at me. "Nicole . . . we're friends. Have been for years."

"It's okay, Dad," I tried to reassure him. "You've been single for a long time. You're entitled to a girlfriend."

His mouth opened, then closed again. He cleared his throat with a short, hard cough. "Nicole and I are just friends. We were much closer at one time." He glanced at me again, questioning, then resumed. "We're friends now."

He seemed to be awaiting a response.

"Seriously, Dad. It's all good." I laughed to try to lighten the moment. "I'm not sure about this furniture, though. I know Nicole meant well. Seems odd for it to sort of come back to its former home. Thanks, though, for the terrace furniture. I know I'll enjoy it."

Dad's expression seemed to be stuck, as if he couldn't follow me into this lighter space. I waited to allow him to catch up. Unexpectedly, he stood. "Good. Glad to hear it. Think I'll take a walk around and check the floors and the furniture. Maybe call it an early night." He pressed his hands together in an uncharacteristic gesture.

I thought I detected a slight tremor in them, even clasped.

"Are you okay, Dad?" I half rose from my chair.

"Good. I'm good."

I could see he was withdrawing. Withdrawing from me and looking pleased to be done with all this frank conversation. I let him go and eased back down into the chair. What had I expected? He'd done pretty well, considering.

The lamp was turned down low, and the light was dim. Areas of the lamplight reflected in the polished floors, and the smell of wax added a nice, fresh spice to the air. I stood and walked to the open windows. I slid them closed, one by one, taking my time and enjoying the peace. I'd give Dad a few minutes alone before checking on him.

He was standing on the back porch. I saw his silhouette and then heard his voice. He was speaking, it seemed, but his voice was too low for me to make out the words. The only word I understood was *Nicole.* There followed a short pause, during which I stopped and even started to back up, realizing I was intruding, eavesdropping, really, on a phone conversation. But then he said, "No, I haven't told her yet." I stayed just inside the door. He added, "I know. You're right." An extralong pause fell, during which a cricket called out, and then Dad said, "Sleep well."

He'd made an excuse to leave me so he could call Nicole privately.

He'd said, "I haven't told her yet." Told *me*? What hadn't he told me?

Dad continued to stare out at the night, and I stepped softly away until I reached the foyer. I was less careful going up the stairs. When I reached my room, I closed the door.

Anger. Resentment. Hurt. It all boiled inside me. I didn't know how to sort it out.

I'd opened the windows earlier in the day, and the breeze touching my hot face was cool and gentle.

A relationship between Dad and Nicole explained a lot about Dad's motivation for moving out here. Had he hoped Nicole would join him in this house? Was I in the way?

Yes, it seemed that I might be the one who was the unplanned, unexpected guest.

I couldn't help wondering—what else didn't I know? Clearly, there were things I didn't know about my father's personal life, and there must be more to know about my mother's.

When I was almost seventeen, Dad had told me Mom had died. He hadn't put it quite that baldly, but he'd kept it succinct. I'd cried in the bathroom, and for many days I had wandered around dazed and silent. Dad had kept a wary eye on me, and my teachers had asked if I was sick. Eventually, my sadness had passed, and we'd gotten on with normal life. After all, what had changed? Not much.

She was gone, but there was more I could find out about her. My mom. It hit me like a bolt. I could do this. Too bad I hadn't tried before Grandma Mary Lou had died.

I could hire a detective. Everyone left tracks. I wanted to know about her early life and her life after she'd left.

I went into the hallway. A faint glow from the night-light cast a small light. Dad's bedroom door was closed. He'd already turned in.

My father had a right to his own secrets, if that was how he wanted it. But if it involved me . . . or my mom . . .

Tomorrow I'd tell him my plan and see what he said.

I practiced in the mirror. "Dad, I'm going to hire an investigator."

What would he say?

CHAPTER ELEVEN

Dad was working in the empty parlor. He had extra lights plugged in and multiple tarps covering the floor. He was standing there studying the tools and looking at the walls.

"Wallpaper removal?" I asked.

"Today's the day."

"Well, you picked a good starting point. The room is empty, and the paper is faded and stained. The worst of the rooms, I'd say." I walked across to where he stood. "Have you removed paper before?"

"No, but it's not hard. I mean, it doesn't seem difficult, and I'm about to find out how hard the actual work is."

"Don't get too involved yet. I'm hungry for a real breakfast this morning, so I expect you to come to the table when I call you."

"I had coffee already."

"For this kind of work, you need better fuel than caffeinated hot water."

"I won't say no, that's for sure. I'm hungry this morning."

I decided I'd wait and tell him my plan over breakfast.

But in the end, I didn't. We were both enjoying the meal too much. No need to risk spoiling it. After I tidied the kitchen, I joined him in the study. He was running a handheld tool over the wall.

"What's that?"

He held it toward me and spun the little wheel by its teeth. "It pokes holes in the wallpaper so the solution can soak through to loosen it."

"Oh." I held out my hand. "Well, let me help. I can handle running this over the walls, surely."

"I have two. Why don't you start in that area?"

I pretended we were working together companionably and let my words flow naturally into that cooperative atmosphere.

"After you told me about Mom, about how you met her and all that, well, I got to thinking that I should find out more about her."

Clack. The plastic body of Dad's scoring tool hit the floor. We both moved to retrieve it, but Dad got there first.

"Why?"

"Why not? She had a life, at least for a while, before she met you and after she left us. I have questions. Curiosity. I may hire an investigator. Probably an easy job for someone who knows how." Inside, I sighed. I'd gotten it said. It was out there now.

He shook his head, set the tool on the windowsill, and went out to the porch.

I stood there feeling about as rejected as I ever had. Was the conversation the other night, when he'd answered my questions, no more than an aberration? Were we back to where I wasn't worth the emotion it might cost him to share those words?

I felt anger growing around the edges, in the prickling along my scalp, in the tingling of my hands and the heat growing in my chest. I was biting my lower lip—actually biting the soft flesh—and I reached up to rescue and protect my lip. My ears rang with the anger, and it felt dangerous.

He was sitting on the porch. I stood in the doorway. The breeze that blew across reached into my head, and I felt my ire slackening, the pressure easing. Was that pity I felt? I didn't want to pity him. Pity was an emotion that opened a person to being manipulated, to being swayed from their course. How often had I buried my face and cried in my pillow instead of forcing the conversation? How long had it taken me to convince myself that that was acceptable? Normal or normal enough? That the present was sufficient without the past as context? Because revisiting the past was uncomfortable?

Dad shifted in his seat. Now, he was leaning slightly forward and looking at the floor. He cleared his throat. "Come have a seat." He gestured toward the empty seat. "Join me?"

I sat but said nothing.

He continued looking at the floor. His hands were on his knees. "It was difficult to discuss your mother with you last night. I thought it would be harder." He let silence occupy the next few moments before resuming. "It was hard, but it was right. I knew it after. It was also incomplete. This part is going to be hard to say to you. I don't know any easy way."

"I don't understand."

"You want to know more about the time your mother was away from us?"

"Yes."

He nodded gravely. "You know it was only about two years between the time she left that last time and when she died."

"Yes, of course. I remember the day you told me. Her heart, you said. I told my doctor about it several years ago, in case it was something genetic. He said my heart is fine." I shook my head. "The fact remains she was somewhere for two years, and I want to find out what I can. I'd like to know that she found happiness. Is that so wrong?"

"No, it's not wrong, and you have the right, but I can't encourage you, Kara."

"Why?" Annoyed, I said, "Frankly, Dad, I don't need anyone's encouragement or permission. I know you don't like to discuss personal things, but we should've done this long ago—as you've already admitted. It would've been much easier when the trail was fresher. Plus,

I'd like to know who she was as a young person. There's bound to be records . . . school records, at least."

Dad rubbed his hands over his eyes, then looked ahead, but not at me. "Slow down, Kara. You're getting ahead of things. Remember what I told you that day?"

"That her heart stopped. She had a heart attack." I rubbed my arms. "That haunted me for a long time. Did she know something was happening?" I stared at his profile. "In her last moments, did she regret leaving? Did she wish she'd come back home?"

"When she left, I tried to find her myself and failed, so I hired a professional investigator. He found her."

"What? You never said a word!"

"He found her about nine months after she left. She was in Illinois."

"What?" My voice was no louder than a whisper. I couldn't believe it.

"I didn't tell you because she refused to return to us. And the circumstances were sad and sordid."

"Sad? Sordid? But you found her? You left her there? We could've gone after her, Dad." My hands were suddenly fists.

He raised his own hand, but gently. "You always liked to imagine that she was happy. I didn't want to spoil that for you. How could I tell my daughter that her mother refused to come home?" He shook his head. "When she died, I had to tell you, but I didn't have to tell you all the details. Details that would help no one, least of all you, and I didn't think your mother would want you to know. Regardless of the decisions she made, she loved you. So in a way, I was respecting her wishes."

"What are you talking about?" My heart was racing. I could feel the pulse in my ears along with a low roar. I rubbed my scar. I didn't want the headache to start, but once everything got revved up, it was almost inevitable.

"Kara. We don't have to talk about this. It solves nothing. Helps nothing. Let your mother rest in peace."

"Just tell me. Tell me what you know."

"You forget, Kara, that she wasn't only your mother. She was my wife, the woman I loved. I failed. She failed too. None of it was your fault, and you have every right to be angry at us, but I always tried. You know that."

I stayed silent. We needed to finish this.

He said, "The detective located her outside of Chicago, near where she grew up. She had no family left there, so I don't know why she went, but she did. She was . . . self-medicating and living in terrible conditions."

"What does that mean?"

"She was using drugs. Heroin, pills . . . I don't know what else. It was the depression, Kara. She could never shake it for long. The doctors had tried different medications on her for years." He shrugged as if trying to dislodge the past from his shoulders. "I remember nagging her to take those prescriptions. Even losing my temper over it. I started staying away in frustration." His voice trailed off on those last words. "And then she left. She ran away.

"The detective notified the police of her whereabouts and condition. By the time I got there, she'd disappeared again. Later they found her in her car, parked at a rest area along the Ohio interstate, gone. Her heart had stopped, but not because of some genetic condition. It was an overdose. And no, I don't think she was afraid at all. I think she fell unconscious—almost like falling asleep—and passed peacefully. When I thought about having to tell you . . . I was angry at her all over again."

He leaned forward. "God forgive me. I did my best, but I failed you both over and over."

~

Almost like the day she left us, I had a weird swirling of buts, what-ifs, questions, and disbelief occupying my brain. It made me dizzy. I hardly knew how I continued to sit upright and not fall flat out of my chair.

That last bit of my universe had worked loose, shedding its anchor, and my world was tilting dangerously. Drifting.

I left my father there on the front porch. I found my cane and gingerly made my way down the slope to the bench by the creek. No deer were grazing here this time of day. Birds were abundant, though, and the squirrels were busy. Butterflies flitted by, and bees buzzed somewhere behind me. I tried to focus, but that drifting feeling continued. I drifted right into imagining Mom's car. The same car that hadn't been in the garage, that I hadn't seen coming or going on our street or in our neighborhood in the days after she'd left or parked in front of the nearby hotels, before I'd given up hope of her returning.

The car that she'd run away in—and died in.

CHAPTER TWELVE

I felt adrift. I told myself I wasn't indulging in self-pity but was righteously hurt and resentful that my father hadn't told me the full truth years ago. If we'd gone after her together while she was still alive . . . my what-if was a fantasy. She'd refused to come home. Dad would never have put me through hearing that in person any more than I would've exposed my own child to more hurt.

As I sat there, still adrift, something drifted into view. Before my eyes, a boat—a small red-and-blue plastic boat with a tiny white plastic sail—floated lightly by, carried along by the currents of Cub Creek.

It was so odd that it struck me as serendipitous—the boat drifting as I had felt myself drifting. It plucked at my misery. I watched the boat go merrily past, mesmerized. A second boat, this one in green, blue, and white, followed a few yards behind it. Despite my desolate mood, the sight of the boats tickled my funny bone and tried to push a smile onto my face.

I heard voices, shouting and happy sounding, and foliage noises. If not for the voices, I might've thought the deer were back and charging raucously through the woods. But it wasn't deer. It was a man with light-brown hair and a little girl with corn silk curls. Seth and Maddie Lyn.

Maddie saw only the boats and kept running along the creek. Seth saw me and paused. The smile was still on my face, and I was grateful.

He smiled back at me, then caught up to Maddie and grabbed her as she was about to jump into the water after the boats.

"But they'll sail away!"

He spun her in the air before setting her back on her feet. He pretended to be winded as he staggered and bent over, putting his hands on his knees. "You're getting too big for that." He spoke directly to her in a more serious voice. "They'll snag down by the big rock. I'll fish them out there."

"Okay." She looked like she was going to chase after them right that moment.

Seth touched her shoulder. "Did you see Mrs. Hart sitting there? Are we just going to run past? I think that would be very rude. What do you think?"

Maddie ducked under his arm to shoot me a shy look, then tugged Seth closer so that she could whisper in his ear.

"Tell her yourself. Go ahead."

Maddie looked at me again. She squinched up her face in what I guessed was a smile. A very shy smile. She came toward the bench.

"Hi, Maddie. Are those your boats?"

She nodded.

Seth said, "Today is a shy day."

"So I see. Today is a gloomy day for me," I said to Maddie. "But not now. Not since I saw those sailboats going by." I leaned forward. "They made me laugh."

Maddie giggled.

Seth said, "You should go sailing with us sometime."

"Where do you launch from? Or rather, where is the port of embarkation?"

He nodded back toward the woods. "At the bridge. Sometimes we go farther upstream, but that's the best spot."

"That's the path to your house?"

"Mom's house. I'm there for now, as you know."

"The boats—you said their destination is downstream? The big rock?"

"I'm sure they've arrived by now."

Maddie pulled at his hand.

Seth said, "Would you like to join us?"

I hesitated. Heaven knows why I did because it sounded like fun. It sure beat sitting alone stewing in unhappiness. "I'd like that."

Maddie danced impatiently, jumping in small hops. "Come!"

We set off. We followed the path that bordered the creek. I had my cane, taking it with me automatically, though it soon became more of a hindrance than a help. It was most helpful in terms of moving low sticker-bush branches aside. It was unhelpful in that it kept catching on unintended bushes and rocks. Once, it caught hard, and I stumbled. Seth grabbed me and kept me from falling. I pretended I was fine and not embarrassed at all as Maddie stooped low to brush the dirt from the knee of my cotton capris.

"Thank you, Maddie."

"What about me?"

"Thank you, Seth."

Maddie went ahead. Seth called out, "Hold up, girl."

She stopped and looked back.

"She's fine, I'm sure, but you never know."

"You never know. That's true about pretty much everything." I stepped over a downed log. "Every time I think I've got things worked out, figured out, it all turns on its head. I have to figure it out all over again."

"But that's good, right? I mean, not all surprises are fun, and even some that end up being good don't seem that way at first. But you can't just fix it, put everyone and everything in its place, and expect it to stay there."

"I don't disagree. In my head, I know that's true. But my heart sees it differently." I slapped at a gnat. "Control is an illusion, right?"

"Best-laid plans most often go astray."

"Waste not, want not."

Seth added, "Look before you leap."

Maddie had stopped and was staring back at us. "Watch me leap," she said, grinning.

She took off running and disappeared from view.

"Maddie!" Seth called after her. He put his hands on my upper arms and gently but efficiently moved me out of the way. "Excuse me," he said as he took off running.

It wasn't far. I caught up quickly, relieved not to have heard a splash or a yell. Maddie's idea of a leap that was worth announcing wasn't all that scary, actually. She made a production of it, though, standing on the bank of the creek, swinging her arms, and then jumping about six inches to a large flat rock. Having reached the rock, she held her arms wide, raised her hands skyward, and declared, "Ta-da!" posing like a gymnast who'd just completed a difficult vault.

Seth said, "No farther. I'm serious, Maddie. Stay there."

"Okay," she said with a groan.

Beyond the flat rock was a much larger one. There was a gap of about a foot between them. It was taller and rounded and looked mossy on one side. I saw the brightly colored plastic of one boat peeking out from the far side. It looked like it was wedged between the large rock and a smaller one on that side.

Seth asked, "Mind if I borrow your cane?"

I held it out to him. "Be my guest."

He stepped onto the flat rock with Maddie and then easily crossed to the bigger rock. He set his knee on a spot and then leaned over, using the cane to fish out the boats.

At that moment, Maddie Lyn moved. She may have only been leaning toward Seth, but I thought she was falling. In that moment, I reached to grab her, moved carelessly, and lost my footing. I saw Seth's eyes widen as my arms flailed. There was no saving me. The creek wasn't deep here. Only about a foot, but the bottom was slippery. I was wet to my waist when I gave up trying to regain my footing and simply sat there on the rocks and sand and sticks with the creek flowing around me.

Seth joined me. On purpose. Without caution, he slipped right over that rock and landed beside me, grabbing my arm and helping me to my feet and getting wet in the bargain.

"Kara," he said, still gripping my arm and helping me up.

"I'm fine. I'm good. Just wet." And only a little humiliated.

We heard laughter and looked up. Maddie was giggling, and her arms were spread wide like wings. Seth said, "No, Maddie—" and she jumped. That gymnast jump again, but without the ta-da. Seth grabbed her before she went under on that slippery bottom. Her feet and shorts were wet, but otherwise she was okay. He stood her back on the rock and said, "Don't move. Promise me."

"I promise." She looked serious.

"I'm so sorry, Kara."

"What?" I'd heard Seth's words, but I didn't understand what he was apologizing for.

"For taking your cane. I'm sorry you fell. I didn't think you really needed it all that much, and I could reach the boats with it . . ."

I held my hand up. "Enough. Thank you. You jumped in after me." I saw the twinkle again and laughed myself. "Help me get out of here."

He helped me up onto the rock and then joined me. We took off our shoes and dumped out the water and sand. Maddie did too. The rock was warm against my legs. It felt good to sit there. It was relaxing, even if my clothing felt a little squishy. I was glad I hadn't been wearing heavy denim.

"I'd better get back and change."

Seth reached down with my cane again and this time came up with the boats one by one. He handed them to Maddie, who cradled the wet boats in her arms while he rinsed her sandals off in the clear water.

When we were put back together, Seth motioned to Maddie, and she stood on the flat rock.

"Okay," he said. "Go for it."

Maddie looked at me, excitement in her eyes. She clutched the boats in her arms and held her breath as she jumped to the bank.

Seth gave me a look. "No sense in making her self-conscious or second-guess herself. Sometimes you make it; sometimes you don't. But if the worst that happens is wet shorts, then it's worth the risk."

Seth and I joined her on the bank. "Ready, ladies?" We nodded, and he said, "Lead the way, Maddie, but wait for me at the bench."

"Okay," Maddie said, already in motion. The word trailed off as she ran ahead of us.

Her shorts were wet and stuck to her bottom. Mine were too. I made sure Seth stayed even with me or ahead of me.

I said, "What kind of bridge? How far is it?"

"It's small. Decorative. Just enough to cross the creek and keep your feet dry." He threw in a little too casually, "If you ever want to visit the Albers clan, just follow the path and cross over the bridge. You'll find us easily. And you'll always be welcome."

My cheeks were hot. I stared straight ahead.

He touched my elbow. "By the way, while Maddie isn't within hearing, I wanted to tell you I think you're right."

"Me, right? About what?"

"What we spoke about the other day. About life moving on without us. I'm not actually out there looking, but I reached out to some contacts. Just to talk, you know."

"It wasn't my business to tell you how to live your life."

"It was good thinking. Frankly, part of the hesitation is that a great opportunity might come along, and then I'd have to make a big decision. Not sure I can do that—not right now with others depending on me."

Just at that moment, the toe of my wet shoe caught the edge of a rock, and I stumbled. Seth grabbed my arm.

"Thank you. I'm fine. Just clumsy."

"The wet shoes. I don't know about you, but mine feel disgusting."

When we came to the downed tree and needed to step over it, Seth was there offering his hand in assistance.

"Thank you." I put my hand in his and stepped up and over the log. He clasped my hand a tiny bit tighter as I found my footing.

"I could show you around the area, if you're interested. Shopping area. Scenic areas. Do you have hobbies? Photography? Anything like that?"

"No outdoor hobbies. Needlework is my thing. I enjoy embroidery."

"Really? Embroidery? I'd love to see it."

I shrugged. "Maybe sometime. I promise that it's nothing remarkable. It's just . . . thread."

He released my hand. The path ahead was smooth and wide as we neared the yard. My hand felt alone.

He said, "Do you mind if I ask you a personal question?"

"I might, but go ahead. I won't answer if I'm not comfortable doing so."

He gave me a strange look. "You always have the most unusual answers. Never a simple yes or no. I wonder if that's intentional?"

"Intentional?"

"Distracting. A diversion." He touched my arm. "Let's catch up with Maddie. If she's left too long to her own devices, she can get into mischief. Might decide to go swimming again."

"Of course." I quickened my pace to match his. "But what was your question?"

He smiled but kept walking, and I realized he didn't intend to answer or, rather, to ask. Aggravating man. But it was just as well . . . no personal questions to stumble over and feel foolish about.

Maddie had settled herself obediently on the bench. The boats were on her lap. I sat next to her and looked away from Seth. I didn't understand my awkwardness. Or was that too silly? Of course I understood. He was an attractive man—I wasn't immune to him. So long as I was careful and didn't offer encouragement, I could enjoy his companionship when he was around, and perhaps our friendship would grow. Like me, he was single, so there must surely have been heartbreaks along the way. He probably had his own reasons to be cautious.

Maddie was saying, "This boat belongs to the princess, and this one"—she picked up the green boat—"this is the prince's boat."

"Do the prince and princess have names?"

Maddie shook her head no.

"Oh." That seemed an abrupt end to our brief conversation. I tried to think of an appropriate response. "But why? Shouldn't they have names?"

She held up one of the boats. "There isn't really a princess or prince. See? It's empty."

"Hmm." I made a show of examining the green boat closely, then pointed toward the plastic deck. "I believe I see the prince right there."

"Do you?"

"Yes, indeed. He is very tiny but quite handsome. What is he wearing? Is that a fancy crown on his head?"

"Yes, it is. Is it gold?"

"I believe so. He's wearing a red cape."

Maddie squeezed her eyes, so intent on focusing on that tiny prince that I wanted to tell her to stop or she'd have wrinkles by the time she turned five. "I see him. I do."

Seth interrupted. "We have to get back. Grammy is fixing us a meal, Maddie. We don't want to be late. Plus, we all need to change out of our wet clothes."

"Grammy's making pancakes for lunch."

"Pancakes for lunch?" I asked, pretending surprise.

"Yes, 'cause I asked her."

"It sounds delicious. Please say hello to your grandmother for me."

With a wave, Maddie Lyn danced away and into the woods.

"She left without you."

"She knows the way. I'll catch up." He gave me a solemn look. "You said you were gloomy. Are you okay now?"

"I believe I am. A little dose of Maddie Lyn was all I needed."

Seth gave a mock bow and pretended to grasp the folds of his cape. "We Alberses are delighted to be of service, milady."

He waved and was off, chasing after Maddie. One of these days I was going to walk that path myself and see what might await at the other end. Perhaps it would be a fairy-tale palace where mothers didn't leave, fathers didn't fail, and a daughter didn't try to hold her own dad to standards she herself couldn't keep.

I went directly upstairs, showered off the creek water, and put on dry clothing. In the kitchen, considering lunch, I almost called out to Dad to ask what he'd like to eat, but I simply didn't have much to say to him. It wasn't deliberate. It was just how I felt. I went about fixing lunch. We needed to eat. I didn't want to punish him. He'd done the best he could do. As had I.

Torn emotionally, I felt as flat as Maddie Lyn's pancake lunch.

I opened a can of soup and pulled out sandwich fixings. Not exactly inspired cuisine, but who cared, really? I didn't. I had every right to be angry at my father. But I'd just had an adventure with Seth and Maddie, and frankly, it felt like a waste of energy and breath to sustain this rift between us, however much he deserved it for not telling me the full truth about Mom's death sooner.

When Dad came into the kitchen, I felt his eyes, his tension, pulling me back toward that unhappy place.

I set the food in front of him, saying, "Please, Dad. Stop worrying over it. Drop the whole thing. Let's move on."

He nodded but didn't answer me. I snuck another glance at him. He looked old.

Was it my fault? I felt guilty, then annoyed.

I had reason to be angry, didn't I? Why did I feel so crappy about it?

We ate, but neither of us enjoyed the meal. Honesty and reality were at odds. And trust was an important part of it. I felt the sharp edges of that old familiar headache and found myself touching the scar, but deep inside I also felt hope because the headache hadn't progressed into flashing lights and crashing sounds. I didn't want to push my luck. I decided I'd lie down, close my eyes, and rest a bit, maybe get a little peace and serenity back. But as we neared the end of the meal, Dad spoke.

"Kara, we need to talk."

CHAPTER THIRTEEN

"Talk about what?" I asked as I gathered up the lunch litter and put the mayonnaise back in the fridge.

Dad spoke again. "Let's take a ride."

"Where?"

"There's something I want to show you."

I shrugged. "No offense, but I think I'm done in. I'm going to lie down for a while."

He cleared his throat. "I think we've both been touched by the same ailment."

I stared at him.

He added, "Close enough to be the same. Will you take a ride with me?"

"To where?"

"I'll explain when we get there. It's not far." He nodded at my bare feet. "Put on some old shoes. It might be muddy."

"Maybe later."

"Please, Kara."

I sighed. "Old shoes, then. I'll meet you out front in, say . . . ten minutes?"

He nodded. "I'll be on the porch."

I paused on the landing. Dad had left the front door open. I could see the greenery outside and feel the breeze. There were times in your life that felt like points of no return. Points of no return might be considered bad things, but not necessarily. I decided to trust my father. He hadn't always been right, but he hadn't always been wrong either. I needed help to get past this . . . this divide. The information he'd withheld from me. The image he'd left me with this morning—that of Mom alone in her car, dying, as people walked past in an interstate rest area. Maybe this was the opportunity.

In eight minutes, I was back downstairs and on the porch. He looked surprised to see me.

"Did you think I wouldn't show?"

"I wondered."

"When have I not?"

He nodded and stood. "I'll drive."

In the car, he repeated, "It's not far in distance, but it's a lifetime away."

"That sounds poetic. And serious."

Dad shook his head. "Not serious. Just truth. An old truth that doesn't matter to anyone but me, but . . ." He tapped his fingers on the steering wheel. "After these conversations about your mom and hearing your questions, I thought it might be good to share it with you."

He added, "Ironically, this may drive you further from me. By my being open with you, you'll see that not only have I withheld information from you but I am also a liar."

My mouth opened. My lips parted to ask, "What?" but I pulled the word back, unsaid. A liar?

Less than half a mile later, maybe only a quarter of one, he pulled off the road onto a wide shoulder area. The woods alongside the road were thick and looked long undisturbed.

"Let's take a walk."

"My cane. I forgot it."

Dad gave me a long look. He said, "No worries, Kara. We'll keep to the path, and if you need assistance, you are welcome to lean on me. Always."

I nodded.

"The road we used when I was a kid starts farther up that way, but it joins this path, so we'll save ourselves a few steps and start here."

"If there's a road, could we just drive there?"

"No, not on that road. Not now or in a long time."

I almost didn't recognize his voice. Dad was rarely upbeat, but this was even more somber than usual. His jaw was tight, too, as he put his hands in the pockets of the light jacket he was wearing. I decided to be quiet and let him get this done.

We walked down the narrow path. It was muddy in spots and crowded by weedy growth. I had to watch where I was putting my feet, and the fronds of plants bordering the path reached out to grab at my jeans and my shirtsleeves, but most were innocent enough, meaning they had no sharp stickers. Still, it was annoying, and I worried about ticks. So far, no mosquitos or gnats had noticed us.

"Dad, what's this about?" I asked. "Are you buying more property? I know you're not thinking of moving again so soon. What, then?"

"It's not much farther." He dropped his hand from my arm. "You've been patient. I don't mean to be mysterious. It's just that . . ." He breathed in deeply, released it, and said, "I always let you think I grew up in Richmond. It was a deliberate choice. I let everyone think that."

"You *said* you did. I remember I had to do some sort of school project . . . third grade, I think. Where were your parents born? Where were their parents born? And so on. Richmond, you said."

He nodded. "I was born here. I grew up out here."

"Out here?" I cast my eyes around. We were still surrounded by greenery. The green seemed to have a special smell, a sharp edge to it. "Do you mean you grew up in Louisa or Cub Creek? Or do you mean literally here?"

"Yes, I lied deliberately and kept the lie in place for over forty years. I forgot I was lying. I was surprised at how easy it is to do that, to rewrite one's reality. When the past came back to find me . . . when Nicole told me the Forster house—your wildflower house—was for sale, I knew it was time to face it." He nodded his head toward the rutted track ahead of us. "Here. It's not much farther." He held out his hand to assist me, inviting me forward. "I haven't been out here in a while. Now that I think of it, while it's unlikely, it's possible that someone, vagrants maybe, could be hanging out here, homeless or camping out. If anyone is around, we'll just leave quietly, understand?"

Now my scalp prickled. Someone hanging out here? Leave quietly? We were truly alone and isolated out here. Was he seriously anticipating trouble?

I looked around. What about wild animals? Snakes? Even hunters? "Dad," I said.

"It's okay, Kara." His eyes seemed to swim suddenly.

I didn't want to see him distraught, not my father, so I pulled my calm back around me. It didn't still the uneasiness inside, but I could think again.

He said, "If you really want to go back to the house, I'll take you. But I think you'll be . . . I *hope* you'll be glad we did this. If not today, maybe someday. It's all ancient history—history I never wanted to speak about. Maybe I was wrong. If you want the details, now or someday, I may not be here to tell you."

"Lead the way, Dad."

I followed behind until the path widened. Over our heads the tree branches arched, creating a canopy that filtered the light. Around us was a strong smell of growth but also of rot.

We emerged into a clearing. Immediately, I felt the weight of despair in the air around us, in the broken house before us, and in the decay.

This was a desolate patch of ground. The small house had caved in. The shingled roof had collapsed inward, held up at the sides and corners by walls that themselves bowed inward. No one could walk through that broken door again, not even if they were willing to risk the whole rotten remains tumbling down onto their heads. Ivy and moss along with some orangey decorative fungus grew in patches and were either holding the disaster together or at work bringing it down. Maybe both.

And yet for all I knew, it had been a home of love and joy. Except I could feel it had not. Too much pain had been left behind here for me to believe otherwise.

I stopped, not wanting to go too near. Dad stopped about the same time, then stepped a little closer, wary of a stray board, and stood and stared. I waited. Finally, he nodded and stepped back to join me.

In a soft but strong voice, he said, "I grew up here."

I looked again. This house could have had only one or two small rooms at most, with a small kitchen on the back. An outhouse lay on its side several yards away, and an old rusty pump was lying near a covered well.

I cleared my throat. "Here?"

He nodded. "I lived here until I was in my teens. Until I left home."

"Your parents . . ."

"And a brother and sister. My parents died long ago. I don't know what became of Lewis and Laura. They were twins. Younger than me by about ten years. Our mother died when they were three or so." In a whispery voice, he said, "About a year after that, Dad told me he gave them away to someone who was passing through." He shook his head. "I didn't believe him. He was being cruel. But because he was cruel, I also believed him. Does that make sense? I was a kid, and they were gone, and I thought maybe that was for the best."

I stared at him in amazement. He'd had siblings, and one day they were gone?

"You just let them leave your life? Just like . . . that?"

"With them gone, I was free to leave, and I did. Later, I tried to find them. I talked to the local authorities. When I had money to hire an investigator, I did that, too, but too much time had passed, I guess."

He stared at me. "It was toxic, Kara. That's the best way I can explain it. From my earliest memories until the day I left." He shrugged. "I didn't know life was different for other people. I accepted my experience at face value. When I was young, at least until third or fourth grade, I thought the other kids in school were putting on about liking their parents. I thought the only real difference between us was that their clothes were cleaner, and that was because they had indoor plumbing. I couldn't fit in with them. I started sneaking off and skipping school." He went silent.

I let him have his silence. I felt dizzy. I *knew* my father's early life. He'd never talked about it much, mostly because he said his childhood was unremarkable—happy enough with middle-class parents who'd tried to help him learn and become responsible by taking jobs at a young age. Was that all fiction? When I'd asked specifically about his parents . . . what had he said? Not much. His mom died when he was in his teens, and his father raised him. He and his dad didn't always get along. His father died sometime after he'd grown up and left home.

How was I supposed to rewrite all that in my head? I couldn't shift my thinking to imagine him living here in this hovel.

I felt the need to sit. I looked around us for an acceptable spot. The best was a relatively recent fallen tree. I touched the bark, and it felt dry and solid. I sat. Dad joined me.

"After so many years, when it didn't matter anymore, you kept lying. You lied to me."

"I never thought of it that way. I created new history. I didn't think of it as a lie. My life as a child, a life I was born to and had no say in, was my business and no one else's."

"How long has this place been empty?"

He shrugged. "Since my father died. About thirty years."

"He died after I was born? Why did I never know about him? Why did I grow up with only you and me?" I held up my hands. "Mom was estranged from her family . . . at least I met them. Your childhood was in this nightmare place. Why wouldn't you share that with people who cared about you?"

"Because, Kara, people who grow up in a nightmare don't find pleasure in talking about it. I spent too much time and effort forgetting. By the time you were grown, what was the point in telling you? All the applicable people were gone. It was old history that didn't need to trouble your life."

"Yet you're telling me now."

"Because it seems like I was wrong. You need to know. I don't know why you want or need to know. Your life wasn't perfect, but far better than many, and the world was open to you. I tried to support you in anything you wanted." He sighed heavily. "I know I'm not . . . emotional. And I don't blame your mother for the choices she made. I'm grateful because I have you. But I know you feel a certain lack." He shook his head. "Maybe I was hoping that if you understood the past, you'd know the things that happened, like our fractured family and imperfect lives, aren't your fault. Nothing is perfect—not the past, not ourselves, and not our present."

"I know nothing is perfect. Niles and I had our problems." I almost expected lightning to strike me for uttering such an understatement. I twisted my fingers.

"For the record, I'll say that my father had a drinking problem, and he was heavy handed. That's all I'm going to say about that." He held up his hand. "Don't get angry. There's more I want to tell you."

An ant was climbing up his pants leg. I leaned forward and brushed it off. He gave me a quick smile.

"By the time I was ten, I was spending a lot of time away from this house." He waved his hand at the hovel. "When I wasn't in school, I'd wander the woods until I was cold or hungry enough to come back. I built a small fort of deadfalls and brush and hid out there sometimes. I stayed away from other people's houses generally, but there was one house that was different. I'd follow the creek and sit in the trees and think that maybe it was *my* house. Silly, I know. When the people who lived there were outside, I'd watch them. It sounds creepy, but I wasn't really spying. I was wondering why my family wasn't like theirs. That's when I began to realize that the other kids in school weren't all pretending about things being good at their homes." He paused.

"It was Wildflower House," he said finally.

He'd called it Wildflower House. Capital *W* and capital *H*—as if it had never been called anything else. I loved it.

"Yes." I smiled. "That's exactly how I think of it. Wildflower House."

"It's a good name." He nodded. "A family lived there. I was no more than a kid myself, but they had a child, only a toddler at the time."

"Did they find you watching? Did you get into trouble?"

He shook his head. "No, but one day the toddler—his name was Stevie—tossed a ball, and it flew right to me, almost as if he saw me there. I was sitting in that bench area, the one where you were sitting the day we moved in."

"The gazing ball area?"

Dad nodded but said, "It wasn't a gazing ball area back then, but there was a bench. The gazing ball and the gnomes, and most of the flowers, came later with Mary and Rob Forster." He paused to breathe, then continued. "So I picked up the ball and stepped out. I'll never forget the look on Rick Bowen's face. He was the father. I give him credit for being cool and a decent man. I was used to rough handling and was surprised when he said hello and introduced himself." Dad slapped at a gnat that was hovering near his face. "I offered my services." He laughed softly.

"Your services?"

"It wasn't as if I had gardening or landscaping skills, but it never occurred to me I couldn't do whatever was asked of me. I was born that way. Never thought I couldn't, you know? For anything? Except maybe being a people person . . . but I can do that, too, if I must. At least for short spells." He laughed again, this time loud enough to startle a bird into taking flight. "He hired me for small jobs and, later, bigger jobs. Most of the money I earned I buried in a jar stashed between here and there. My father started asking questions about where I was disappearing to, so I told him I was picking up odd jobs. I gave him some of the money. I imagine he used it to buy more liquor."

"Did you help landscape the property?"

"Nothing that grand. I weeded and trimmed, raked the leaves, and cut the grass." He looked embarrassed. "I shouldn't say this aloud; it sounds so pitiable. But I pretended I lived there. I worked that yard and pretended it was mine. That I was some sort of friend or relative and I'd been asked to live there . . . oh, I only pretended in my head. I never said it to anyone, and in the reality part of my brain, I saved up my money and waited for the right time to leave and go to the city and make my own life.

"Kara, that house and the people who lived there were my only touchstones of sanity when I was growing up. They even asked about my grades. I tried harder in school so I wouldn't have to lie to them or disappoint them."

"This is so sad. I'm sorry you didn't tell me before, but I guess I understand."

"It was a lifetime ago. The Bowens moved away, and then the twins disappeared. There was nothing else to hold me here."

"Did you keep in touch with them?"

"No. When I moved to Richmond, I cut all ties here. Never came back. And then, after you left for college and I wanted a smaller place, a place closer to my office, I met Nicole. She was living in Richmond at the time, too, but our past, being from here, was coincidental. Over time, I told her some of it. I guess it gave us a bond."

"How did you find out about your father's death?"

"The sheriff tracked me down and called."

"Do you know what he died of? Where he's buried?"

"He's buried at the cemetery in Mineral. Mom made the arrangements for them both before she passed. I remember that argument. She'd used the money her parents left her to prepay for the plot and all that. My father was irate." He sighed. "As to what killed him? Life and poor choices, I'd guess. Simple meanness."

What was worse? I wondered. The good parent who left, or the bad one who stayed? Still . . .

"I'm sorry, Dad. I'm trying to understand, but even with everything you went through, how could you walk away without knowing where your brother and sister went?"

He started to speak several times. Each time his breath hitched. He blinked and coughed, then tried again.

"It's okay, Dad."

"No, it's not. Give me a minute. I may never have another chance like this to explain myself. Will never want it, more like."

He drew in a long breath and released it slowly. I'd learned that from him. How many times in the grip of stress had I done that myself?

"I told you I talked to the authorities. Later, when I had enough money, I hired an investigator. But in between . . . well, I knew a fella who owned some dogs. Special dogs. Cadaver dogs."

There was a long moment of silence between us. I didn't breathe at all but waited.

"I asked him for a favor—to take those dogs out here and let them roam." His voice choked off. He was staring ahead of us, but he wasn't seeing the fallen house.

"Did they . . . no, they didn't, right? Because you hired the detective later."

"That's right. Found nothing." He pressed his fingers against his eyes, then dropped his hand. "I never ever want to live through such as that again. Never. Do you hear me? I hired that investigator later, and so

I thought of doing that when Susan left . . . and he found . . . you know how he found her." He shook his head. "I can't do that again. Ever."

I sat quietly, thinking about being the child of someone who died of being mean, who'd done something with two of his children, whose wife had likely died grateful because it meant escape.

I took my father's hand. He accepted mine and tightened his own around it.

Dad continued, "When Nicole told me that the property was going on the market, it seemed . . . not like fate, but rather coming full circle. It was a chance to live out what I pretended all those years ago. To take on, a lifetime later, the best part of my childhood and put the bad parts to rest. Plus, I'm at that age—stepping over sixty and catching a glimpse of what the rest of my life will be." He glanced at me. "I worked hard at my business and took pride in it. I didn't want to walk away from it, but running that business wasn't all that I ever wanted to do. At one time in my life, I just wanted safety and security. And opportunity. Then I wanted a wife and a family—one that was free of what I'd grown up with. I thought there'd be more to my life than tires and a failed marriage. A person wakes up one day and wonders what their life would've been if they'd taken a different path. Yet I never saw another path. And didn't, not until I had the chance to return home. Almost home, that is."

He sighed. "Maybe explaining all this to you isn't just about giving you the information but also about facing it down myself. I didn't know I needed to face it down. Choices. Memories. Unacknowledged scars."

Dad squeezed my hand. "Are you okay, Kara? Remember, this is all in the past, and I've had a full life since with few regrets."

"It's sad."

"Sad." He nodded. "Yes, for my father's sad, miserable life. For the misery he inflicted on my mother and their children during his time on earth." There was a pause; then he said, "I know I wasn't the ideal father, but I hope I didn't cause you misery."

For the first time in perhaps forever, I leaned against him, impulsively, and put my arm through his. "No. You were a good father and provider. I always felt safe with you as my dad."

He made a small noise, almost like a little grunt. I took it as a positive response. I reached up with one hand and touched my eye, surprised to find it damp and teary.

"Do you have any good memories of him?"

"Maybe. There were moments of light, of near goodness, but it made the rest hurt even more. The waste. You know what I mean? The potential that was squandered."

I sat up and pressed my shirtsleeve against my eyes. "So now I understand why you wanted that house, huge and old as it may be. It makes more sense to me now. But you can't rewrite history, Dad."

He laughed a little. "Well, that's debatable. Seems like politicians and media do that all the time . . . but personal history? Well, people change. Or remember what they want to remember *how* they want to remember it. I'm not trying to do that. A person must respect their past, even an unpleasant past, because it's part of them, of what made a person who they are. I thought I came to terms with it long ago and then shut it away. Until this came up between us, about your mother. The past is what it is, but I also think a person can see their past through new eyes, eyes of experience and understanding, instead of remembering it only as the child saw it."

"I suspect that child saw through fairly honest eyes."

"Honest but not objective, and not with an appreciation of the misery my father carried that ruined his life."

"Maybe that's the biggest triumph."

"What?"

"That you didn't let a miserable start ruin your life."

"No, but . . . a kid doesn't choose where it starts its life. You're just born there, and you don't know any different, and you do the best you can within whatever situation you're given. I did that until I saw other ways to live. And then I made a different choice. A better choice for me.

"Sometimes I think if I'd forced myself to review my childhood objectively years ago, maybe I could've been a better husband and father."

I said, "I've heard you say before that no one is perfect. So you aren't perfect, but you did well. You're a very strong person. I've always known that about you."

He didn't look at me, just stared ahead at that fallen house.

I added, "I'm not strong. I always wanted to be strong like you." I regretted the words and the puny voice they were spoken in as soon as I said them.

This time, Dad shook his head and looked down at his feet. "I'm strong. I am. And no, Kara, I wouldn't describe you as strong."

His words hurt. I didn't say so aloud, but I felt the pain keenly.

Dad waved his hand at the woods around us. "People build houses to last, to be strong. And these trees, they are strong. If a strong wind blows, they'll fight it and face it down because that's what they do. But if a strong enough wind blows, they'll fall. Flat. They won't get back up." He scratched his cheek. "Being strong has value. I'm strong. I always have been. I have always thought of you as resilient." He nodded as if confirming his own words. "Resilient. You've been knocked down a few times, but each time you get back up and move forward again."

"Do I? It doesn't feel like it, Dad. Maybe I've been knocked down too many times."

He smiled and looked at me. "I didn't say you always got up fast."

"Ha ha. Funny. Or not funny."

"You're better. You might not be where you want to be yet, but you are well on your way."

"With your help."

"You would've managed it with or without me. That's who you are. I hope I've eased the way for you a little. I haven't always done that. I wanted to but didn't know how."

I put my hand on his. "You did good, Dad." I added, "Mom wasn't strong either."

"No, she wasn't."

"Would you call her resilient too? Ultimately not resilient, of course, but if the depression and medications hadn't changed her?"

Dad sat in silence for a long time before answering.

"No, she was never resilient. She was all emotion. She laughed, she cried, she danced. She was the most beautiful, enchanting person I'd ever known. Maybe that can't be sustained. I think she burned out." He looked away. "I'm not saying it well. If I'd been able to give her what she needed, understood how to help her, it might have been different. I'm sorry, Kara, that you lost your mother."

"I found her wedding portrait in one of the boxes. She was so bright and lovely. I wish I remembered her that way. I'd like to." I paused before asking, "Would you mind if I hung her portrait? Maybe in the hallway or the sitting room?"

Dad cleared his throat. His voice came out almost hoarse. "That would be fine. Wherever you think best."

"I'm not like either one of you, am I?"

He reached over, and this time he took my hand in his. "No. And yes. I think you got the best of both of us. My logic, my drive, and your mother's heart and spirit." He squeezed my hand.

I didn't know what to say. If that was what he thought, then I was afraid I'd let him down. He might not know it yet, but one day he would see the truth. Unless I could change the current state. Get back on track. Find a job and make my mark.

We sat in silence. The house shingles were a kind I'd never seen before. They looked almost like little pebbles glued to a backing. The roof shingles were black. I couldn't guess at the material. A front door.

Two windows were set in the front on either side of the door. A concrete slab peeked out from under the house, from where the house had collapsed forward and into the tangle of greenery and fallen sticks. I wanted a closer look. To fight the green growth and see what was behind the house, to get a feel for what this life had been like. But not here, not in front of my father. Exercising my curiosity in that way, in the reality of his painful memories, wouldn't be appropriate.

"What about this property? Who owns this house, this land, now?"

"Does it matter?"

I shrugged this time. "I don't know. I was thinking that if this represented bad memories for me, I'd bulldoze it. The debris doesn't need to sit here like a reminder or a shrine. Put these old ghosts to rest." I thought of that Emerson poem again: "They called me theirs, / Who so controlled me; / Yet every one / Wished to stay, and is gone."

"Past is past, Dad. You taught me that."

"True enough. Not always so easy to accomplish. At any rate, I pay the taxes on the property." His breath sounded ragged again. "Plus, not knowing for sure about my brother and sister . . ." He took his hand back and ran it over his face.

He'd kept ownership of the property, but when he'd finally returned to Cub Creek, it hadn't been to this sad spot or even to visit his father's grave. He'd returned to the Bowens' house. Later the Forsters' house. Now our Wildflower House.

"I was imagining you as a child sitting in the grotto watching the Bowen family."

"The grotto?"

"That's what Seth calls it. Where the gazing ball was."

He nodded. "The Forsters changed it a lot. It didn't look like a grotto back when I was young." He sighed and slapped at a small black insect that had landed on his cheek. "I think the bugs have found us."

"One more thing, Dad, if you don't mind?"

"What's that?"

I shook my head. "After meeting Nicole and seeing the two of you together, I thought you must have wanted to move here to set up a new life at this house because you wanted to be near her. I thought I might be in the way." I let the statement . . . not quite a question . . . hang there, waiting.

Dad scratched his scalp through his short hair. He shook his head slightly, too, and I couldn't tell whether he was upset that I'd brought up Nicole.

"Nicole and I had our time. Now we're friends. She's a lot younger, in case you hadn't noticed."

"Is that irony or sarcasm?"

"Just honesty."

"Honesty. Dad, if I'm being honest, I have to admit that it bothers me that Nicole knows certain things, like about your childhood, that I don't. Or didn't know."

He smiled gently and took my hand. "A loving parent wants to protect their child. Anything I might not have told you was only for that reason."

I nodded. We stood and retraced our steps toward the road. I saw something moving through the brush as we walked. It moved quietly but swiftly. An animal. "Dad, did you see that?"

"What?"

"Some kind of animal, I think."

He waved his hand. "It's harmless. Animals do live in the woods, Kara. You rarely see them because that's their nature. They either sleep during the day, or they stay undercover. It's all about survival. Most aren't even curious about you, except in terms of how to evade you."

"We're the predators?"

"The food chain, Kara. Everyone's on it. Humans along with other living creatures. Regardless of our place in line, we are just renters on Earth. Tenants."

"Are you okay, Dad?" I tossed aside all thoughts about woodland creatures. "You sound short of breath."

He nodded. "I'm fine. Just ready to be home."

We all had our limits. Mom had. Maybe Niles had too. Had I reached mine yet? At times when I was in the hospital and even during my recovery, I'd thought so more than once. Now, as we caught glimpses between the trees of the road ahead, I knew better. My limit, or my perception of it as having been reached, was grossly premature. Despite the craziness of the last few weeks, my footing in this life felt steadier than ever. My shoes might be muddied, but the trip had strengthened me.

Why? Because sometimes the things you didn't know could hurt you by preventing you from understanding. Not everything could be understood, but information, no matter how hurtful when it was revealed, could make all the difference. The problem was this: How did one know when it was good to share it or a selfish act?

"Coming, Kara?"

Dad was waiting beside the road. I cast one look back and then shook off my darker mood.

"You bet. Got distracted for a moment."

As we climbed into the car, I said, "Dad, thanks for sharing this with me."

He nodded but didn't speak. I guessed he'd run out of words.

I smiled and returned his nod as reassurance, and we drove home in silence. At first, I stole a few sidelong glances at him, questions forming in my brain, trying to find voice. But I sensed he didn't want to discuss it. Not now. Maybe not ever again.

When we reached the house, I said, "I'm going to start supper."

Dad caught up with me as we climbed the porch steps. "Early for supper, isn't it? Seems like we just had lunch."

"It is early, but I think we can both use some calories. We'll replenish some of that energy we just expended out there. After we eat, we'll get back to work on that wallpaper. I'll help you."

"I've been thinking, Kara. Why don't we hire someone to remove the rest of the wallpaper? We can put our energy into other projects. Leave the paper removal to the professionals."

I leaned against the doorframe, the screen door propped open against my arm. I controlled my facial expressions as I cheered inside, *Yes, yes, yes*. Smoothly, and without a hint of gloating, I said, "It's a big job—that's for sure."

He nodded. "We can't do the removal or painting in some of the areas, like the stairwell, anyway. We'll get someone in. Nicole gave me some names. Maybe I'll make a few calls while you're cooking?"

"Sounds fabulous."

CHAPTER FOURTEEN

The contractors who advertised they could remove wallpaper from old house interiors and restore and paint the high-ceilinged walls arrived in white vans with logos on the side or drove up in huge pickup trucks hung with ladders and filled with metal scaffolding pieces. These contractors came to the door one by one, and Dad invited them in, saying, "Hello, I'm Henry Lange. This is Kara. We'll show you around and explain what we want."

Each came inside and did their thing. Some measured; some didn't. Some took one look at the place and said they weren't the right folks for the job. The last one was Moore Blackwell, a tall, gaunt man with thick dark hair, olive skin, and a worried expression. He looked this way and that, gazed up at the high ceilings and the stairwell, asked a few questions and made notes, and seemed morose throughout the whole visit. At one point, he stood and stared at those cabbage roses as if they were sending subliminal messages directly to him.

I started to speak, but Dad motioned me to stay silent.

Finally, Mr. Blackwell turned to us and said, "Handy that it's so empty. Did you have a particular starting point in mind?"

"The main floor?"

The man nodded. "We'd cover the floors. They're in excellent shape, especially considering the rest." He cast a long, sorrowful look at the parlor wall and the ripped paper and abandoned tools. His was the most recent in a series of baleful stares directed at our failed effort.

I couldn't take it. I blurted out, "It looked better before we tried to do it ourselves." I cast a quick glance at Dad, and he frowned.

The man smiled at me. "I've seen it before. Nothing wrong with doing it yourself, if you can. Even better to recognize when to bring in help." He scratched his cheek. His heavy five-o'clock shadow had arrived a few hours early, and the scratching sounded like nails on sandpaper. "Fact is I won't know for sure how best to proceed until I get started. Judging by the age of the paper, there's probably not many layers beneath. Beyond that, we'll have to see how it's stuck to the plaster. Might remove it. Might remove what we can and plaster over. Can't say for certain till we're into it. Want to be sure you understand that. This ain't an exact science."

I appreciated that he didn't judge us on our failed attempt. I was relieved and didn't know why. I wasn't the person pushing this project. At least I'd had the willingness to try. No, wait—that had been my father. My dad had tried. I'd dragged my heels the whole way, all the while saying I was supporting him.

My thoughts were interrupted when Mr. Blackwell asked, "What are your plans for this place? A bed-and-breakfast or something like that? They're getting popular in the Louisa area. There's a new one opening in Mineral."

I frowned this time. "Out here? In this wilderness?"

He raised his eyebrows. "Mineral is a town, ma'am."

"I do know that. I'm speaking of Cub Creek. And I know this area doesn't look like a wilderness to the people who grew up out here. I meant no offense. But . . . well, there are lots of trees and no other houses in sight."

"No offense taken, ma'am."

I continued, "A bed-and-breakfast would make more sense in a place where people could go and *see* stuff. I mean stuff other than trees and unkempt properties and roads to nowhere." I smiled in apology. "Sorry. I wasn't expecting all that to come bursting out."

Mr. Blackwell looked confused.

My father said, "Kara is used to the city. This seems middle of nowhere to her."

The man gave a short laugh. "It's getting more crowded all the time. Where it's empty, they sell the timber and then try to turn the land into a subdivision. You're only a few miles from the interstate to the south and Mineral to the north. I get what you're saying about a city B and B, but my sister's husband's cousin owns a place in the Tennessee mountains. Named it Blueberry something or other. Calls it a getaway. A retreat. Says folks like to get out in the country and relax. That's not my business, though, and I'm not trying to tell you how to manage yours, but the point is sometimes the intent should figure into the destination, the end result. Course, if you and your husband are planning on just plain living here, that's fine too."

I'd gotten lost somewhere in all his words.

Dad spoke up, surprising me. "My daughter."

"Oh. You never know, right?" Mr. Blackwell closed his notebook and shoved his pencil down inside the spiral binding. "I'll send the estimate, and if you're happy with it, we'll set a date to start."

~

I folded the tarp as I cleared away the mess we'd made attempting to strip the wallpaper. I was so glad to cast off the responsibility for that task. Funny how Mr. Blackwell thought Dad and I might be setting up a bed-and-breakfast or some sort of retreat. A retreat. I laughed out loud. I could use a retreat . . . or maybe I already had one and didn't properly appreciate it yet. I laughed again, imagining myself as a hostess.

I tucked Dad's tools into the large storage closet off the mudroom, then swept and dusted the wooden floors as I thought about Dad and how he'd interacted with those contractors. I'd never seen him in action like that, so to speak. I was impressed.

By keeping me out of his tire business, I suspected he'd cut me out of so much more—because that was where he'd lived most of his life. Not with his home as a focal point or a touchstone but his business.

I could've been part of his life. I would have liked that. By the time I'd been approaching adulthood, I'd been absorbed in college and falling in love. Maybe he hadn't been the only one in our family who wasn't always available.

~

The moon looked different out here. It hung, big and bold, outside my bedroom window. It cast silvery reflections over the landscape and inside the room too. I lay in bed waiting for the exhaustion of the move and the work we'd been doing to wash over me and bear me off to dreamland. But that sleep—the sleep of a well-earned rest—eluded me tonight.

My head was on the pillow, and my hands lay idle on the covers, but my brain was busy.

I asked myself again—what was I doing here?

Helping Dad? He didn't need my help. Not with the house and not with his life. He had Nicole. Likely, other friends too. It was so odd, but I'd rarely seen my father interacting with people like neighbors and tradesmen. I was surprised that he behaved like a regular guy. Not like someone who was stunted emotionally or who avoided interaction. Of course, it was mostly superficial interaction or business related, so maybe it was the nature of the interaction that shut him down rather than avoidance in general. He'd greeted the contractors, smiling and shaking their hands and discussing the work he wanted done like some men discussed their families or hobbies. Easy breezy. Dad was cool and relaxed with these people, and I felt like an idiot among them.

Was it this place? As strange as this house, this moon, these new friends seemed to me, maybe Dad *did* belong here. I didn't belong. Life was passing me by while I was hanging out here in the country.

But I *could* belong. I felt it. I sensed it when I walked these floors, when I saw the sky and the trees and the green world beyond the window glass—and felt safe.

I pushed the covers aside and went to the window.

The moonlight dappled the waters of Cub Creek. On the far side, the forest was dark and thick. Between there and here, where I stood at this moment, stretched a fantastic landscape made mysterious and full of potential by the magic of the moon.

I had always worried that I was like my father. Cold. Afraid of emotion. Wary of disorder.

Perhaps I should've been more concerned about being like my mom.

Echoes of Niles again. I shivered. I recalled what Niles had said and how it had set me off. He'd found a fear, a tender spot, and had ruthlessly jabbed at it.

I acknowledged to myself I felt a bit of jealousy over Nicole's relationship with my father, mostly because I hadn't known about it. I'd been effectively excluded from that part of his life too. But despite myself, I liked Nicole well enough. Probably helped along by the fact that I liked her mother without reservation. My own mom would've been about Mel's age. Mom wouldn't have been anything like Mel Albers with Mel's wiry strength, her brash talk, but I'd never really known who my mom would've become. I'd been without her now longer than I'd been with her. A sad marking of the passage of time.

What was it that Dad had said about re-seeing one's history through eyes with greater experience? He'd been speaking of his own childhood when we'd been sitting in the woods on that downed tree, in that sad place where he'd grown up. He could see his past through adult eyes now. Not necessarily a truer view, but likely a more balanced one. I could do the same. And I could recognize depression. Lots of people suffered from depression. What Dad had said before about Mom's post-partum depression made sense. Had the treatments helped or made it worse? Like throwing a pharmacy at a guinea pig. In the end, how could you know whether the patient was still sick or now suffering from the treatment?

I turned away from the window, my hand on my throat. I was parched and greatly in need of a glass of water. I walked down the hall-way, bypassing the back stairs. They were too dark and too steep for a nighttime stroll. I paused outside Dad's door, listening.

Not a sound. Not even a snore. I continued to the stairs. By now, I knew which steps were most likely to creak. Step one, step two, avoid the creak by stepping near the end of the tread on three. I held tightly to the railing. I'd left my cane downstairs. It wasn't much good for descending stairs with anyway. Plus, my thigh was much better. Not perfect, but this move had done more for my post-accident ailments than those last months of physical therapy had seemed to accomplish.

In the kitchen, my cane was hanging on the back doorknob. I gripped the crook and flipped the door locks.

The last time I'd done this had been the first time. I'd stayed on the porch. On this trip I admired the night view and listened to the soft, subtle sounds and steady rhythm of the cicadas or whatever kinds of insects were emitting that steady hum, and then, assured, I stepped carefully down the steps to the terrace. I didn't want to fall out here. If I reinjured myself, it would be a lonely, maybe scary, and certainly uncomfortable night before someone found me.

Between the moon and stars overhead and the reflected light moving on the surface of the creek, the night hardly seemed dark at all.

I kept to the grassy walkway yet felt every stick and stone poke at the soles of my bare feet. The grass was damp and icky. *Such a tenderfoot!* I laughed silently at myself. Near the end, where the flower field gave way to that area of lawn near the creek, I paused again as small lights suddenly appeared near the flowers at about eye level.

These lights weren't impersonal beacons of the universe but fellow creatures. Deer. They lifted their faces from their nighttime meal. Their eyes picked up the moonlight and other night lights and glowed with a greenish tint.

What did I look like to them? Standing there, transfixed, I began to hear other sounds. Nearby, a tree groaned. Something, perhaps an owl, disturbed the upper branches with a slight swoosh. A small creature scurried through the deeper shadows of the tree line. There were splashes in the creek as a living animal jumped in.

The scent of the flowers was strong. The wildflowers' scent was softer than most hothouse flowers, it seemed to me, but out here in the greenhouse of the night, their tangy sweetness toyed with my nose. I fought a sneeze lest I disturb the peace.

Perhaps the scent, though not obvious, had called to me through the open window. Maybe that was why I hadn't been able to settle into sleep.

High above, the stars were strong in number and brightness. I recognized the Dippers and some other constellations. I could reach up, I was sure, and touch Orion's belt with my fingertips.

I was holding the cane with one hand, but my other hand, the one that wanted to touch eternity above, felt empty. Empty. I pressed that hand to my heart.

When I was a child, I walked with my parents. I held my mother's hand. My father's hand.

When I was a teenager, I shook off those hands. I needed mine free to find who I was, to find my balance of personhood.

When I fell in love, I held Niles's hand. We clasped our hands tightly together and found our way to marriage. If death hadn't ended that marriage, life would have. I didn't doubt it.

What did they say in the service? Giving one's hand in marriage? Yes, that was it. Supposedly until death did us part—and it had.

The reality was that if the accident hadn't happened, and if it had come to a choice between Niles and my unborn child, I would've helped Niles pack and wished him well.

I pressed my hand to my belly. Would I ever have that chance again?

But more than the child who hadn't been, I missed the human connection. The hand held, the hug, the kiss.

How many worn or lonely people through the centuries had stood beneath a night sky and felt the same? I sought the right word. Loneliness? Not quite. Incompleteness, maybe? I felt a kinship with them. Some may have found what they yearned for. Others settled for what they could get. For some, it may have been too sad to go on.

I wasn't sad. But I hadn't found what I yearned for either. I remembered thinking about the stages of my life. Maybe I'd been wrong. Stages implied a relatively clear end and beginning. Maybe seasons of life? Though trite through overuse, it was probably the better descriptor. Maybe that was why it was so overused. Because it was true. I smiled into the night.

Did I belong here? No. But being here felt like a gift. Perhaps a temporary one, but that was life too. Even the stars, so long in their places high above that they spoke of forever, would one day lose their light.

An owl called in the night. What did he call for? Maybe I knew.

I whispered to the deer, "Good night." Gently and quietly, I turned and made my way back to the house.

~

At breakfast, Dad said, "I haven't seen you working on your needlework flowers since we moved."

I shrugged. "I've been busy."

"I'm glad. Not that there was anything wrong with it."

"But I did it too much?"

He grimaced. "Sorry. Yes. I know you're grown up and don't need me telling you how to spend your time."

"No worries, Dad. But don't be disappointed when you see me pick the embroidery hoop back up again."

"Actually, I had an idea related to that. Those flowers you put on the mantel in the sitting room made me think of it."

Those flowers? Yes, I'd cut a few, leaving the stems long and arranging them in a vase. The wildflower field was packed. It could spare a few for an admirer . . . me.

Dad was saying, "Those tall blue flowers. The big canvas?"

"What?" I shook my head. "I'm sorry, Dad. I was daydreaming."

"I was just saying that the flowers outside won't be around forever, right? I was looking at the ones you put on the mantel. I thought about the needlework you did . . . especially the big one with the tall blue flowers."

"Yes, I know which you mean. The delphiniums."

"We should get it framed. It would fit on the wall above the fireplace. Maybe frame some of your other embroidery too."

I was astounded. Wordless. He'd paid that much attention to the crewelwork—close enough that he could differentiate between them? Had even picked a favorite to frame and hang over the fireplace?

Dad forked another bite of eggs into his mouth. He was looking at me, waiting for a response.

"Sure. That's a good idea. A great idea, actually."

He cleared his throat. "We could maybe use those colors to pick a rug for the room. What do you think?"

"Dad."

"What, Kara?"

"I never knew you were interested in decorating."

He looked surprised. "I'm not. I was thinking, though, that we should find some rugs for these front rooms. It's easier to do if you narrow the population to choose from. For instance, we could base the choices by aligning to something else. But the flower picture solves a few problems—like something pleasant to look at—and the style and color inform the rug styles. Come winter, those floors will be cold."

I sat back in my chair with a smile.

"What's so funny?"

I started to explain but then backed off. "I'm glad you like my needlework. I wonder where I should take it for framing? Richmond, maybe."

Dad gathered the last bits of breakfast onto his fork. "We'll ask Nicole. She knows good places to buy rugs and to get framing done too. Especially any that might be local. I like to support local merchants, if possible."

Ask Nicole. Of course. Nicole was the fount of all useful knowledge. Then I mentally smacked myself for such petty-minded snark. Nicole was my father's friend and ex-girlfriend. She wasn't my rival, and there was no call for me to behave like a jealous teenager. I had already acknowledged and accepted that.

"And birdhouses," he added.

"What?" What was he talking about now? This was the strangest conversation.

"I want to hang birdhouses and feeders. Remember how we had them in our yard when you were little? You enjoyed watching the birds."

He was smiling. I didn't want to dim his fun, but I couldn't help myself.

"I remember the bird feeder . . . the one outside the kitchen window. Mom liked it."

He gave me a blank look, a thinking expression, the kind a calculator might give you if it had to stop and think when solving a particularly gnarly problem. He shook his head. "You did too."

I sighed and stood, ready to break this off before it got too gloomy.

"Kara," he insisted, "you were always asking me to refill it, seemed like every time I turned around."

"Because no one did, Dad. Mom liked to look out at it, but she wouldn't fill it. I asked you to, but you were always in a hurry to get to work or late getting home from work. I wasn't tall enough to reach it." I kept going. "Then winter arrived. It cracked. Even then, it was left hanging there."

His complexion flushed.

That sharp tongue of mine—I regretted it. "That doesn't mean we won't enjoy them now. And now I'm tall enough to fill them myself. I think it's a good idea."

"Are you sure, Kara?"

I nodded and picked up his empty plate and utensils. "I'm sure. Maybe wind chimes, too, for the porch."

He pulled a small pad of paper from his pocket along with a short pencil. It was the kind of pencil golfers used to record strokes. He peered at the paper, then put it on the table and wrote tiny letters on it. He picked it up and read it again, smiled, and said, "Got it," as he slid it back into his pocket.

"My list," he said, patting his pocket. "I'll take care of the bird-house, feeder, and chimes." He pointed at me. "Can you handle the framing and the rugs?"

"Framing, maybe, but you'll have to come along for the rugs."

"Good idea. We'll do it together. We'll take care of that later this week. Deal?"

"It's a deal, Dad."

I saw the relief in his eyes. Another conversation successfully completed? Maybe. I couldn't resist teasing him. "With all the flowers out there, birdhouses and feeders make sense. We already have the garden gnomes. I believe we're still missing a gazing ball."

His blank look was back, but then something changed. Perhaps he was reading the twinkle in my eye.

With great solemnity, he pulled out his list again and began to write on it. He said, "One . . . gazing . . . ball." He tapped the pencil against his cheek, then said, "And pink flamingos."

I looked at his face as he bent over the pad of paper. Was he teasing me? Or was he serious? No, he couldn't be. A vision of a yard full of plastic pink flamingos did me in. "No pink flamingos."

"No?" He paused, holding his pencil over the paper.

"No, Dad. I must draw the line somewhere. I'm drawing a hard line and stamping it as final regarding pink flamingos. We will make do with gazing balls, wind chimes, and garden gnomes."

"Well, if you're sure."

He hadn't cracked a smile throughout the exchange, and he still didn't as he turned and strolled out of the kitchen.

He called back, "What's for supper tonight?"

"Pink flamingo," I muttered.

"Interesting menu item." But he kept moving and didn't return.

I stood there, rinsing the dishes and asking myself, *Who is this new Dad? This new Henry Lange?*

A stillness came over me. I continued staring out the window, wondering. He'd unburdened himself about my mom, our family, his friends, and even his dreadful childhood. Was I finally seeing the real Henry Lange? Now freed of his secrets?

Did I feel the burden of them now? His shared memories? Had he shared them with me, or had he effectively shifted the weight of them to me?

Maybe he truly was rewriting his history—taking the sting from it by crafting a hopeful present and a better future out of the best parts of it. I needed a magic pen of my own to plan my future.

CHAPTER FIFTEEN

Dad said, "Blackwell's crew is coming a week from Monday, first thing in the morning. We should have everyone over sometime this week before the house gets torn apart."

"Torn apart? That sounds awful. Who's everyone, and why do we want to have them over?"

"Nicole, Seth, Mel—the people who've been helping us make this move work. Anyone you want. Mr. Blackwell's crew will start in the parlor first. Between the start and the finish, things are going to get very messy, so let's have them over before."

"Are you sure about this?"

He nodded. "I am."

"We should include Maddie, too, if she won't be too bored."

"What about Victoria?"

"What about her? She isn't an Albers."

"You know she wants an invite. Get it all handled with one meal."

"If Victoria's in Richmond visiting her mom or something, maybe. I wouldn't want her to think we expect her to drive down from Northern Virginia."

"That's up to you. I get the idea that you aren't sold on Victoria these days. Seemed like you two were good friends before."

"We were. Are." I grimaced and shrugged. "I don't know. I met her about the time I met Niles. Maybe that's it. She reminds me of those times."

"Of losing him?"

I nodded. "Yes, that, plus other things . . . like things that didn't go quite right between us. Niles and I were having problems."

"Every relationship, every marriage does."

"True, but if all I have left of Niles and our time together are memories, then I'd rather remember the good ones." I waved my hands as if dispersing the syllables I'd just uttered. "That doesn't mean I don't appreciate her thoughtfulness. She came to visit me in the hospital, at home, and even here. In fact, when she was here before, that day when Mel was cleaning the furniture? I was supposed to set something up for her to come back and visit us, but I just never did."

"Give it time. You'll find your friendship again. You just have to find your new life."

I smiled. "True. I keep thinking I'm moving forward, and I guess I am, but I still don't see the path. Sometimes I feel like . . . well, like I'm floundering. I think I've gotten lazy, especially when it comes to getting out there again."

"Be patient, Kara. You're young yet. You have a lot of life ahead of you." He added, "Can I tell them?"

"About the thank-you dinner?"

Dad rubbed his hands together. "This will be the first time we've had dinner guests, ever, Kara. It'll be fun."

I shook my head but couldn't help absorbing some of his excitement. "Tell them we're keeping it casual and simple. When you agree on a date and time, let me know."

Less than an hour later, Dad came walking through. He paused when he found me in the kitchen. I was using the laptop at the kitchen table. When he came over to where I was sitting, I lowered the lid, enough for a little privacy. He didn't seem to notice.

He said, "Tuesday at six p.m. That works best for everyone. Is it good for you?"

I sighed. "Not the weekend? Tuesday doesn't give us much time."

"We're keeping it simple, right? Up to you whether you want to check with Victoria."

"Odds are she won't be able to come, especially with such little warning. She has a job, after all." I looked at Dad again. "Are you sure Tuesday is good?"

"That's what Nicole said. Weekends are her busiest time, so . . ."

"All right, then. I'll let Victoria know, in case she can work it out."

"Do you want to go to the grocery store? Or shall I?"

I didn't feel inclined to drive anywhere. "Why don't I make you a list? I suggest kebabs."

He looked a little sad. Had I let him down in some way?

"Dad, if you don't want kebabs, tell me. No problem."

"Kebabs are fine. I just thought you might like to get out and see the area."

"Not today. Soon. Besides, you'll be going out today anyway for other things."

"All right, then. Make a list. I'll run by the store in Mineral." Dad glanced at the laptop. "Is the internet working okay?"

"Yep. I'm doing a little surfing."

He nodded. "Not my business." He paused and shared a knowing look with me. "Of course, you always did enjoy online shopping. While you're at it, see if we can order some curtains. My windows feel . . . open." He walked away with attitude as if to show he was cleverer than I'd realized.

I lifted the laptop lid. No shopping was going on. I'd found some of Seth's old newspaper columns and was reading through them. The variety of topics was interesting. The common denominator was the human-interest story, as he'd said. One was about young men on the street and resources in the downtown Richmond area that offered them assistance. Another dove into charitable activities like church groups feeding the homeless in a city park. Yet another was about an art exhibition at the Virginia Museum of Fine Arts.

He was talented. I was glad I'd encouraged him to consider his profession and his future. If he found the right job, then the rest of the pieces of his life would fall into place. Which was exactly what would happen for me if I kept trying. I just needed to get that first piece set.

I closed the laptop and ran my hands over the smooth metal of the lid.

It seemed to me that Seth was the kind of guy who took responsibility. He assumed the roles that his loved ones needed him to fill. He wasn't a guy-of-all-trades because he was lazy or couldn't stick with something. He was needed. I didn't doubt it. But not as needed as he'd been. If he wanted to do something else, even the type of job he'd had before, then his time was now.

~

Tuesday morning, as I finished showering and returned to my room to dress, I heard the noise of a mower at work through the open window. I peeked out. Far below, Seth was pushing one down the grassy path that bordered the wildflowers, moving down toward the creek.

I dressed quickly in a T-shirt and capris. I left my long hair to dry on its own because the wet felt good as the breeze touched it. I took a quick look in the mirror.

Yes, the scar was still there at the hairline, but fainter. Really, not too bad. I fluffed my wet hair over it with my fingers and went downstairs.

I took my coffee cup out to the back porch. I stood there as Seth worked his way up the slope. Finally, he noticed me. I waved. He continued pushing the mower, and the roar prevented conversation until he was closer, and he put it into idle.

"Good morning, Kara," he called out.

"Good morning, Seth. You're at it early. It's looking good."

He cupped his hand to his ear. "You said I'm looking good?"

"Ha ha," I said. But yes, I did think he was looking pretty good. Not that I'd say it aloud.

"As to working early," he said, "I have plans later today. I've been invited to dinner at a friend's house."

"What a coincidence. We're having friends over for dinner today."

Seth grinned. "We're looking forward to it. Mom said to tell you she appreciates the invite. Maddie won't be coming. She's staying over with a friend tonight."

"Are you sure? She's welcome. Probably not much fun for her, though."

"Trust me—she'll be happier spending time with her friend."

I smiled. "I can believe that." I stepped back from the railing. "Sorry to have interrupted you, but I couldn't resist."

"You couldn't resist?"

"Oh, I guess that sounded odd."

"Not at all. In fact, it's not the first time I've been called irresistible. Though I wasn't cutting grass that time."

"I didn't mean it quite that way."

"No?"

"No. It's just that every time I see you, you're working—cutting grass, fixing windows, and such. You are that Seth-of-all-trades guy. But I found some of your blog posts and articles. Human-interest topics. I enjoyed them, especially the ones about second chances and those about local artists."

"Ah." He started to speak, paused, and then started again. "I'm glad you liked them. Unfortunately, human interest and heartwarming are the first things to go when budgets get cut. Besides, I'd like to do something a little different. I told you I've been putting out feelers in the industry again? It's too soon to know if interesting opportunities will arise, but we'll see."

"I'm glad. You are a talented writer."

His flush deepened, and it wasn't just from cutting grass.

"Sorry to have interrupted you, but as I said, I couldn't help myself." I smiled. "I'll see you later."

He nodded. "Looking forward to it."

~

There wasn't much cleaning for me to do. Mostly, I had to cook and set the dining room table. I ran the dust mop around the empty floors. It was almost fun, satisfying in the simplest way imaginable. I shined up the sitting room and dining room windows, and I hung Mom's wedding portrait on the sitting room wall. It was temporary, of course, since these walls would be stripped of their paper after the parlor was done. It was sad and also lovely to see her there.

Her eyes seemed piercing but warm. Her gaze had a recent feel and brought back memories. They came at me in a rush, and I almost took it back down. I needed to remind Dad and give him a bit of warning.

~

It was a sight—the pretty linen and shiny dishes on the table versus the utter lack of any kind of interior decoration except for ancient wallpaper and the dull, tarnished chandelier overhead. It was like a bright island in an otherwise empty—and now dust-free—landscape. It would make an interesting, if eerie, painting. On impulse, I picked up my cell phone and took some photos. As Dad said, we were marking the start of the official renovation. This room, this whole house, would look very different in a few months.

I experienced an odd moment then. It crept over me demurely, politely reminding me that I was just passing through here. This was my father's house, and the decisions were his. My life, my future, were elsewhere.

I thought of wildflowers and children. No one chose where or to whom they'd be born. We had to manage where we began. Like wildflowers. I'd survived a lot, and Dad wasn't perfect, but he'd done his best. I'd thought I'd made the choice to go to college, to fall in love with Niles, to find that job in DC. In retrospect, I suspected I'd just followed what had seemed the most natural, most expected course and had tried to fit myself into it. And had ended up back with Dad.

But this time, being here or choosing not to felt like a true choice. I did have the power to stay or to go—and the power to decide when the time was right. My father had done the same. He had made and remade his life.

"For now, I'm here." I said those words aloud and felt a strange reassurance. I stood straighter and tugged at the hem of my shirt as if in punctuation.

I went outside and selected blooms that were still pretty. I arranged them in a crystal vase and placed it on the fireplace mantel in the dining room. The wallpaper above the mantel had an imprint left behind—the shape of something, either a mirror or a painting, that had lived in that spot for many years. Before long, the proof that anything had ever hung here would vanish along with the old paper.

Satisfied with the dining room, I considered what to wear this evening.

This would be a casual dinner. I didn't want to overdo the dressing up—which was good since I still hadn't gone shopping to update my wardrobe. Besides, these were Dad's friends more than mine—with the possible exception of Seth—and I was just helping him host.

The menu was set. I would assemble the kebabs ahead of time, and Dad would cook them outside on the grill. I had the side dishes all ready to heat in the oven and on the stovetop. I looked at my phone. Time.

I had plenty of it. Dad was due home at five p.m., and our guests were due at six p.m.

I chose a silky top to go with my slacks. I applied a little makeup but kept it light.

After a last check in the kitchen—yes, everything was ready to go—I walked outside. The weather was amazing. The air was warm, but the humidity was low, and the breeze kept it all stirring gently—the perfect weather brew.

From the porch I looked down at the field of flowers. They were still beautiful, though slightly past their prime. It was a little sad that the physical and emotional rush I'd first experienced when seeing them had lessened. Now they'd become more a piece of the whole—a piece of the quilt of the whole landscape: the house, the bushes and trees, the special sitting areas, and the creek. I wished the sweeping view was something I could frame to hang on the wall and admire in the winter, to remember how glorious it had looked when the flowers were blooming and bright with promise.

I leaned against the porch post. The flowers shifted in the breeze, and several birds lifted from the copse where the birdbath was. One diverted from the others and flew across the creek to a low-hanging branch. That tree was dead, its trunk a cold gray color, and it had a stark, sculptured quality to it. The bird perched there, and for all its tiny size, it trilled out a song as if singing especially to me.

"There you are."

I turned to see Seth on the terrace with a smile on his face. He was holding a large brown paper bag. The grocery store kind.

"You're early."

"I am. I came ahead in case you need help. Mom will be along shortly." He walked across the terrace to the porch steps. As he climbed, he said, "Nicole will be on time, she said to tell you. She's with a client and will come straight from there. May be a minute or two late. She wanted to warn you, just in case."

"No problem. Dad's grilling. We won't start until she gets here."

"Beautiful day for a cookout."

"Well, strictly speaking, Dad will cook part of the meal out on the grill, but we'll be eating inside."

"Are you okay with me being here early? If it's a problem, I can disappear for an hour."

"No, you're welcome. If I looked distracted, I'm just trying to match up all the bits and pieces in my head. You're early. Nicole may be late. Dad isn't here yet, though he's supposed to be. Nor is my friend Victoria. We're old college friends. Victoria combined this trip down to join us for dinner with a visit to her mom in Richmond, so I'm sure she'll be here anytime now."

"Lots of moving pieces."

"But not really a problem, right? Not for a casual, friendly gathering. And yet this feels like a dinner party that may fail to launch."

"Fail to launch?" He laughed. "There's food, right? And at least two of us are here to eat it." He shook his head. "I'm sorry. I don't mean to make light of the effort, the prep, or anything else. Henry and Nicole will always pay attention to business over pleasure. You know that, right?"

I shrugged and tried not to smile too broadly. "I do know. They are different in appearance and age but very similar at heart."

"That heart similarity—interesting way to put it—is probably a big part of what attracted them to each other in the first place. Business oriented and not overly emotional. But it's not really sustainable in the long term, not as a relationship, is it?"

I was listening and didn't answer. It was probably a rhetorical question, anyway.

Seth continued, "I don't think I'm giving away any secrets. They were involved, then not, then involved again. Your accident—and this will sound bad, but I promise it's not meant that way—was something of a blessing for them. They were talking marriage. They put that discussion aside when your dad rushed to your bedside, and by the time you were improving, the 'marriage fever' had passed."

"I had no idea. I ruined it for them."

"No, and I mean it. It was a good thing, and I think they both knew it then—and still do. They are better as friends."

"How did I not know all that?"

"How could you? Unless your dad filled you in, how would you know?"

"Maybe he would've. I was busy with marriage, with my job, and then with the accident and the aftermath. But I don't like the idea of him keeping secrets from me." I shook my head. "Not fair of me to say that. Dad doesn't really keep secrets as such. He just avoids some subjects. If they'd set a date, I'm sure he would've told me. He has always been uncomfortable in in-between areas. For him, it either is, or it isn't."

"Secrets are tricky, for sure. Like with Maddie. It's not really a secret that Patricia is gone, but no one talks about it in front of Maddie. We tell ourselves there's no need to burden her with worries she can't understand or do anything about. Maybe the truth is that we're afraid of being asked questions we might not know how to answer."

"What about her father?"

"Never in the picture. Patricia and Maddie lived with Mom. Maddie was only two. I was in Richmond then and doing what I did with writing for the newspaper and online blogs and all that but barely making a living."

He cleared his throat, then said, "Patricia's death was pretty devastating for all of us, but Mom and Maddie . . . Nicole became Maddie's legal guardian. Mom did most of the caregiving. She did a good job, but it took a toll on her. Finally, I came home, and we all worked it out together, resorting our lives. Over time, it has worked well, except . . ."

He shrugged. "Except this can't be my life indefinitely. I think we all know that. You and I have talked about some of this. I'm talking to some former colleagues. I'd appreciate it if you didn't mention it to anyone. I know Nicole is a little worried that I'll decamp and leave them to manage alone. Now that Maddie is older—out of the infant and toddler stages—she's pretty easy to care for. It's the diligence, the need to be ever vigilant, that's hard on Mom."

"I understand. This isn't where I thought I'd be at this time of my life either. Please don't misunderstand. I appreciate all that my father has done for me, but I'm not living my life. I'm living someone else's." I looked at him. "You too. I think."

"Maybe. Nothing's holding you here, right? Your dad enjoys your company—I can see that—but he doesn't expect you to stay here with him, does he? I know that you were recovering, but you look good. No, not good. Great."

It made me a little uncomfortable that he seemed so knowledgeable, so easy, with my personal details, but then I'd asked him personal questions, and he'd answered without reservation.

"I'm good. Much better, anyway. I have some lingering challenges. I worry sometimes that I'll never be up to returning to the life I lived before."

"Were you happy before? You said you liked the city, but what about the rest of your life?"

"That's a difficult question to answer." I looked for my cane, realizing I must've left it inside. "I had a good life."

"You still do, I think. Different, I'm sure, but still good. I'm very sorry for your loss. Your husband. You're right: We both know something about grief and loss. And change."

Our interesting chat had turned solemn. I didn't want to continue this discussion.

"I can see I've made you sad. Let's change the subject."

"Please."

"So let's talk about Maddie. Hard to go wrong there."

"She's a very sweet child."

"She is. She can talk a streak, though, if something captures her attention. Asking a million questions. Wanting to chew on it over and over. I think she gets that habit from my mom."

I let the conversation lapse for a long moment. I pretended to be staring at the view, but I was having trouble moving back into an easy conversational exchange. Was it the mention of my accident, my marriage? The child I hadn't had? I'd lost that pregnancy early, but it had felt real to me.

My scar ached a little, but just from tension. I would shake this off.

"I'm sorry, Kara."

"No," I assured him. Not wanting to call attention to the scar, I said, "Only a headache. I get them from time to time. Sort of a hangover from the accident."

"Why don't you find a quiet spot and relax for a few minutes? I'll sit on the front porch in the shade and wait for your father to show up."

"He went shopping for a riding mower. How long can that take?"

Seth laughed as if I'd said something silly.

I shook my head but couldn't resist a small smile. "What is it with guys and lawn mowers? Really, tools of all kinds. Even when they haven't the least clue how to use them. Dad has dragged tools of every kind into this house over the last few days. He talks about supporting local businesses, but he seems to be dedicated to personally keeping them in business."

Seth laughed. "You're right. But owning a riding mower is special."

"Must be. What's delaying him?" I looked around and patted my pocket. "I left my phone inside. He's probably called and is wondering why I'm not answering." I looked at Seth. "Maybe he's had a problem and needs help?"

I headed straight into the house. My limp was suddenly back, and slight though it was, it made me feel damaged. Seth had come inside right behind me. He couldn't help but see, and my limp increased.

My phone was on the dining room buffet. One missed call. Dad. He'd left a voice mail.

I looked at Seth as I listened, then said, "He's on his way. Apologies and all that, but he found a great deal." I set the phone back on the buffet. "I think he must've found a mower he wanted. If so, and if he figures out how to make it work, then you've lost a paying gig."

He gave a mock sigh. "Breaks my heart. Who doesn't love cutting grass in Virginia in the summer?" Seth glanced around. His gaze hesitated briefly on the papered wall in the parlor that had been messed up and then around through the dining room with its odd contrast of decent but everyday dinnerware on crisp white linen, in this once-upon-a-time fancy, formal dining room, now dingy, tired, and long out of fashion.

I said, "It's sort of a mash between the past and present, isn't it? A battle of wills between a past that won't let go and present-day, everyday reality."

Seth stared. He frowned slightly, then smiled ever so interestingly. Finally, he nodded and said, "I like that." He looked around the room again. "Except in this case, the past surrendered already. The reconstruction—the literal reconstruction—is now in progress. You two have your hands full, I think."

"My father does. It's his house."

He grimaced. "Yes, though it's going to be a big, empty place for him when the work ends."

"It's the same for him as for us. If he doesn't like where he is, he's free to move on. He'll take a loss, maybe, but that's life's balance sheet."

"Maybe you're right. I'll have to think about that one." Seth's shifting stance told me the conversation was changing. "At any rate, it looks good in here—will look even better after the work is done. And it was nice of you to invite us over."

His words and tone had that polite, dismissive see-you-later sound. Except I guess he couldn't go because he was my guest, albeit early.

"My pleasure. I appreciate all that you and Nicole have done to help Dad and to make this as good a move as it could be."

I sensed between us a sudden awkwardness, an uncertainty of how-do-we-get-out-of-this-gracefully kind of bubble. A clear bubble. The air between us was so sharp that I felt like I was seeing Seth for the first time . . . really seeing him.

Suddenly, he clapped his hands. Just one clap. He had my full attention, but that wasn't the intent, apparently, because he said, "Where'd I leave the bag?"

"Bag? Oh, that's right. You arrived holding one. Did you set it down outside?"

"I must've left it on the porch." He raised his hand. "I'll be right back." He grinned as he said, "Wait here. It's a present."

I waited, curious.

Seth returned immediately. He was holding that brown grocery bag. It was distorted as if the object inside was much wider than the bag was designed to accommodate. The bag was tearing.

He held it up for me to see. "It's a tough fit. I'll take it out for you."

Seth pulled a frame from the bag. It was an old frame, wooden with some brushed-on gilt decoration. He dropped the bag and kept the frame's picture, if there was one, turned toward him. He said, "For you and your dad. Mostly for you." And held it out for me to take.

Puzzled, I accepted the frame.

It was the house. Our house. Long before Dad was born. Young women in long white dresses posed on the wide steps of the front porch. A few looked very young. Flanking them were a couple of older women in dark, eminently respectable, and uncomfortable-looking dresses. All long dresses, except for the youngest girls, and high necked. Long hair in curls. The older women, surely the teachers, had their dark hair up in buns. The older young women wore their hair up in that fluffy style I thought of as Gibson girl.

There was no date. Turn of the century, surely.

"Sue had it. I talked her out of it."

I stared at his face. His expression was one of delight.

"Thank you. I would like to say much more, but I don't know the words." I added, "Dad will love it."

Seth frowned. "He might be interested, but I doubt he'll love it. It's really for you. I only said it was for him, too, so you wouldn't feel awkward."

I gaped. "But you just said . . . you were worried about me feeling awkward about accepting a gift from you? But now you're telling me that's exactly what it is?"

"Do you like it?"

I nodded. I felt flushed. Seth was confusing me. He was getting past my defenses, and I didn't know how to stop him.

"I do like it." I walked away to hide my face. I sat in my chair, still looking at the photograph. I touched the glass covering the faces. "Each one looks like a real person. Each woman's face has a story."

"Uh, well, they were real people."

"No . . . you know what I mean." I grimaced. "These women stood on my porch." I pointed toward the windows through which we could see that porch. "Out there." I sighed. "Students or teachers at the girls' school."

He smiled. "You like it."

"Of course I do." I stood. "I'm going to take a closer look later. For now." I set it on the mantel, next to the blue vase, and leaned the frame against the wall. "I'll hang it when I figure out the best place." I turned back to Seth. "Thank you again. I love it."

Dad arrived soon after. As soon as he was in the door, I said, "Come see what Seth gave us."

My father stood at the mantel and peered at the framed picture. "This house?"

"Yes. Seth got it from Sue Deale for us."

Seth said, "I saw it when we were there picking up the furniture."

"Thanks, Seth."

Dad was still staring at the photo's details, and I felt a bit of triumph.

"It's fascinating, isn't it?"

Dad said, "It certainly is interesting from a historical perspective. For instance, look at the details of that woodwork along the apron of the porch roof." He looked my way. "Maybe we should try to recreate that?"

When I didn't answer, he said, "I'd better get that grill going. Are the kebabs ready, Kara?"

"Yes."

He walked out. I stood there, face to face with Seth. Seth grinned.

I shook my head. "Woodwork? That's what he saw?"

Seth moved closer and spoke in a low voice. "Guys are different. In fact, people are different. Not necessarily good or bad. In fact, I would argue that the very difference in perception is important. No one person can anticipate every potential problem or account for everything. We contribute our different skills and talents to the effort. That's what having a team is all about."

I raised one eyebrow in doubt. "A team?"

He nodded. "You and your father make a very good team."

"Sometimes," I said. "Right now, my team member is waiting on the kebabs."

"Draft me, Kara. Put me to work."

I pretended not to understand the "draft" reference. Seth already had a team—the Albers team. I reminded myself silently that sometimes teams traded players. I'd never heard of them successfully sharing players.

"Thank you again, Seth. Give Dad a hand. He doesn't have a lot of experience with grilling—at least as far as I know. And don't let him put the food on to cook until after the guests arrive. As you said, Nicole may be held up."

~

Victoria arrived by car. Soon after, Mel arrived on foot. Nicole drove up right after that. I handled the introductions.

"Hi, Mel. Hi, Nicole. Mel, you've met Victoria. Nicole and Seth, this is Victoria. Victoria and I have known each other since college." I touched Victoria's arm. "Mel is Nicole and Seth's mom."

Victoria said, "So pleased to meet you all. It wasn't easy getting the time off on short notice, but as I told Kara, I wouldn't have missed this for anything."

She'd already hinted to me that she'd gone to extra lengths to get the time off from work. Not knowing the details, I didn't want her to launch into the story in front of my guests. To divert her, I said, "You remember Mel from the last time you were here?"

"Of course. Absolutely. So glad to see you again."

Mel nodded. She didn't exactly smile, but she accepted Victoria's impulsive hug.

I thought I had managed the introductions well enough and was ready to move on. "Seth? Will you let Dad know that everyone is here?"

"Will do."

Nicole walked into the sitting room and remarked on the view of the dining room, then spied the blue vase on the mantel. "Oh, how lovely. The perfect spot. I hope you like it."

I smiled my thanks. "Yes. It's beautiful. And locally made? I appreciate your thoughtfulness."

Mel winked at me. Almost a wink, anyway. I knew she was counting words.

"And this old photograph. This is a treasure. Nice to have for the history of the house."

I touched the glass again. Even Nicole hadn't felt those women's eyes, hadn't taken in their faces. "History, yes, but I think there are many stories—each woman's own story. Long gone, but each one had a story and dreams."

"And discomfort," Victoria said. "Can you imagine wearing those awful garments? The collars alone would strangle you. And I'll bet there's some sort of corset under those dresses."

Victoria was Victoria. She was practical. She lived in the now, but not like my dad. She was all feeling and reaction. Sometimes she was exhausting.

"You're missing the point," I said. "I'll explain it later."

Victoria ignored what I'd said. "Your house is still empty. The dining room is the only room with enough furniture. You need things on the walls. Give it some personality."

"There's furniture in the sitting room."

"Two chairs and end tables?" She sounded unimpressed. "At least there's a TV."

"We'll get there. There's no rush." I shrugged and tried to look easy and pleasant about it. "If we waited until the house decor was perfect, we'd never get to have our friends over to say thank you and to enjoy each other's company."

I saw a frown flit across Victoria's brow. She knew she'd been corrected.

"Of course," she said.

"And to that end, we've kept it simple and informal. If you'll excuse me, I'll fetch the ice and drinks."

Mel was quick on my heels. "I'll give you a hand."

I'd chosen to put pitchers of ice water and iced tea on the table, along with a frosty bucket of ice. I handed the ice bucket to Mel and brought the two pitchers in myself. By then Seth was walking into the house bearing a dish of roasted brussels sprouts and baked potatoes. He rushed back outside. This time, he and Dad both returned bearing plates of kebabs, meat, and fish. The swirling aromas filled the air around us, and no one had to be asked to take a seat.

Nicole said, "Henry, I didn't know you could cook like this. And Kara, the tea is delicious. Could you pass the lemon, please?"

Everyone was laughing and in good spirits. At some point, Seth saw Mom's portrait on the wall. His gaze paused on it, but he didn't mention it. Victoria noticed his shifting attention and asked, "Who's that, Kara? Is that your mother?"

Everyone went silent.

"You never talked much about her. She's quite pretty."

Mel squirreled her head around for a quick look and said, "She certainly was a beautiful bride. I can see that. Now, on *my* wedding day, they had to hunt my groom down. He went missing that morning . . ." She launched into a funny story. By the time she concluded with "We were both a sight when we finally said our 'I dos,'" the weirdness had passed.

Victoria said, "You lost her so young. I never understood what happened. What was her name? Was she sick?"

I shook my head. "Susan, and yes, she was young. I had Dad, thank goodness." I shot him a quick smile, remembering what Seth had said. "We've made a good team."

"And Niles," Victoria added as a sour expression twisted her lips. "He's gone too."

"Yes. Niles too."

Victoria looked at Seth and said, "We three were good friends. Kara, me, and Niles. At college, the three of us were always together, and we even found jobs in the same area after graduation."

I would've tried to ignore Victoria since she was determined to keep running her mouth, but Dad had a weary look on his face—so different from when we'd all sat down to enjoy the meal.

"Victoria, can you give me a hand?" I stood.

She looked at me.

"Now?" And I walked past her, giving her a friendly thump on the shoulder, signaling her to follow.

CHAPTER SIXTEEN

I took Victoria straight out the back door. Even outside, I kept my voice low. "What are you doing? Why are you bringing up things that make my father sad? And no one else knows what to make of any of it, because none of them ever knew Niles or my mom, not at all, and they have no idea what to say to any of this. That's our business—ours, being mine and Dad's business. So drop it."

"I'm sorry, Kara. I didn't think. It's hard being with you and your father and not thinking of . . . of people we've lost. I'm so sorry."

"Talk about something else. Talk about the weather. Talk about your jerk of a boss. But not about our personal issues, and certainly not about my tragedies. Got it?"

"Yes, yes, I'm sorry. I mean it. What can I do to fix it?"

"Nothing. Just don't say those things. You can carry the dessert out, and don't let on we've just had this conversation."

She nodded swiftly. "Sure. Of course."

Victoria did look chastened. I hoped she really did understand and could control herself. There was no excuse. She knew better, and she'd better do better, I thought as I shut the refrigerator door, or she'd answer for it big-time.

"You really do need new appliances, Kara."

"They work. That's enough for now." I handed her the chocolate pie. "I'll bring the rest and come back for the dessert plates."

Victoria did behave, and Dad's color improved. The mood grew mellow and relaxed, and Victoria launched into a story about a trip she'd taken with her aunt. They'd gone to Charleston and had stayed in a bed-and-breakfast. I zoned out, trying to quietly recharge myself, until I heard her saying, "Just like this house. But smaller." Victoria turned to me. "You should consider something like that. Have you?"

I said, "Having strangers in and out all the time? I don't think so."

"It wouldn't work with the house as it is. You'd have to install more bathrooms, and some of the rooms should have private baths. The grounds . . . you'd need to clean those up a lot."

"Victoria." I held up my hand. "Stop. For one thing, we are in the middle of the woods here. Quaint and historical cities have B and Bs for tourists. Even small towns with some sort of tourist draw may have them. But I can't offer that here. Even if I could, it's not my house or my choice." I said it with a smile and a certain exaggerated, dramatic flair, and everyone laughed, but I drilled my stare straight into Victoria's brown eyes.

Her cheeks flushed. "Sorry. You know my brain is always full of ideas."

Nicole said, "Actually, it's not a bad idea, Kara. I have ideas I can share with you."

"Not today, please." I sounded harsh. I tried to back it off. "You all know I'm moving on at some point, getting back into the workforce. Dad couldn't run something like that even if he wanted to. Maybe with a partner." I shrugged and immediately wished I could pull those last words back, because Nicole gave Dad a *look*. A real look, and Dad returned it.

Things went on awhile longer, but soon our guests were making the usual remarks preparatory to leaving. I stood, and with everyone's help we moved the dishes and leftovers into the kitchen.

"Thank you all, but I've got it from here. I owe a special thank-you to Mel."

Mel looked at me.

"Thank you, Mel, for making that furniture shine. I resisted bringing the furniture back, true, but tonight I realized it belongs here. You made that happen. Thank you."

It was dark outside as Nicole, Seth, and Mel drove away. Victoria lingered on the porch with Dad and me.

"I'm sorry," she said. "I didn't want to get into apologies while your friends were here. I don't know what possessed me. Sometimes my brain and my mouth run away with me. I say the wrong things."

Dad said, "No apology needed. No harm done."

"I know the topic of Mrs. Lange and Niles, too, weren't appropriate for a dinner party or your guests. The portrait is lovely, though. I think that's what did it. Kara, you look so much like her. It kind of threw me and got me started. Again, I'm sorry. I'm very grateful you invited me—that you included me."

I had no words. I simply nodded.

Victoria went to the railing and leaned against it, her arms crossed. "You can't know this, but to be included, to be wanted, means the world to me. Things aren't going so well for me at work or with my family these days."

"I'm sorry, Victoria."

She shrugged and looked aside. Her eyes glittered. "It's the usual—you know. But for a while I thought it was getting better. My brother has problems, and Mom focuses on him. She wants me to listen to her complaints but keep my mouth shut." In frustration, her arms came uncrossed, and her hands became fists. "We're all adults, right? My brother should live his own life. Mom should have a good life of her own. If not now, when? Right?"

Dad said, "Some problems aren't so easily solved. Sometimes it's best to let them work themselves out instead of forcing confrontation or solutions—solutions that are artificial and won't last."

She gave Dad a long look. "I wish it was different, but it is what it is." She stood again. "I'd better be getting on the road . . . going back to my mother's house. I was planning to stay there tonight."

Neither Dad nor I disagreed, though my heart urged me to.

She sighed loudly. "It's just that I'm not eager to, you know? I was thinking about moving back to the Richmond area so I could be nearer to Mom, but now it's so stressful at her house. At any rate, I'm going to cut my trip short and head back to Northern Virginia. I should anyway. Fred, my boss, wasn't all that happy about me taking time off again so soon. Don't judge me, but I told him it was a family emergency." She gave us a bright but rather sad smile.

Dad broke first, saying, "Why don't you stay here tonight rather than making the drive? The guest room isn't fancy, but it has a bed."

Victoria smiled. "If you can throw in a pillow and blanket, I'll accept gladly."

My heart sank, and yet I knew Dad was right. I wanted to tell Victoria that she needed to mend her relationships with her family while she could. That Dad was wrong. She shouldn't wait and hope, and she shouldn't run away, either, not while there was a chance. But that was my own sad experience speaking.

"I have a stash of extra toothbrushes, and I can loan you pajamas."

For a moment, Victoria looked stricken; then she crossed the space between us and threw her arms around me.

"Thank you so much. Thank you both. In many ways, you two are the family I never had."

What could a friend say to that? I patted Victoria on the back and shot a look at Dad, but it was nothing like the looks Nicole had given him earlier in the evening. In response, he shrugged and nodded. I knew he was right. This was the least I could do as a friend, for a friend.

~

We cleaned the kitchen—the three of us—and when we were done, I said, "Let's get your bed made, Victoria. Dad looks done in with all this sociability. I know I am."

Among the furniture that had returned to the house was an iron bedstead. It fit an old-fashioned full-size mattress, which had given Nicole an opportunity to get rid of a mattress set she didn't want. The mattress and box springs she'd sent over looked new, so I could hardly complain. And here it was, set up and in place, as if fate had known we would need accommodations for an unexpected guest.

I gripped the window sash and worked the window open. It stuck a bit, but once I had it moving, it moved well.

"You might want to close the window, at least partway, before going to sleep."

"That breeze! It's wonderful."

I hadn't gotten around to making the bed yet, though I did have sheets that would work with a little extra tucking. I dug those out of the linen closet and found a decent-looking blanket and a pillow. Together, Victoria and I made her bed. I took the opportunity, away from Dad, to bring up the subject she'd skirted earlier.

"What exactly did you tell your manager?"

"Oh." She shook her head at me. "I know I shouldn't have. I told him Mom was sick and needed me. That it was an emergency."

"Doesn't that bother you? I'm glad you could join us for dinner, but besides being dishonest, saying something like that is too much like tempting fate."

"Tempting fate? Not at all. It's just a story that serves a purpose." She looked at me dead-on. "I had a boss once who said if I needed something—like time off, for instance—I needed to ask in a way that made it possible for her to say yes. So that's what I did. If I'd asked Fred to give me a couple of days off because my best friend was having a dinner party . . . well, the way I look at it, I would've been putting him in a very awkward position. So I was really thinking of him and being considerate."

Best friend, she'd said. I was still stuck on those two words and not really listening beyond that. We had been, right? Yes, we'd been best friends in college. But loyalties could shift. Mine, along with most of my time and energy, had shifted to Niles. I didn't know where those feelings were hiding now.

Victoria added, "I'm glad you understand."

She wanted more. I knew that. Maybe a few brief words confirming the best friend status. I couldn't give it to her. She let it pass.

"Besides, Kara, there are things I want to discuss with you."

"I'm tired. No discussions tonight, please."

"I'm serious. I know you don't agree and don't even want to discuss B and Bs and such, but just let it simmer in the back of your mind. You'll thank me one day."

"Huh . . . well, time will tell about that. For now, I'll get you a toothbrush. The toothpaste is already in the bathroom."

I wanted to be alone. I had enjoyed having company but hadn't planned on an overnight guest. We descended the grand staircase, as Victoria called it. She paused on the lower flight of stairs and looked back up. "I feel like I'm on one of those big cruise ships, you know? The ones with those grand staircases? *Titanic*, right? Or maybe it's more like the old mansions—Biltmore or . . . I know! It's like the Maymont mansion in Richmond or Swannanoa in Afton. Or no, Swannanoa is marble and is arranged differently, but it has that gorgeous stained glass on the grand staircase landing. Have you ever seen it?" She kept rattling on without waiting for a response. "But you need something special, like maybe a table with a lamp, a small ornate lamp, I think, to give it a tiny dash of elegance."

"Slow down, Victoria. You're getting ahead of yourself—and of us too. For now, we're dealing with wallpaper. Removing it."

I expected to find Dad in the sitting room watching his news shows. The room was empty and dim and lonely looking. I crossed the foyer and peeked into the parlor. His workman tools were there but no *him*.

Victoria called out, "He's out back, Kara."

She'd gone to the kitchen and was at the window. I went to the back door.

"Dad? Want anything to drink? We'll come out and join you."

"How about a cup of decaf? Instant is fine."

"On its way."

Victoria asked, "I'll go out and keep him company?"

"Sure. I'll join you as soon as the water is hot. I'm making tea for myself. Want some?"

"Whatever you're having is fine with me."

The screen door slammed, but softly, and through the open window I heard Victoria greet Dad, thank him again for inviting her to dinner and for the offer to stay the night. She continued blathering on, and I tuned her out, wanting to reset myself, recapture my thoughts, and determine my own mood.

It wasn't Victoria's fault. I was alone too much. Moving out here . . . well, maybe it wasn't the best thing for me. Dad had provided me with an even better hiding place than before. I'd been burned by the world, and that was the truth. I wasn't the first, and I wouldn't be the last, and I needed to pull myself together—put on my big-girl heels—and move forward with my life.

Somehow, though, it seemed that the life I'd known before the accident no longer held the same appeal for me. Had it ever? Maybe. Or maybe I was just following along in the wake of others. Taking the usual road? No, not quite that. But . . .

The kettle whistled, startling me back into the present. I hurried to set up the mugs with coffee or tea bags, as the case might be, and had them out to Dad and Victoria in a jiffy.

"Ladies, I admit I'm worn out. I couldn't resist the evening quiet."

The fireflies were out among the flowers and in some of the higher reaches of the trees. The cicadas were calling. The night was peaceful. Except for Victoria.

"You need a firepit."

Dad laughed and shook his head. "Maybe so," he said.

"You could make it an extension of the terrace up here or put it down by the creek. Though I suppose that ground down there could get damp, especially in the wet season."

"Victoria," I said. "I've just realized you're in the wrong line of work."

She smiled. "You mean I should be in the hospitality industry?"

"I was thinking more about interior decorating and staging. You seem to have a feel for setting, especially dramatic ones."

Dad eased forward in his seat and rose slowly to his feet. "I'll leave you gals to visit. My day is done." He paused in front of us. "Victoria, I hope you'll have a restful night at Wildflower House. And Kara, you did an amazing job hosting our friends today. With that, I bid you both good night."

"Good night, Dad."

"Good night, Mr. Lange."

"Call me Henry, Victoria. You're an adult now." He waved and went up the steps and into the house.

"He's so sweet," Victoria said.

I raised my eyebrows.

"I didn't say he was perfect. Who is? But he's steady and respectable and has a stylish sense of irony. I can't say even half of that about my father."

Stylish sense of irony?

"Victoria, sometimes I can't tell when you're serious and when you're joking."

She laughed a little. "It's easy being a parent . . . at least as far as I've observed. Oh, they say how hard it is, and I wouldn't know personally.

We wouldn't know, right? But judging by my parents' feeble attempts with my brother, seems to me that the best I can say about their parenting skills is that their early benign neglect has led us to the current situation. And it's all on Mom to deal with." She put her mug to her lips and downed the remaining dregs as if it were a shot of liquor. "Being a *good* parent? Now, that's something different. Especially belatedly. It's much harder on everyone."

"I'm sorry, Victoria. I know you hurt for them."

Her voice softened. "They were tougher on me. I don't know why, and I resented it, but maybe, in retrospect . . ." She left the sentence unfinished and changed the subject. "Do you think you'll marry again—I mean, assuming you meet the right guy and want to try again?" She dropped her volume and said, as if being clever, "Like maybe Seth." She smirked. "Not that I'm pushing you. I'm thinking about myself mostly. I'd like to have children. Try that parenting thing for myself. What about you?"

I caught my breath, reset my sudden tension, and replied calmly, "Sure. I'd like that."

"Well," Victoria said, "we aren't getting any younger."

Closing my eyes, I rested my head back against the cushion. I felt depleted. A little broken too. Victoria couldn't know what my pregnancy had meant to me because she didn't know about it. If she'd been different or had a more compassionate personality, I might've told her, but no. It was history anyway. Done and past. And private.

"I'm beat. I need to call it a night too."

"It's been good, Kara. Really nice hanging out here. I think this place is great."

I sighed. For me, this day was done, yet she seemed intent on prolonging it. I said, "It's growing on me, but it isn't a place I can see as a long-term daily kind of life."

"Well, your dad's not going anywhere anytime soon, so you don't have to make decisions about that now. In fact, I sensed that he and Nicole have . . . I don't know . . . something special between them."

No, I told myself. *You won't discuss your personal business with her. Don't discuss your father's personal business with anyone.* I said only, "They are friends."

"More?"

"Just friends." I stood. "I'm beat. If I don't go up now, I'll have to sleep out here. I'm past the age and size when someone could carry me up."

"Let's go, then. I have a book I'm reading. I'll dig into that before going to sleep."

"A book?"

"On my phone." She pulled her cell phone from a pocket and waved it at me. "My life is on my phone." Victoria laughed a little when she said that, but it had such a lonely sound it caught me off guard.

"Are you okay?"

"Hey, I'm just joking," Victoria was quick to add. "It's all good."

"Lots of people say they can't live without their phones."

"But not you?"

"Are you kidding me? I'm always losing it or forgetting my passcode."

Victoria held the screen door open for me. She said, "Keep it simple. That's what I do. Keep it simple. Like 5-4-3-2-1. Hard to mess that up."

~

Victoria left early the next morning. I was surprised. I'd expected her to delay and maybe even hang around for lunch. But no. She was up, dressed, and on her way out when I emerged from my room.

"Drive carefully," I said, trying not to show my relief.

"No worries. I'll tell Fred that Mom recovered extra fast and that I came straight back to get to work. Might even earn me a few brownie points." She laughed. "Seriously, thanks for dinner and for putting me up. I enjoyed the visit." She groaned. "I need to get on I-95 before the worst of the traffic. You know how it is."

She drove away. I realized I was going to miss her. But not as much as I'd missed my peace and quiet.

Later that morning, I heard the screen door shut and then footsteps coming up the hall. By then Victoria was long gone, and the steps were too heavy to be hers anyway.

I spun around. "Seth? I thought you were Dad."

"Sorry to disappoint you," he said, but he was grinning. "I saw him outside. He told me you were in here."

A mixture of feelings whooshed through me. Was I glad to see Seth? Yeah.

"Are you going to ask me why I'm here?"

"Okay. Why are you here?"

"Remember that landscaping company I recommended?"

"The local one—Mitchell something or other."

"Jim Mitchell is here. He's talking to your dad about cleaning up that front area between the house and the road. Thought you might want to weigh in." He waved his hand. "I know you say you want what your father wants, but you have an opinion and ideas. Some pretty good ones. Your dad views this kind of work from a different perspective. For instance, you might find he bulldozes the whole front acreage."

"What?" I jumped forward.

"Not saying he will, but just thought you might want to help him decide."

I crossed my arms and leaned back against the counter again. "You've got good sense. What do you recommend we do with that mess out front?"

"Clear out most of the low growth. Spruce it up along the driveway. Knock down the dead trees. For the growth up nearer the house, do some real pruning and landscaping. Fill in the potholes, and put down fresh gravel."

"I disagree."

"You disagree?"

"That's what I said. Not gravel. Asphalt."

"It's a long driveway. That'll be costly."

"It'll be worth it in terms of convenience."

"Over time, upkeep will cost more than gravel repairs too."

"Don't care."

"Then you'd better go out there because Henry might think otherwise."

"Okay."

"Sorry I can't hang around. I made the intros, but I need to run. I promised to take Maddie over to a friend's house. Nicole is working and will be late, so it's on me. Have you got this?"

"I've got it." On impulse, I reached out and touched his shirt. "Thank you."

Seth touched my cheek. His fingers strayed near to my temple and found the thickened flesh near my hairline. He brushed against the scar lightly, then slid his fingers down to my chin.

For a moment—a breathless heartbeat of a moment—I thought he was going to kiss me. My lips were still shaping themselves to respond when he said, "I'll be back."

He slipped out the door, taking a piece of my heart with him. I held on to the countertop, staring out the window as he crossed the yard and disappeared into the woods.

If he had . . . yes, I would've kissed him back.

With a deep breath, I pulled myself together. Mitchell's Landscaping was out there with Dad. I needed to be out there too.

I was pretty sure I floated down the hallway. I was cocooned in a glow. It was too soon to call it love. But perhaps I was ready to consider love again?

"Kara. This is Jack Mitchell and his assistant, Will Mercer." Dad looked at the second man, asking, "Did I get that right?"

"Yes, sir."

Jack Mitchell was a nice-looking man. Well dressed and obviously intelligent in his manners and speech. He looked more suited to office work. Maybe that was why he was the business owner. His assistant, Will, was broader in the shoulders and looked built for heavy work. He was a little shy because he kept looking away and at the ground—anywhere but at me.

Mr. Mitchell turned to me. "Your father wants me to review his plans with you."

"Oh? Thanks, Dad. I'm happy to weigh in. Are you going with asphalt?"

The discussion continued, but frankly, I was only half-engaged. The glow remained, and I was remembering that Seth had offered to show me around the area. We hadn't taken that any further. The next time I saw him, I was going to suggest the time was right.

~

Later that day, Seth knocked on the door. When I opened it, he said, "We never did go on our tour of Mineral and Louisa."

Surprised, and recalling my own thoughts on the matter earlier in the day, I asked, "Are you suggesting now?"

"Not so quick, Ms. Kara Hart. Don't go making assumptions."

His eyes were twinkling. I didn't see anything amusing in this. Only confusion.

"Well, then, Mr. Seth Albers, please state your purpose. What brings you to my doorstep reminding me of an unkept promise?"

He offered his hand. I accepted. He led me out, assisting me over the threshold with great care, then escorted me to the swing.

"On the contrary, I want to be certain I do not disappoint. I want to be sure of your expectations."

"Expectations? I have none, sir, so no worries."

This seemed to set him back. He gave me an extralong look before he began again.

"We'll have to change that."

"You are welcome to try." That was about as daring as I could manage. I almost apologized for being so brazen and was tempted to call my words back. Before I could, the twinkle in his eye turned slightly more serious.

"I have news."

"News? Good?"

"I hope it is. It has potential, but nothing's certain yet."

"What? Tell me."

"Remember we talked about having our lives interrupted and getting back to them? About finding a job in my field instead of taking care of everyone else? Mom and Nicole have things under control now. Maddie Lyn loves me, and she'll miss me, but we always miss the people we love, right? Those feelers I put out? I got some interest."

"Interest?"

"I'm pretty sure I'm about to get an offer from a public relations firm. It's the real thing. I heard from them this afternoon. But . . ."

"But?"

"There's good news and not-so-good news."

"Bad news?"

"Not bad, but inconvenient. The firm is in California."

"Oh." I felt a frown growing on my face and tried to dispel it.

Seth placed his finger lightly on my forehead, then moved it gently and slowly across, just above my eyebrows. I held my breath and felt my frown evaporate. He smiled and dropped his hand.

"They are suggesting that I can work remotely after I learn their workstyle and their clientele."

I took his hand in mine, squeezing it. "I'm so glad for you. I don't want you to leave, necessarily, but this sounds like a great opportunity, especially if you can do the job from here. From Cub Creek. Did you tell your mom and Nicole yet? How do they feel about it?" I'd meddled in their lives—perhaps unintentionally, but I had. I was relieved that this could work out well for everyone.

"They are happy too. Apparently, I was underfoot a lot."

I dropped his hand and gave him a hug and a smile. "I doubt that." I shook my head. "I'm glad for you, Seth. A little sad for the rest of us."

"So the thing is, Ms. Kara Hart, I'd like to take you out to celebrate and make good on my seeing-the-town offer."

"It will be my pleasure to celebrate with you."

"Excellent. We'll go on Saturday, if that works for you? Sunday afternoon, if you're already busy on Saturday."

"Saturday is yours."

"Wear comfortable shoes. It's a big county."

I laughed. I couldn't help it. Seth laughed too.

He glanced at the time on his phone. "I promised to pick up Maddie Lyn from her playdate. I'll see you Saturday at ten a.m.?"

"I'm going straight in to mark my calendar. Saturday is all yours."

And I did. Seth left, and I went, all but floating on air, straight to the kitchen and wrote on the calendar square for Saturday in big letters, "Seth."

A little later, when Sue Deale knocked on the front door and offered me a piano, I didn't even blink in surprise, because it was that kind of day—the kind when you smiled at the gifts you received whether they made sense or not—and said thank you.

"It works," she said. She pointed behind her at the pickup truck in the driveway. A trailer was hitched to it. "It's in there. Needs tuning, and it's old, but it does work. Figured we'd swing by and offer it to you since your dad was happy about that other furniture. Otherwise, Johnny says the next stop is Goodwill. Says it's wrong to let the piano languish and become unusable."

I looked back at the truck. An older man was sitting at the wheel. He nodded and waved. I waved back. Looked like two men were crammed into the narrow back seat. Such an odd sight and an unexpected event. Laughter bubbled out of me.

Sue said, "Guess this doesn't happen every day, huh?"

"No, ma'am, but I'm glad you thought of us. I don't play. Maybe it's time I learned."

"Well, I always did think a piano gives a house a certain flair whether it gets played or not."

"How would we get it up here and in the house?"

"No worries about that. My Johnny brought along two helpers." She shook her head. "I just knew, you know. And hoped. Mary loved her music. Felt to me like the piano was coming home. Could almost hear it singing her favorite tunes."

So Mary Forster's piano and its bench seat joined us at Wildflower House. Dad walked in as the men were getting it situated.

"What's this?" he asked.

"We have a piano."

He frowned. "We do?"

"Sure, Dad. It missed the other furniture. It was lonely, so Mr. and Mrs. Deale brought it home."

He nodded. "Okay. Sounds good." He paused. "*Does* it sound good?"

I shrugged. "I have no idea."

"Well, okay, then. Why don't we put it over in that corner in the sitting room? Might look good at an angle in that spot."

And it did, of course. It fit perfectly.

~

I arose the next morning to birdsong. It was Thursday, and I had a new item on my task list. I pushed through my closet, taking another look at the current options.

A day in town—a day-long date with Seth on Saturday—didn't require fancy clothing. Most of what I already owned would be satisfactory. But I didn't want to be satisfactory. I needed something special. And I didn't have much time to find the right outfit considering I had to travel a distance to shop.

"Dad?" I called out as I walked down the hallway and saw his empty room. "Dad?" I yelled again as I descended the stairs.

"Here, Kara. Everything okay?"

His voice came from the kitchen. I joined him there.

"Do you know where I left my keys? Do I have enough gas in the car to make it to Richmond?"

"Richmond?" He frowned, confused. "You're going to Richmond?"

I smiled. "I am. I have a little shopping to do."

"You're good on your own?"

"I can handle it." Impulsively, I leaned forward and gave him a quick kiss on the cheek. "No worries. I've got this, Dad."

And I did. I made the drive with no problem, ended up at the Short Pump mall, and earned blisters walking most of its immense square footage. I was loaded with bags. This was a Kara redo, and it felt long overdue.

~

Late that night, while lost in deep sleep, I awoke to the lights of an oncoming truck, already huge and growing immense with unbelievable speed. Not only were the headlights bright, but sounds of rending came with them, accompanied by big tires rolling hard enough to set the asphalt to vibrating. I came to consciousness in violence and fear, with my mattress still shaking beneath me. I rose so fast from my bed that I tangled in the covers. Like someone who hadn't fastened their seat belt before a collision, I was thrown to the side and over. I hit the floor with sharp, jolting pain.

I lay on my bedroom floor realizing those last artifacts, the lingering dregs of my trauma, had returned. The light-and-sound show. My punishment for the accident.

My elbow hurt. I touched it. The arm worked, so nothing was broken. My thigh hurt. I was fully awake now but devastated that the pain, so long absent, had returned with such force. And for no reason, I thought. It had been a good day.

I closed my eyes and pressed my hands to my face. Tears slowly squeezed past my lids and lashes and ran down my cheeks. I didn't want to go back to this. Going backward. Back to misery. Not again.

As I lay there in self-pity, light touched my eyelids, and a softer boom echoed. I was on the floor near the open window. I moved my hand away from my face and saw I was looking up and out through the window as a light show played—not in my head but across the night sky. Sharp lightning strokes played from cloud to cloud, dancing across the night and setting off thunder. The fine hairs on my bare arms rose and tingled, not from the lightning directly but from the cool air and the charged night.

Mother Nature's handiwork—not my failure. Thunder and lightning—not my damaged brain and psyche backsliding.

I sat up slowly and gingerly knelt by the window. My thigh still hurt, along with my elbow, but the night breeze was cool, and the windowsill was dry.

This wasn't a thunderstorm. Heat lightning. Earth was going about its business, resetting its electrical balance.

I prayed. I gripped the windowsill, and for the first time in a long time, I said a prayer of gratitude as I huddled there.

Gifts, I thought. I'd received so many recently. Maybe it was okay to be glad, to be grateful, to put nearly a lifetime of fear and guilt aside. To hope for release from the past and let the future welcome me.

CHAPTER SEVENTEEN

Friday morning, I awoke to a roaring sound. The rough mechanics of it, plus a faint smell of gasoline, entered my bedroom through the open window. The morning sun streamed in.

The roaring changed in volume as the machine moved away and then returned. Finally, I was faced with the reality of either giving up sleep or disrupting it long enough to rise and close the window—well, not much of a choice, really. Either way, I wasn't likely to get back to dreamland.

After the electrical storm during the night when I'd climbed back into bed, I'd slept soundly, and this morning I felt as fresh and clear as the air the storm had left behind. Languid and relaxed, I stretched my legs and feet before dropping them over the side of the bed and bringing the rest of my body upright. My thigh felt good. My elbow was sore, but not bad. Hope was good medicine.

I stood at the window. As always, my eyes sought the flowers below and, beyond them, the creek. The sun sparkled on the moving water, the ultragreen of the grass, and the flowers raising their colorful heads . . .

The roaring grew louder. I realized the noise was coming from the side yard. The mower, Dad's newest and most expensive toy thus far, was taming the wilderness—that tangled mess of bushes and weeds on the side of the house. I hoped he'd use it in the front yard too. Not much grass out front, but he'd gotten the cart attachment, and he could use it to pick up all those downed sticks and assorted debris.

I grabbed a quick shower to help tame my bedhead hair, then pulled on capris and a light cotton shirt. One never knew who might drop by, after all. For being so isolated, we seemed to always be greeting folks or sending them on their way. Generally, it seemed to be the Alberses. That was okay by me.

Like a kid worried about giving up her training wheels, I carried my cane but didn't need it. I rarely did now. I kept my hand firmly on the stair railing and never missed a beat. Last night was behind me, and it felt like so much more was too.

On the lower landing, I looked around at the warm, burnished floors and the about-to-be-stripped-and-painted foyer and parlor, and though the furniture still wasn't right, and there was so much yet to do, I knew—*I knew*—all was well and getting better all the time.

The mower started up again, and the sound lured me to the kitchen. Dad had left coffee for me, and I poured myself a cup. The air in here was stuffy, so I opened the back door and the windows. I saw Dad riding his mower. He was wearing a hat to shield his head and the back of his neck. He drove across the yard from side to side, near the house, and when he turned, he made a new pass across the flowers.

A pass across the flowers. With the mower. I was stunned.

They bowed, bending their rough stalks and brave petals before the bright-red, shiny-new mower as they fell beneath the noise and wheels and blades, as someone, my father, reached into my chest and yanked out my heart with searing pain.

Lights flashed. Before my eyes? Or in my head? I know I screamed because later my throat hurt, and my ears rang for hours, but no one heard my cries over the sound of the mower moving with dreadful intent across the wildflowers.

I flew down the porch steps, crossing that wasteland between the house and my father. I descended upon him in anger, shrieking at him to stop, to stop killing my flowers.

My fists hit his arm and his shoulder. His expression was one of angry surprise, then confusion. He recoiled, then yelled back, pushing me away, but I couldn't understand his words because my head was filled with blinding red rage. The mower noise and the forward motion finally stopped, but not in my head. It seemed to go on and on. Not ceasing. Not easing. Driving me to continue stumbling alongside. My bare feet hurt as the soft soles were stabbed by the sharp, ragged stems. He grabbed my arm and half rose as if to dismount. I pulled away roughly, upsetting his balance. He released me to catch himself. I heard my name and other words, first spoken, then shouted. I backed away.

"Stop it. Stop. What are you doing?" I screamed at him. I didn't want an answer. Only to accuse. "They were beautiful. Why did you have to destroy them?" I yelled the harsh words as I backed away.

"I'm sorry, Kara. Listen—"

"Fix them. Put them back. Until you do that, I don't want to hear your voice."

Dad struggled to get his leg free of the mower. Something was caught, perhaps his pants leg, and in that interval, I ran into the house. I was done, I told myself. *Done.* Back to the city for me. Back to the normal world. To a nine-to-five life and a paycheck and utility bills and everything that went with that.

The noise in my head was so loud that when I reached the kitchen, I paused. My breath was coming hard and hot, and my lungs ached. Due to my heart that had been ripped from me? From the beauty and the joy that had been cut short? Had never had a chance to live its life? To thrive and laugh?

Flowers. Just flowers.

I rejected that. *Not just flowers. They were special to me, and he knew that.* My father—and Niles, too, even my mother—rejection was all around me, and I could do some rejecting myself. I slammed my fists against the table, rejecting the pain inside me. I threw a chair across the room.

Dad grabbed my arms. I tried to shake them off. He slid his arms the rest of the way around me and pulled me backward against his chest. He spoke with a low voice. "Kara, sweetie. It's okay. It's okay."

I struggled against him. "It's not okay. It can't be. You know how much they meant to me."

"They're flowers, Kara. Wildflowers. Listen to me." It sounded like his own breath was coming with difficulty. I made myself stop struggling. When he released his grip, I'd throw off his arms and go. I'd run straight upstairs and start packing. There wasn't much that I'd need to take with me to start a fresh life. One more restart.

Dad was making shushing noises. Then he was speaking again.

He said, "They are wildflowers and getting past their season."

I rejected his words. "They are still beautiful."

"You can't keep them. They don't live forever. They are past their season, and it's time to cut them back."

"No."

He removed one arm and used it to pull out a kitchen chair. He maneuvered me into it.

"Sit, please. Let me get you something to drink."

I did sit, and I stayed seated. The tipping point of the anger, that murderous rage in which any action was justified, had passed its peak. I was shaking. My knuckles were rapping against the table of their own volition. I pulled my hand away from the wood and hid it in my lap.

He drew a glass of cool water from the tap and brought it to me. "I should've warned you."

"You *should've* left them alone."

"Kara, you're seeing those flowers as they were, not as they are. They need pruning just as most growing things do."

"That wasn't pruning."

"Cutting them back is pruning for them."

"You don't know. You don't know anything about flowers. All you know is that you wanted them out of the way, and you could use your new mower to do it."

He opened his hands and held them palms up. "Is that what you think of me?"

I glared at him. My head felt abuzz. Like the mower was still roaring in there. I rubbed my forehead but refused to touch the scar.

"Kara. Hear me. Do you believe that I would deliberately destroy something knowing how much it meant to you? I thought you knew how flowers grew. Everything has its season."

"They were in your way. You didn't like them."

He sat silently and waited. If there'd been a newspaper nearby, I suspect he would've picked it up. I stared at him and felt myself calming.

They were flowers. Dying flowers.

My heart was resuming its normal pace—not torn from my chest after all.

"When I saw you and the mower and what you were doing, it upset me."

He nodded.

"I . . . I . . ." I closed my eyes and felt the brain buzz diminishing as the water cooled my body, and quiet fell around us.

"It was so loud, Dad," I whispered.

"Well, it's a lawn mower."

I opened my eyes again and recognized him. He was there. My father. Not some monster.

"Dad . . . I . . ."

"It's okay, Kara. I apologize for not telling you ahead of time."

"I'm still angry about the flowers, but I'm sorry I flew apart like that." My hands were back on the table. The shaking had stopped. I felt drained. Embarrassed at my irrationality. My two-year-old give-me-my-toy-back fit.

Dad put his hand over mine. "I'll wait. It won't hurt to let you enjoy the flowers a little while yet."

"Seriously?" My eyes prickled. I didn't want to cry. I didn't want to behave like a manipulative child. I pressed my lips together and forced my eyes to stay open, to recall the tears.

"Seriously. Mind if I finish that one row to keep it neat? Then I'll cut down the grass sides and by the creek. The grassy areas."

I nodded. "I'm sorry, Dad." And I cried.

He touched my hand, then my cheek. "It's okay, Kara. I understand."

"Dad, I lost my temper. I didn't mean to. It all blew up inside me."

"I know."

"That's not all of it. I'm talking about with Niles. That night. I got so angry, so irate, that I wanted to hurt him, I—"

"I know, Kara."

"How could you know?"

"You told me when I was with you at the hospital." His voice gentled. "You were mostly out of it, in shock and pain."

"I told you?"

"You said it was your fault he'd died."

I put my hand to my throat. The muscles seized up and tried to choke me.

"I'll say it again, over and over, if necessary. The accident wasn't your fault. The truck hit you. It crossed the median, and it was a case of you and Niles being in the wrong place at the wrong time."

"I know that. I do. I was in my lane. But if I'd been watching . . . if I'd been paying attention to driving instead of . . . maybe I could've avoided the collision."

"Not likely. Everything moved too fast."

Silence sat with us. So much was foggy from that time in the hospital . . . in the aftermath.

"What else did I tell you?"

Dad frowned. "You were mostly out of your head in shock and grief. I didn't bring it up again. I thought you would one day, if you felt the need, and we could discuss it then. The coward's way—I see that now. I told myself it was the best way." His own eyes reddened. "You know that I am uncomfortable . . . discussing emotional things . . . but if you want to, if you need to, I can do that for you." He closed his eyes, too, as I had when I'd needed to calm down. When he opened them, he said, "You asked me about the pregnancy. The doctors had already told me . . . it was over. I shared that with you. But you were still coming out from the anesthesia. I doubted you'd remember we'd spoken of it. You never asked again, so I let it go."

He cleared his throat. "I'm going to have a drink of water, too, and then finish my work. We can chat this afternoon, talk about anything you want, if that works for you?"

Dad filled a glass with water and drank it down; then he turned to me. He gave me a small smile, but a sweet one. It was off kilter, slightly crooked, and I found it endearing.

"Later is fine."

"So you're okay now? You can manage?"

"I am. We'll manage, Dad. Just fine."

"Good." He nodded and went to the kitchen door.

I called out, "Wait, Dad. I need to talk to you. I don't understand why I lost it out there. My reaction was . . . extreme. My other issues from the accident seem so much better. Maybe it's the brain damage? The noise of the mower, maybe? You know how light and noise affect me sometimes."

Dad returned to where I still sat at the table.

"Kara. You were seriously injured in the accident, and I know that noises sometimes bother you. I don't doubt that's connected to the accident, but . . . I mean this with love, and I'm only telling you because it's time. You're ready to hear it. You don't have brain damage."

I reached up to my scar. I touched it. "It's real, Dad. I've worked hard to learn to manage with it so I can find a job, rebuild my life and all that. The injury . . . the doctors said . . ."

He touched my hand and touched the scar. "Your head was injured. You needed stitches, and you did have a mild concussion, but the serious injuries were to your arm and leg. The doctors said you had injuries to your head and you needed stitches, but not brain damage." He took my hand and pulled it away from my face and held it in his. "I'm not trying to diminish anything you've suffered or experienced, but you can get past this, Kara. Your brain is fine. You are afraid of reengaging with the world, and that's natural after what happened. Don't let it hold you captive."

He released my hand and sat back, the animation leaving his face, and again he offered that crooked smile, but this time it looked sad. "You are stubborn and persistent. Perhaps more so than anyone I've ever known. You don't surrender. I admire that about you. Remember when I said you weren't strong but that you were resilient? I was wrong."

"Wrong?"

"You are resilient. You are also strong. In some ways, I envy you, Kara. You *did* get the best of both your mom and me."

As he stood, he seemed to be searching for words. He gave a long sigh, then said, "I want to thank you for your help with this project. I appreciate your passion for it, Kara. It wouldn't be the same without you here."

I think I nodded and muttered a thank-you, but otherwise I hardly noticed him leaving. I was dazed. *No brain damage?*

If that was true, what did it mean? That my sensitivity to noise, to light, was all in my . . . in my head? As in *imagined*?

He didn't say that they weren't real. But that there was no brain damage. Emotional instead of physical?

I pressed both hands to my face. I couldn't think about this anymore today. I'd pull out the medical documents later. I'd find the notations about the brain injury . . . head injury . . . and show him he was wrong.

Every bit of me, muscle and bone, ached as I rose from the table and went to the kitchen sink. I leaned over the faucet and splashed water on my face.

The thoughts kept intruding. Could I have gone back to work long ago? Was Dad right? Had I just needed to get past the fears?

It was more than that. I knew something had changed in me, more than release from fear . . . more than I could explain, perhaps.

It felt like pity. Not for me. But for my father. How hard it had been for him to raise a child alone. Meeting someone else's emotional needs could be exhausting . . . and yet I hadn't pushed. I'd modified my own wants and needs to accommodate his shortcomings, and sometimes I'd blamed him. Perhaps more than I'd even realized. I'd let him off the hook because there was no point in doing otherwise. For him, that had probably been the right thing to do.

For me, no. I should never have accepted that pale life. That graytone existence.

When Niles had said I was as cold as my father, he was wrong. I didn't doubt that now. No one could have as much fire and anger burning in them as I did, even if it was sometimes misdirected, and be missing an emotional cog in their brain.

Could Dad be right? About the brain damage?

Maybe it didn't matter. In fact, if he was right—if the damage was emotional rather than physical—then it was possible that it could be undone or overcome.

Could I have gotten that so wrong? I had my medical records. I'd find out. Unless . . . maybe I'd choose to just go with this new idea and not try to verify it. My hands shook a little. It felt . . . so . . . I couldn't pin down the word. Revolutionary? Really? To me, it was.

Suddenly, I was flooded with lightness. Almost what I'd experienced when I'd seen the field of flowers. That lightness of being, of being flooded with joy. It was a heady experience. Dizzying.

Dad knew what had happened with the accident. It wasn't my fault. Sometimes bad or unfortunate things happened.

And yes, those were just flowers out in the yard. They'd grow back. If not, Dad and I would throw down more seed. Easy to fix. Seth would help us figure out which seed was best.

I stood, suddenly needing to tell my father that we were good, that he could finish cutting the wildflowers. We really *could* manage. And then I noticed the silence.

He should still be mowing. Maybe he was down by the creek. It wouldn't be so loud from there. Had I heard the mower start back up? I'd been deep into my feelings and my own thoughts. He could almost have driven that mower right through the house, and I wouldn't have noticed.

From the window, I saw the mower, still shiny, out in the field about where it had been when I'd stopped him. Had Dad been distracted by something? Someone? Maybe Nicole or Seth was out there. I smiled to myself. Probably. The world felt different. Not just myself and my world but my universe.

I smoothed my hair and dabbed at my eyes. The lashes were damp, but my face was all smiles. I went out to the back porch.

"Dad?" I called.

It was the absence of a response that gave me pause. A small moment of alarm. All the while I told myself he'd probably gone around to the front of the house.

Just beyond the mower, an area of flowers wasn't standing with the rest. Among the well-ordered ranks, they looked disordered.

"Dad?"

The lightness spilled out of me. My legs gave way, and I nearly fell down the steps. The forward motion got me going, and I scrambled back to my feet. I ran toward the mower and those flowers.

He was there on the far side, on the ground and unmoving, as if he'd crumpled in the act of reboarding. He'd planned to cut the rest of this row. He'd said so.

I fell to the earth beside him, thinking he was gone and gone and gone. I rolled him onto his back. There was an ugly twisting, drawn-up expression on his face—a more extreme version of that sweet smile he'd shared in the kitchen. My fingers found his jaw, his neck, and pressed into it. I tried his wrist too. I believed I felt a faint pulse. Unless I was mistaking mine for his.

"Dad."

I needed a phone. I found his in a small secure tray on his mower. I dialed 911. Frantic with shock, I was afraid I wouldn't be able to speak, but when they answered, my voice rose in anguish: "My dad, he's dying. He's unconscious." I ended in a near scream. "Please hurry."

They took my address and then asked other questions while assuring me help was on the way.

There was no color in Dad's face, but his lips still had a faint tinge of rose. Maybe he was breathing. I put my cheek to his face. Was that his breath I felt? Or false hope? It was hard to tell.

"They're coming, Dad. Hang in here with me." It could be his heart, but I was sure it was a stroke. But strokes could be treated if help was given fast enough.

"Hang in with me, Dad."

My hands were useless. They didn't know CPR. They couldn't even reliably find a pulse in his wrist or his neck, though I tried over and over. Finally, I grabbed his shoulders and shook him. I pressed my hands to each side of his face and yelled at him to fight. As I waited for help, desperate to hear sirens and see people in uniforms running around the house armed with medical tools and a stretcher—people who had useful hands and the knowledge I lacked—I cursed this wilderness we lived in. Wildflower House and Cub Creek were not worth the cost of the distance between my father and help.

A man's voice came to me from a distance. He was a first responder who was off duty and who lived in the area. I answered his questions as best I could, but as the sirens sounded and more help arrived, I found myself standing back, away, my hands held out before me, rigid and unable to close. They were caught in the memory of my flesh on his flesh, mine warm against his . . . his cooling . . . and knowing it was done.

I knew before they told me. There was no fight left to be waged.

CHAPTER EIGHTEEN

Mel said, "At least he didn't outlive his friends." She was right about that. He'd sold the business he'd spent his life building and moved into retirement in the country only weeks before his death.

Henry Lange had lasted less than two months at this house. His dream.

I'd never made funeral arrangements before. I'd lost people, yes, but the arrangements had always been someone else's responsibility. Nicole, pale as a white swan's feather, drove me into Richmond and sat, silently waiting, while the funeral director talked me through what was needed. There was tradition. There were choices. In the end, it wasn't all that difficult, but it was nearly impossible. Knowing Nicole was capable of stepping in and checking the boxes if I faltered gave me the composure I needed to get it done. The date we chose for the service was Wednesday.

Dad would've been pleased to see us supporting each other. I didn't doubt it.

I contacted a few people directly to inform them, and I contacted the new ownership at Dad's old business and the one employee I knew well enough to call to make sure anyone who cared received word of his passing and the details about the service.

Victoria drove back down from DC when I called. I was glad to see her. Nicole had been helpful, but I couldn't tie her up for days on end.

Besides, while Victoria had liked my father, she'd never been in love with him. Being around Nicole, remembering that she and my father had almost married, became too much for me. When I asked Victoria how she'd managed more time off, she hugged me and told me she'd worked it out and I wasn't to worry about it. I didn't. Frankly, it was a relief to share the trip back and forth from Richmond with her as I prepared for the service. It was also a relief not to be alone in the house, especially at night, when there was no one anywhere nearby. At night, the house echoed in on itself, almost like a vacuum—sucking out the noise, the light. I hadn't noticed it when Dad had been there with me, but I knew it would overwhelm me if I was there alone. So Victoria showed up and offered her help, and I welcomed her. During the visitation at the funeral home, she stood at the main entrance greeting people as they arrived and welcoming them. So many faces, and almost all were strangers to both of us. But Victoria could talk to anyone. It was a talent I didn't have.

Seth stayed in the background. He was there, always in sight, but at a distance. I felt his support and appreciated it. I owed him. In fact, I owed the whole Albers clan. Except for Maddie Lyn, they made the trip into Richmond to be there for Dad. And for me.

Dad had kept his personal and business lives segregated, compartmentalized. I knew a few names, but not their personal stories or their faces. That was okay. Most people were content to offer their regrets over his loss, and no one expected the daughter to be performing well. I used that as my shield—not to protect my own reputation as a reasonable human being but to protect my father's. None of these people would understand how he could be such a presence in the business and know each and every one of them so well but not see fit to insert even their mention into his family's life. These were kind people, hardworking people. Some of them were local. Others came from out of town. I appreciated the effort they made to pay their respects.

One of the few faces I knew from Dad's business days was Olive Bernard. She'd been Dad's administrative assistant for as long as I could remember. She and I had actually met once long ago, and she was a kind woman. She came directly to me, hugged me, took my hand in her two warm ones, and said, "I'm so sorry, Kara. Your father was an amazing man in many ways, and you meant the world to him."

"Thank you," I said. That was what everyone said on such occasions, but I knew she meant it kindly.

"I remember when you won that spelling bee . . . what was that? Fifth grade? Everyone in the office heard about it. Same with your many successes in high school and college."

Dad had bragged about me? In the office?

I was so surprised that the words just slipped out. "I didn't know. He talked about me?"

"Oh yes, dear." She leaned closer and dropped her voice. "He was normally very reticent about personal things, but he loved talking about you. He was so proud of you."

"Thank you. I appreciate you sharing that with me."

She patted my hand. "It was sweet of you to put your own plans on hold to help him with his dream." She shook her head. "I admit I thought it was a little crazy . . . I mean, uprooting his life, leaving his business, to move to the country? No one can truly understand the heart or the dream of another. But your father was a determined man. Once he set his mind to something . . . well, it was good as done." She glanced around us. "I'll let you speak with the others. I'm so glad I could be here today and so glad I could speak with you."

People came and went. Suddenly there was a lull. I stood there with that half smile on my face, ready to receive the sympathy of the next mourner, and there was none. People were nearby but grouped together and chatting among themselves or speaking with Victoria or moving past the baskets of flowers to approach the table where Dad's urn was displayed with a few framed photos. Over the low music that was playing in the background, I overheard a woman say, "Yes, that's his daughter."

Another one said, "No, I don't think so. Isn't his daughter the woman standing by the door? The one who welcomed us when we arrived?"

The first woman laughed. "No. A relative maybe. Or maybe he has two daughters . . . but she isn't Kara. Kara's the thin woman with the long dark hair. Right over there."

"They both have long dark hair."

"Okay. The one with the long *straight* hair. Not the curly."

She pointed and saw me looking, and I smiled as if I hadn't overheard. But it hit me wrong. I wanted to be grateful. I had been very grateful for everyone's help. But Victoria being mistaken for Henry Lange's daughter—it twisted inside me painfully. How would most of these people know otherwise? If some were confused, then so be it. I couldn't be both at the door and here, nearer the remains, too. Where was the harm anyway? Except for the Albers family, I'd never see any of these people again.

During the service, Victoria sat next to me, and I let her stay. Seth, with Nicole and Mel, took the seats directly behind us.

After, I did my best to show my appreciation to those who'd attended, including providing an abundance of food in the fellowship hall of the church we had attended on and off through the years. Dad worked many Sundays, and I didn't like to go alone. Plus, I'd lived out of town during the years I was married. But the pastor was kind and officiated at the funeral. The ladies of the church provided a delicious meal, and I made a donation to their weekly dinner program.

Dad would've been proud. The funeral had been well ordered, and every person had played their part. Including him and me. We were a good team whose season had ended too soon.

CHAPTER NINETEEN

Victoria had settled into the same room she'd used before. She asked my permission to move a small nightstand from Dad's room into hers, and I told her that would be fine. Dad wouldn't need it. That thought brought home a sad reality—I couldn't stay here, not indefinitely. It had been one thing to be here with my dad. But I couldn't live his dream. Even if I had shared his dream, I didn't see how I could stay in this big house day after day, night after night, with only the echo of my own voice for company.

I could get a dog. But aside from providing security, a dog's companionship wasn't the same as being around other people. I wanted to scream. I wanted to cry. I didn't because Victoria would hear. She'd want to offer comfort and advice, and she'd drone on and on. And I was angry. I bumped my shin walking into my dark bedroom and nearly started throwing things. I didn't because that would draw Victoria's attention too.

I wanted to be alone, right? No, I didn't want to be alone. Not at all. I fell onto the bed, still clothed. Too empty and too full—empty of what I needed and too full of what I couldn't define and didn't know what to do with. Anger, grief, all rolled up into abandonment. Could a thirtysomething daughter feel abandoned? My father had offered me help, a haven, and I'd tried to help in return . . . instead of moving on with my own life. That wasn't his fault. That was mine.

It was a dark night, and as the clouds moved away from the moon, the night's light seemed to grow all the stronger. It soothed me in some way that I couldn't explain, but I fell asleep, still in my mourning dress and my makeup streaked and ghastly—though I didn't discover that about my makeup until morning when I ventured near a mirror.

I stood and tried to remember crying. My pillowcase looked almost as bad as my face, so I must've. I dropped my clothing, including the black dress that I never wanted to see—much less wear—again, and stepped into the shower to wash yesterday away. Inside, I was still boiling with hot, unsettled currents that didn't bear close inspection. I knew they, like the grief, would pass over time. The best cure was to move on. Sell this place for whatever I could get for it, return to the city, and never look back.

When I had myself together and looked reasonable—the shadows were dark under my eyes, but no one would think twice about that on the day after one buried one's father—I went down the hallway, sure that Victoria was already up. She was. I smelled the aroma of breakfast wafting up the stairs. I followed it to its source.

"Victoria?"

She looked up from scrambling eggs. "There you are. I was thinking I might have to start yelling up the stairs for you." She carried the frying pan toward the table. "Can you grab the toast and put it on the plates? Here are the eggs. I hope you don't mind them plain?"

"No, that's fine." I ran my fingers through my hair, not sure whether I was angry or hungry or what. "I'll get it."

Victoria had the table set for breakfast, and a jar of jam was next to my plate along with a stick of softened butter.

"You made breakfast."

"I did. I'm not much of a cook, but you need to eat real food. Me too, for that matter. Have a seat."

We did sit, and we ate. I discovered I was famished.

"Thank you, Victoria. I didn't know I was hungry." Between bites, I apologized to her. "I'm sorry for taking your help but not asking if you need to leave. What about your job? I don't want you risking your job for me."

"I had to be here, Kara. You must know that."

"I appreciate it, but I've taken advantage of you. Do you have to be back at work on Monday? Sooner? Do you need to go see your mom before driving back up?"

"I told you to let me worry about that. I have a question for you. What do you have planned for today?"

"Today?" I frowned. "Rest, maybe? I don't want to think today. Not about anything."

"Maybe get some rest, but you really need to engage—engage with something. You are a project manager, Kara. Find a project to manage."

"What are you talking about? Are you telling me to get a job?"

"No, silly. I'm saying you already have a job."

I shook my head, feeling more confused than ever.

Victoria groaned but with good humor. "Come with me, Kara. I'll feel like I'm pointing out the obvious, but you've had other things on your mind, I know."

"Come where?"

Victoria leveled her gaze and fixed it on me. She said, "What are you going to do?"

I sat back, wanting to get out. Out. Be anywhere but here.

"I'm not deciding anything today."

"Listen to me. You are probably thinking of selling and leaving. You don't want to be stuck in this house alone." She nodded. "See how well I know you?"

"Okay."

"But you have an opportunity. Right here, Kara." She took my hand and tugged.

I stood. "Okay, what?"

Victoria pulled me down the hallway. On the parlor side, the stripping of the wallpaper was still as messy as we'd left it. The work had been put on hold, of course, while I buried my father. My heart felt like it broke a little more seeing this.

"Remember what we talked about at dinner? Even your friend Nicole thought it was a good idea."

I backed away, waving my hands in the air between us. "Don't start that again. I don't want to run a hotel, even one that sounds cute and chic."

"You're missing the point, Kara. You can have people in and out as much as you want. You don't have to keep the place full of people, but just enough so you don't feel so isolated. There's so much potential here."

Victoria ignored my pushback. "Wildflower House. Name each guest room after a flower. You could even host weddings in this fabulous great hall. The staircase is a bride's dream. And garden weddings or parties. You just need to cultivate—" She broke off to laugh a little. "I didn't mean that as a pun, but it works, so let's go with it. Cultivate a list of caterers and such. You provide the location, and someone else can coordinate the details."

"I'm not a hotel keeper, and I'm not a party planner."

"But that's the point. You could have an assistant. A partner. I could help you, Kara."

Despite myself, despite knowing Victoria meant well and I should appreciate her heart even if I wasn't buying what she was selling, I backed away a few steps. I felt breathless. A little light headed. I put my hand to my head and found I'd backed right up against the stairs.

"Not now, Victoria. It's too soon. I can't talk about all this."

"But you need to think about it before you do something crazy like sell it at a loss. I'm guessing, but I'm sure your father left enough money for the renovations you'll need to do . . . and to keep you going while you're getting the business up and running—"

"Stop!" I yelled. "Just stop, Victoria. I can't do this now." I turned and walked up the stairs, practically pulling myself up by grabbing the handrail and leaning into it. I felt old. Discouraged. And now besieged by a person who was trying to help me. She had helped me, but it wasn't all selfless. Victoria had motives. She always had her reasons—or *a* reason—she used to push what she wanted to accomplish. I made it to my room, thinking the same was true of me. I'd been happy enough to use her while she offered what I thought I needed, but now I just needed her to go. I felt ashamed of that, but it didn't change anything.

~

Early that evening, strains of music filtered up the stairs while I was resting. Hearing the music brought me back to the beginning. To the first day here. To seeing the flowers. The light. To hearing music that wasn't really playing, except in my own head.

I sat up in bed. I'd dozed off hard and deep and felt foggy. I listened, recognizing the instrument as the piano downstairs. The music was "Simple Gifts."

Stepping carefully to avoid the squeaky boards in the hallway and the stairs, I followed the melody. Victoria was seated at the piano. Her back was to me. She was playing. I walked toward her and stopped. Her fingers faltered on the keys. She pulled her hands away, and the last chords died.

"I didn't know you played piano."

"Lessons when I was a kid. I don't play often enough to do it well."

"Sounded amazing to me. Why that song?"

Victoria pointed toward the sheet of music. "This one?" She patted the bench. "I found it in here with a bunch of old music." She stood and moved aside.

I lifted the bench lid, and yes, there were sheets of music. The edges of the papers were frayed, and the paper had yellowed with age.

"I didn't realize."

Appalachian Spring and "Simple Gifts" were well known, commonly heard and played music. I didn't choose to see it as anything other than what it was—an intersection of lives, perhaps past and present, wherein for long or short moments we shared pieces of it. No more and no less than that.

Just a simple gift of solace.

CHAPTER TWENTY

As I walked down the hallway, I noticed Victoria's bedroom door was open. The covers had been tidied and the pillows plumped, so it all looked neat. Victoria had left a few items on the bed and nightstand.

A breeze blew in through the open window, and the gust caught a paper on the nightstand and sent it sailing onto the floor. Instinctively, I went after it, picked it up, and returned it to the nightstand. Victoria had left a slim book, like a journal or address book, on the nightstand, and it made sense to slip the paper into it lest it blow away again. I don't think I intended to snoop, but I was hiding a lot of things from myself, so maybe I did and just didn't admit it to myself. When I slipped the paper into the front of the book, I saw Victoria's neat handwriting. I had never kept a journal of any kind—too personally revealing, perhaps, or too painful or whatever—but clearly Victoria had, but it wasn't what she'd written in the book that caught my attention. It was a photograph that she'd wedged between the pages. A photo of herself and Niles.

I stared. It wasn't so odd, really. She'd been friends with both of us.

But this photo wasn't from our college days. I recognized Niles's haircut as one he'd gotten shortly before the accident. It had been more . . . modern, more stylish . . . I didn't know quite what to call it. But that longer hair on top with the shorter cut on the sides hadn't fit in his routine, business-oriented style before. The cut had looked good on him, had reminded me of some movie star or other. And Victoria . . . the two of them looked . . . cozy. His arm was around her. His fingers rested comfortably at her waist.

This photo had been printed on cheap paper. As if from a phone. I slammed the journal closed. I put it on the nightstand with such force that it made a slapping noise. I pulled my hands back, weaving my fingers together like one big fist, and clasped them together over my heart.

I heard Niles's voice from that dark night saying he was seeing someone.

He'd been impatient when Victoria had called as we were about to leave for our anniversary dinner. Was that when his mood had soured? If I thought about it in detail, I was pretty sure that would be the moment.

Now I heard Seth's voice. His voice seemed to weirdly entwine with my memories of that last evening with Niles. But Seth's voice was real. It was the present time. His words came up from below—from somewhere out front—and entered through the open window. From the porch, I thought. I heard his voice and looked out to see him descending the steps. He stopped beside his car.

How long had he been here? I hadn't heard a car, so he must have arrived at least before I'd left my room. Victoria hadn't told me he was here. But now I heard her voice, light and lilting, as she walked with him, and they stopped to chat.

I saw them clearly, and though I couldn't hear every word, I heard the tone and read her movements. My heart ached as it turned to ice. Ice kept the rage contained. But it made me shiver; even my jaw shook. I scanned the room, realizing I was looking for her phone.

It was there on the bed. I punched in her code, and it opened. *Keep the code simple, she'd said. 5-4-3-2-1. Simple.*

I opened the pictures folders and thumbed through them. The selfies of Victoria and my husband—there were only a few, but their faces were close together and smiling. Recent photos—that haircut was like a time stamp.

The voices drew me back to the window. I watched Victoria's body language—her hand touching Seth's arm, her hip thrust in his direction, her hand fluffing her hair. I told myself that was just Victoria. Just Victoria. She was friendly that way.

Had she been friendly that way with Niles? Until he'd been friendly back?

No. It was ridiculous. Victoria and Niles . . . no.

I went straight for the stairs and through the foyer. My fist hit the screen door, and it swung back with such force the sound blasted out like a gunshot as the doorframe hit the house.

Both Niles and Victoria looked up at me.

I gasped. *No, not Niles. Seth.* Seth was standing there.

I pressed my hand to my forehead and unintentionally hit the scar. I pressed my fingers against the scar and drew my finger down along it. They stared at me.

Seth reached me first. "Kara? You look awful. No, sorry, I mean you look like you've been through . . . your father's death. Come inside. Let me help you."

He took my arm as if I needed support to walk, to make it back inside. Maybe I did. I felt disoriented, as if too much was happening too fast and I didn't know how to tell up from down or real from fake. I shook inside. My teeth chattered. I tightened my jaw and stopped the disintegration.

Then we were in the kitchen. That awful kitchen with its nasty walls, stained linoleum, and filthy cabinets.

Seth sat me at the table and went to the coffee maker. It was on the counter. Victoria must've started it this morning. He kept glancing over at me as he located the mugs and poured out the dark brew.

"Do you take sugar and cream?"

I didn't answer. He looked over at Victoria. She shook her head no.

Yes, Victoria was there. Not to be left out, I supposed. She wanted to be where the interesting action was. The interesting people. The interesting male.

I closed my eyes and sipped. Seth moved near to me, and I saw that he'd set a pastry on a plate and laid a fork and folded napkin next to it.

"I picked these up in Mineral this morning and brought them over. I thought you might need something extra."

"Thank you, Seth. And thank you for everything you did yesterday too." I sounded almost normal.

"I was glad to help. Thanks for letting me be part of it."

His voice was soft, and the words were spoken low, such that it seemed privately done. Just the two of us. Then Victoria said, "That's what friends are for, right?"

She wanted her own recognition. And that icy heart in my chest said to my brain, *And she'll get it, too, in due time*, but aloud I said, "I've heard that song."

Both she and Seth smiled, heartened because I'd made a pitiful joke. Maybe because my improvement let them off the hook a bit. I wasn't quite so needy after all. They could do their thing. Move on with their own lives.

Seth said, "I brought a couple of the smaller arrangements—the ones that can be kept—back here in case you want them. I hope I did right. Nicole thought I should ask first, but I donated the fancy floral arrangements to a couple of churches. They'll enjoy them. Was that okay?"

"Of course. That was good. I'm glad you thought of doing it."

Seth added, "Take it easy this morning. Rest. I'll be back at lunch-time. Mom made some food for you. She's a decent cook, so that's a good thing." He paused and checked the time. "I'll be back in a couple of hours. Is there anything you need me to bring you? Pick up at the store?"

"No, thank you. I'm good." How polite I was. I was grateful too. How could I blame Seth for anything? But the whole time we were speaking, I was very conscious that Victoria was nearby. Her presence nearly curdled my insides. I was like that coiled rattler—full of poison and waiting for the right moment to share it.

CHAPTER TWENTY-ONE

I remembered those college days—meeting Niles in class and Victoria in the dorm and the many study groups and social meetings during which Niles and I had grown close. Those days had formed the foundation of our relationship and set the tone for our love, our married life. We were people in love and focused on each other. My time had shifted away from spending time with friends like Victoria to being with the love of my life—Niles—or so I'd thought at the time. Niles and Kara. Everyone had known we were a couple. They'd said our names together like our future with each other was a given.

We'd thought Victoria would find her own person, but the guys she dated didn't seem to stick. The two of us had been too often the three of us. Neither Niles nor I had known how to leave her behind when she'd invited herself along. For some dates, though, I'd been clear with her—Niles and I had plans for just us. She'd understood.

After college, when she'd found a job not far from where Niles and I lived and worked, it was natural that we'd continue our friendship. We'd had several college friends in the area at the time. Over time, some had moved away, and others had simply fallen away into new relationships or new lives that revolved around children instead of hanging with old college buddies. But Victoria had been there. I'd introduced Victoria to all the single guys I knew. Some of those relationships had been more successful than others, but what I found, over time, was that Victoria seemed to resent me—not so much for fixing her up with blind dates but for the failure of those dates, the failure to succeed in terms of a lasting relationship. It was my fault because if she'd never gone on those dates, she wouldn't feel hurt, wouldn't feel the pain and embarrassment, and wouldn't feel rejection.

Niles had said to stop matchmaking. She'd find the right guy on her own. And it seemed she had. Even if he was already taken. And mine. I couldn't blame it entirely on Victoria, though. Victoria couldn't have "found" him if he hadn't made himself available.

And that left me, on the rainy night of our sixth wedding anniversary, stunned to discover my husband had been unfaithful, and all the little things, the annoyances he'd expressed, the late arrivals home, him not being where I expected him to be—all the little bits and pieces had begun to assemble in a whirlwind in that moment before the semi had hit us, which had then scrambled and scattered them all over again.

Until today.

Today, it all made sense.

Victoria. Victoria and Niles.

I forced a deep breath into my lungs.

Seth touched my cheek, saying, "I'll be back before lunch."

Victoria said, "I'll walk him out. Stay there and eat. You'll feel better."

I watched her walk with him, her butt giving that extra twitch and her arm finding an opportunity to brush against his.

The screen door slammed, and then there was a short delay before I heard the car door open. Another delay happened as I waited for the sound of it slamming shut to cover the distance from the front door to the kitchen. Seth and Victoria. What were they chatting about?

Discussing themselves? Talking about me? Poison nibbled at the thawing edges of my icy heart.

Victoria walked back into the kitchen wearing a smile. "How'd you sleep?"

I sipped my coffee. I did my best to steady my voice and my backbone without letting the building violence inside take me over. When I felt steady and in control, I said, "Pack your stuff and leave."

Her smile hardly slipped. She frowned slightly as if not understanding my words.

"You heard me. Get out. Don't come back."

"What . . ." Victoria looked around us as if she'd find an explanation there in the kitchen with us. "I don't understand."

"I'll keep it simple. Leave."

"Kara, did I do something wrong? Did I offend you?" She pressed the flats of her hands against her chest. "I'm sorry if I did. I assure you it was unintentional. Please tell me."

I sipped my coffee again. I picked up the fork but didn't touch the pastry.

"Kara. You are overwrought. I want to help you." She waved her arms. "I *can* help you. Let me." Her smile had vanished now. She looked toward the foyer, and when she turned back toward me, her expression was saying something else. "Is this about Seth?"

I stayed silent.

Shock and disbelief lit Victoria's face. "Seth? Really? Is that what you think? I'm after Seth?" Her cheeks flushed a bright, rosy red.

Victoria tried to move closer to me, but I stood and pushed her away—I pushed her face away from mine and walked off. She followed me, saying, "He's a nice man and wants to be your friend. He hasn't done anything wrong. Neither have I."

I paused at the base of the main staircase, cupping my hands tightly over the decorative newel post, clutching the wood to prevent me from using my hands against her, against her face.

Victoria stopped, too, but her mouth didn't. Her protests kept coming as she gripped the other newel. "Why are you kicking me out? Why are you angry with me?" She leaned into the post, holding it tighter, saying, "What's wrong with you?"

"Niles." With his name, I gave her a look that I hoped contained enough warning to make her end this now. Before I lost control. I might be justified in throwing her out bodily—and I assessed the option and was pretty sure that with the level of adrenaline surging through my body, I could—and it might feel glorious in the moment, but it wouldn't feel good in the aftermath. So I held on to that newel post for all I was worth and let the threat and the promise fill my eyes.

"Niles what?" She frowned, and then her expression shifted as her eyes widened. "Are you serious?"

I fixed my stare on her. "I'm right, aren't I?"

"No!" Her response was explosive.

Her lips moved and her jaws flexed, but I read guilt in her eyes.

She said, "You always did have a mean streak. I tried to overlook it and be patient, but it's hard to always be the one who has to turn her cheek, to be the one who forgives." She ran halfway up the flight of stairs and stumbled. As she recovered her balance, she said, "He met you through me, remember? I knew him first. But did I cause a problem? Did I try to interfere between you?"

I didn't answer. I was struck that she didn't hear the irony in her own words.

"Did I?" she repeated. "No, I didn't, though he was technically mine first. And I didn't do anything wrong this time either. You should be thanking me, not making accusations. I tried to help you both."

Laughter burst from me in loud, rude guffaws. Victoria stood there, shock in her face. Her fingers gripped the banister so tightly they were a ghastly white against the dark wood. I couldn't help my reaction or prevent the noise from happening, but I reined it back in as quickly as possible. Between the last bits of coarse laughter, I said, "Did Niles know he belonged to you first? When he asked me out? When he proposed? If you think he felt anything more than a little friendship, it was just another fantasy for you. Another rationalization for why your personal life didn't work and no one wanted to be around you. And when my marriage had troubles, as all marriages do, did it justify your pathetic choice to steal my husband?"

"I didn't steal anyone. I begged him to work things out with you. He said those six years with you had been pure hell." Her cheeks had gone from red to maroon. She hit her forehead with the palm of her hand and made a guttural noise that sounded like a groan of frustration. "It's no wonder people leave you, Kara. One way or the other, they leave because they just can't take you anymore. You think you know me? You think I'd do what you're accusing me of? It's obvious you don't know me at all."

"I know you entirely too well. And for way too long."

Her breathing was ragged. Her chest rose and fell, almost with violence. I wondered if she was going to pass out. If she did, what would I do? Not much, I told myself. Not anything.

Victoria closed her eyes and drew in a long, deep breath. Slowly, she opened them. She squared her shoulders and stood taller. She said, "You are physically unable to hear what you don't want to hear—whatever doesn't fit with what you believe or want to believe—no matter how sane or crazy it is. Well, guess what, Kara? You'll get your way—as you always do. I'm leaving, and I'm glad of it. Be happy alone. You were born to be miserable. Have fun with it."

She paused again and looked back down at me.

"Think about this, Kara. What if you're wrong? What if you put all the pieces together and thought you had the answer, only to discover, when that last piece slid in, that you were wrong? Totally wrong?" She shook her head slowly. "Would it even bother you?" Her voice grew soft. "I wasn't a perfect friend, but I was a good one. Probably the best you'll ever have."

"If that's so, Victoria, then please tell me about those photos of you two together."

"We were close friends—but just friends. I knew he was having an affair. I told him to break it off. To talk to you. To be honest."

"You're a good friend to me? That's not what those pictures say. Can you honestly say you didn't want him for yourself?"

Victoria glared at me, outraged. I forestalled any further response from her by saying, "A friend, a good friend, an innocent friend, would've told me the truth about my husband instead of leaving me in the dark . . . instead of protecting him—or worse. Whatever you did or didn't do . . . I don't care. You and I are done."

She ran the rest of the way up the stairs. I heard her footfalls as she moved quickly around her bedroom and then in the bathroom. I stood in that same spot, at the base of the stairs with my hands tightly gripping the post, until she came back down, and neither of us uttered a word as she stalked past me and straight out the door. I heard her car start and the gravel crunching under her tires as she drove away.

How much of what she'd said about Niles was true? I couldn't tell. She'd used those words to hurt me, not to prove honesty. And I'd done a lot of that right back at her. As to what she'd said about me and my personality—well, that might have some truth to it. I'd heard it before, hadn't I?

Dad had said more than once that no one was perfect. I agreed with him. We had to do the best we could with the imperfections we came with, with them or in spite of them.

A pain shot through my chest, in my heart.

I turned and leaned back against the newel post. There was no one here. Only me.

I hugged my arms together, trying to find some small comfort. I'd been left behind before. More than once. I should be good at managing that state by now.

~

The hallways and rooms felt empty after Victoria left. I told myself I was glad of the peace. I told myself all the usual crap—my life was my canvas, and I could paint it any way I wanted, or it wasn't about what happened to a person but rather how they responded to it. Those sentiments felt too airy and prone to emotionalism and cliché. I was in a more bottom-line frame of mind. The reality was that I was my father's sole heir, and he'd left me enough money and other assets that, within reason, I could live without worry for a long while. But did that mean I wanted to throw my financial security into this money pit of a mausoleum? To what purpose?

Better to sell it. Even if I took a loss.

This was Dad's left-behind dream. I had my own future to consider now. It was up to me to look out for myself.

Feeling empty of anything worthwhile, I dropped heavily into Dad's chair. My own chair was nearby, and the walnut cabinet was next to it, holding my needlework projects. The projects were as abandoned now as they'd been since the day I'd started prepping for the move. They would continue to wait until my interest reengaged. For now, I couldn't think of a reason to do anything, or even to *be*—no raison d'être, as they said in fancier circles.

I rubbed the scar, feeling the slight ridge of flesh and the tingle around it as I pressed my fingertips against it. It was a reminder that I was real. That I had had a real life at one time. That life hadn't been perfect, but it had been self-directed, hadn't it? At least it had had purpose.

I felt weighed down by the sense of having behaved badly. Unfairly. I'd allowed my temper, my hurt pride, my dark suspicions to get the better of me.

Suppose Victoria was truly guilty? Guilty of cheating with Niles? Betrayal. Disloyalty. If so, I would've sent her away . . . which I had. She might've deserved whatever ugliness came her way, but I didn't have to indulge in such low behavior. I could've simply sent her away . . .

Suppose Victoria had been guilty of being a poor friend—but of nothing more than that?

It didn't matter, I told myself. Any attempt to reach out, to perhaps offer her some sort of apology, would sound only like an invitation back into my life. I didn't want that. Either way, she had failed me badly.

I sighed, but the sound was ragged in my chest. I pushed the doubts and regrets away. Or tried to. I looked around, wishing for rescue. Or diversion.

Next to my father's chair was the small chest he used as a side table. He also used it to hold magazines or books he was reading. He'd left a large plastic bag behind it. The shopping bag was forgotten, hidden behind the chest and the back of the chair. I imagined Dad walking in, the front door slamming behind him as he kicked off his outdoor shoes. He'd walked over here to stash the bag out of the way. He would've told himself he'd be back shortly. Maybe he'd been thirsty or whatever, but then he'd forgotten and hadn't come back for the bag. Life or death had intervened.

I lifted the bag up over the chest and set it at my feet. At the top of the bag were several plastic pot bases. Like terra-cotta pot bases but without the pots. These were larger than dinner plates.

I held one in each hand and stared. Maybe he'd left the pots themselves somewhere else? Maybe in the car? Or mistakenly left at the store?

Bees, I thought. They'd been on Dad's pocket list. Thirsty bees.

These would be about the right depth.

Just now, I wasn't concerned about bees. I put the plastic plant saucers aside, balancing them on top of the side table.

A largish square box was at the bottom. I worked it out of the bag. The box read, "Gazing Globe Mirror Ball—Silver."

I held the box. Its corners poked my arm and my chest. I closed my eyes, and a few tears marked the cardboard before I pulled myself together. I opened the box and pulled out the globe. Stainless steel. Yet it looked almost liquid.

The box fell to the floor as I stood. I held the ball up, catching the daylight streaming through the windows, and watched the swirling highlights meet and merge with the reflections of the shadowed corners of the room. I was almost twirling with the gazing ball, suddenly remembering that day when I'd danced on glossy wood floors and then had met Seth.

Hugging the gazing ball, I ran down the hallway, through the kitchen, and out the back door. I made myself blind to the mower and to the wildflowers and hurried down the grass path to the grotto nook. The branches of the trees draped themselves forward, reaching for the daylight and disguising the entrance to the stone steps. Careful of my footing, I stepped lightly down to the pedestal. I brushed the stray leaves from the vacant bowl and set the silver globe, Dad's gazing ball, in its place. Then I backed away. When I felt the bench behind my knees, I sat. I watched the globe. The colors of the grotto were captured in the ball, as were the shadows, and they moved and reformed as the breeze shifted.

But that was all it was. A gazing ball. No matter how long and hard I stared, this was no more than a silver globe reflecting its surroundings. It had been an item on Dad's list. He'd made a list and fulfilled it. It was as simple as that.

There was no comfort or inspiration here.

I put my hands to my face and cried.

CHAPTER TWENTY-TWO

Maybe my heart shattered as icicles were prone to do when they fell. Or maybe my heart had melted clear away and no longer occupied its former place in my chest. I felt empty. Bereft. As Victoria had declared I'd be, I was lost in aloneness. The state of being alone felt like a brittle husk, an empty shell in which only an occasional shiver rattled me from head to toe. I was occupied with nothing and no one. I sat in my chair next to the walnut cabinet and couldn't remember the project I'd been working on that last day—the day that my father had announced he was moving. Where had I left off with my threads and needles? Those needlework projects seemed to belong to a former life. One I had no power to reclaim.

In my first life, I'd had a mom. The second stage of my life had been spent with my father and the third with Niles. The third had ended in pain and grief but had led to recovery—the fourth new start—and to Wildflower House, only to end in yet more grief. Did I have heart enough to face a new life? A fifth attempt? Alone?

I sat until I could stand the emptiness no longer, and then I walked out to the back porch. The flowers were truly past the best part of their season, but they still had beauty in my eyes.

Dad's mower sat in their midst like an ironic time stamp. It marked the moment between moving forward and the time switch in which everything had stopped so fast that time had collapsed in on itself. My time. My life. I grasped the railing, unable to move forward or backward.

"There you are. Lost in your thoughts? I called your name, but you didn't hear me."

Seth touched my arm and moved closer. I wanted him to move closer still, maybe to steal some of his warmth, his life, for my own. I may have leaned toward him without consciously realizing it because his arm came the rest of the way around me.

He said, "I'll pull together some lunch. You need to eat."

I shook my head. "There's a ton of food. Your mom gave me several casseroles."

"I'll heat it up for you. I recommend the rigatoni."

"Not right now. I'll eat later."

"You're still in shock, Kara. Grief is normal."

I breathed and felt my lungs shudder as I expelled the air. Seth tightened his arm.

"You don't understand."

"I lost my sister Patricia, remember? And my dad when I was a kid. Everyone experiences grief differently, but I do have an idea of what you're going through and must still go through. Grieving isn't a one-day process. Not a once-and-done kind of thing."

"It's not just about Dad."

"Okay. Talk to me. I want to hear."

I shook my head.

After a pause, he asked, "Where's Victoria? It helps to have an old friend around."

I flinched. I tried to hide it by looking away, pretending the sun was in my eyes. "I sent her away."

It was a much longer pause this time. He said, "I don't understand."

"It's a long story. I don't want to discuss it." I crossed my arms but let Seth's arm remain around me, his hand resting on my shoulder. "I'm sorry. I just don't want to talk about it."

I felt his grip slacken, but he didn't move away.

"Okay. If you change your mind . . . if you want to talk, I'm here." In a low voice, he added, "There's something I want to talk to you about if you feel up to it?"

No more, I thought. I was full up with unhappiness. I moved, breaking the physical contact.

"Kara?"

There was a long moment, and we both stared out at the yard, the flowers.

I said, "I'd like to rest awhile. Then I have some things I need to take care of. Can we talk later?"

"Okay."

"Also, not today but soon, I need to speak with Nicole. Maybe she can represent this house again. I'll be putting it back on the market."

"Kara, I know this is a difficult time for you, but don't move too fast. You know what they say—don't make big decisions while you're grieving."

"I'm sure about this, Seth."

"I'll tell Nicole, then, if that's what you want."

"Thank you."

He turned toward the steps. As he descended, he asked, "Is the key still in the mower?"

Instantly alert, nerves firing and ready to fight, I said, "Why?"

If he heard the warning note, he didn't react to it. He was already down there beside the machine, his hands touching Dad's mower. I called out, "Stop."

He looked up with a question in his face. "The porch is tall enough to shelter it. I was going to move it under there, under cover, instead of leaving it sitting out here where . . . where it's just sitting out here. In view. And exposed to the weather."

He was trying to be sensitive and thoughtful and helpful. I didn't want it. I rejected it. But this was Seth, not Victoria—that husband-stealing false friend—so I tried to soften my tone. I failed.

"Just leave it. Right there."

He stepped away from the mower. "I'm not sure you should be alone. Why did you send Victoria away?"

I saw suspicion in his face and heard it loud and clear in his voice. When I didn't answer, he said, "I'll go. I'll send Nicole over to talk about the house."

"Not today. Today I just want to be alone."

"Are you . . . okay?"

"Don't worry. I'm just fresh out of conversation. Wednesday . . . and the days that came before it, preparing for it took all my words, all my energy. And the two days after . . ." I felt those ugly words, the ones born of anger and resentment, stirring me again. I didn't want to unleash those on anyone else . . . especially not on people who were inclined to be friendly and think well of me and who'd never done me harm.

"Okay. You have my number. Call me."

I nodded.

He came back up the steps. He put his arms out and pulled me into a hug. A hard hug and a brief one. He released me. "Call me if you need me," he repeated. And then he left.

I sat on the top step of the porch. I replaced his arms with my own, hugging myself, asking, What was the value of loved ones and even friends? Was that value worth the agony of losing them? Of being left, one way or the other, behind?

If we hadn't been here, buried in the country, Dad might have had the stroke, but he would have been around other people, smarter people, people who were less self-involved such that they might have noticed one of the warning signs and could've called for medical help quickly. Dad might still be alive to dream his dreams—rather than dying in the pursuit.

CHAPTER TWENTY-THREE

Each day had gotten a little warmer and the air thicker. Today was the worst. I considered turning on the air conditioner, but in this huge house? It felt like a waste since it would only be for me.

I'd buried my father just over a week ago. The week had begun in sorrow but was made bearable by the loving support of friends, both new and old. Then it had gone downhill fast—without restraint—as if none of the goodwill had meant anything at all. Looking back across the week of days, it seemed to me like a mash-up of sorrow upon sorrow, with regret and lashing out thrown in as a bonus. It was almost more than I could bear.

With the windows open, the flow of air was good. I was looking forward to nightfall, when I could reasonably consider the day done. My bedroom benefited from the best of the breeze, and so the AC was less necessary, but that afternoon, as the humidity ratcheted up, I reassessed. I closed the windows upstairs, then went down to check the ones on the first floor.

If the sunset brought cooler temps with it, I could always turn the AC off and reopen a few windows.

I thought about everything and nothing as I went through the house. The wood floors were smooth and cool beneath my bare feet. With the light growing dim, the wallpaper looked old fashioned but in good shape, except for the project area—the abandoned area. Mr. Blackwell had called, asking if I was ready for him to get to work. I'd put him off. "I'll call you later," I'd said. But would I? It seemed unlikely.

Seth had telephoned. He seemed to accept that I was okay. In fact, this day had seen a steady stream of people invading my grieving space. Nicole had called, advising me not to put the house on the market before I discussed it with her. Even Mel had shown up on my porch this morning. She'd knocked on the door until I'd answered. I'd invited her in, and we had chatted. I'd kept my head on straight and managed a reasonable conversation, and she'd seemed satisfied, too, and left.

I was okay, but I was alone. I didn't know what to do. If I let the not-knowing get the upper hand, I'd shatter into a million pieces, and there'd be no one, certainly not my dad, to help me put my life together again as he'd done after Niles's death.

Niles. It had hurt so badly to realize my husband had cheated and apparently felt justified. Many years before that, Mom had left for reasons I'd never really understood. Both times, Dad, in the best way he could, had picked me up and brushed me off and crafted a life for us together.

I'd reached the sitting room windows and was carefully lowering the sashes when I noticed how dark it had gotten inside and out. Had I missed sunset somehow? The dark color above the treetops was a strange, uneasy shade, as if the sky couldn't decide whether the clouds should now be a dirty gray-green color or something closer to eggplant. My arms tingled. I ran my hands along the bare flesh and felt the goosebumps. With some urgency, I resumed closing the windows, determined to beat the rain.

That first day, there'd been a brief rainstorm. I remembered how the squall had blown in across the treetops and the open area of the creek and had swept up the slope of the yard. The trees had moved, bowing before the wind, and when the rain had come, it had washed the dust from the flowers, restoring and deepening their colors.

After I'd secured the last window, I went out to the back porch and knew immediately that this storm was different. I heard the distant rumble of lightning, but stronger energy rode swiftly in on the wind preceding the storm. The flowers swayed and jerked as a rush of big but isolated raindrops blew across the yard. The trees, as much as I could distinguish between their mass of green in the near dark, thrashed. The source of the distant thunder was suddenly and shockingly over the creek. Violent, vivid streaks of electricity ripped the dark sky from top to ground. As the sky was lit briefly by the lightning, I noted the backdrop of clouds was no longer a solid bank but seemed to be an agitated, writhing mass of smoky swirls. The brief spate of rain would soon be replaced by a downpour. Was I safe here under the porch roof? Another cloud-to-ground bolt struck in the nearby trees. The electricity radiated out. The hairs on my scalp and arms rose.

I had my answer: it was dangerous to stay.

I stayed on the porch anyway, compelled by the fading memory of bright lights against my eyelids, now briefly meshed with relentlessly oncoming headlights, and the blue-and-red strobes—which could not compete with the white fire now slashing down from heaven. Nature's bright lines marked my vision, burning out the old and artificial—the artifacts of my prior life—before vanishing themselves.

I raised my arms to the storm, to the breeze running before it. It was the clearest, cleanest air I'd breathed in ages. That air touched my skin, and I leaned forward, trusting the porch railing not to let me fall. I wanted the rain to come down hard, to wash my face, to rinse away the last week and maybe even longer ago than that. The flowers, too, turned up their bedraggled faces, seeking the sustenance. But as the rain grew heavier, splatting against the mower and smacking at the porch, I retreated into the house after all. I held the door open and stood just inside.

How many rainstorms had this house withstood? The wind whipped through the trees and bent the flower stalks, but they stood again. Like me, I thought. Each new iteration of my life tried to knock me down—and sometimes did—but each time I got back up.

I was slower getting up now, it seemed to me. Less eager to risk the next slap down, the next heartbreak.

But as Dad had said, I did get up. Resilient, he'd called me.

The sky was growing lighter, losing the preternatural dark. That sense of something hellacious in the offing was passing as everything around me turned eerily dirty green again. The wind stopped, and so did the rain.

The storm was already done.

Then a piece of ice fell from the sky. A chunk of it. About pea size. And then another.

In those first moments, I didn't understand. I saw the flowers twitch and jerk again in a weird dance, and beyond them, the water in Cub Creek seemed to be spitting and spurting. Suddenly the sky was raining ice. I flew from the doorway to the porch and down the steps. I was there among the flowers as the hail fell. I swung my arms wildly with some crazy idea that I could shield them with my body. I picked the flowers up as they fell. I tried to make them stand. But unlike when the wind had bent them and then released them, this time Mother Nature threw small ice bullets from heaven itself to destroy them.

Pea-size ice gave way to golf balls. They slammed into the metal of Dad's mower with such intensity that I stopped and stared, seeing the dents appear, and then they hit me too. I put my arms over my head, my palms facing the sky, but the onslaught continued, stinging my flesh. As I backed away, with some idea of fleeing into the house,

I tripped and fell. I huddled in the mud along with the flowers, trying to protect my head.

It didn't last. The larger hail subsided to small bits and then stopped altogether. I relaxed my arms, but I didn't get up. From my vantage point on the ground, I could see clearly around me. The flowers were down. And I was down with them.

~

A little time later—I don't know how long—from a distance, I heard my name being called. A man's voice. In that first moment, I thought of my father. But no, it wasn't my father. I thought of Niles. Not Niles. I didn't want it to be Niles, even if that had been possible.

Seth. Yes, it was Seth. All the more reason to hide myself among the wrecked flowers in the shared camouflage of mud and trampled greenery.

But he kept coming, and his voice grew louder. I heard him climb the steps, open the kitchen door, and yell into the house. I realized I must become an adult again. I must get up whether I wanted to or not, but before I could, Seth spied me from the height of the porch.

"Kara!"

His shoes were loud on the steps. Apparently, he didn't fly as well as I did. The words danced through my head like a gentle joke. Not really funny, but now that there was a witness to my embarrassing situation, I wanted to pretend it was okay—that I was okay—until I really was. If I ever would be. Had I ever been okay?

I tried to stop him short of the field, pushing up and raising my hand toward him, saying, "Wait, you'll get muddy." But he didn't stop. He plunged right into the morass of me, broken flowers, and mud.

Ugly red marks covered my arms. My clothing was slathered in dark, wet ooze.

Seth stopped short of hauling me to my feet. "Are you okay?"

I nodded, and a heavy hank of mud-coated hair slapped my face. I pushed it back and felt the mud smear all the worse.

He reached toward me.

"No. Stop."

"What? Why?"

"You'll get muddy."

"Oh, shut up," he said, half under his breath.

"Don't tell me to shut up. I was thinking of you."

"Let me help you."

But that mud was slick, and when he moved forward, bending toward me, he kept coming. He caught himself with his hands and only fell to his knees.

"Warned you." I pushed up to a full sitting position. Things hurt. The specific aches were undefined and more of a vague throbbing.

Still on his hands and knees, Seth asked, "Why are you out here?"

"I wanted to save the flowers."

He stared at me, his eyes trying to read mine. "Is that a joke?"

"I suppose it is. But not at the time. When that hail started falling, it seemed to make sense." I reached toward him. A stick of some sort of squashed greenery had attached itself to his cheek. "Hold still." I snagged it. "Got it." I held it up for him to see. He couldn't see the smear of mud I'd left behind.

He looked away. He bowed his head for a second; then with one hand, he touched my chin, then the back of my head, my muddy hair, and pulled me toward him. Our foreheads touched, then our cheeks, then our lips. It was a brief, gritty kiss, and my heart tried to beat right out of my chest. I moved forward. His arms went around me.

"Kara. You're okay."

"I am. A little bruised under the mud, I think."

He nodded.

"Did you come over here to check on me?" I smiled. "Because of the storm?"

"Yes. But it wasn't just a storm. There were reports of a tornado touching down in the area. I came to see if you were okay."

We helped each other to our feet and held on as we stepped carefully out of the muddiest part of the wildflower field.

Wildflower field? No flowers were left. I sagged against Seth. He didn't seem to mind. As we reached the grassy area of the yard, the walking grew easier, but still we didn't let go of each other. I gripped a handful of his shirt.

"Is everyone okay at your place?"

"Yes, we're all good. Don't get too many tornadoes in this part of the state. With you being alone and all that . . ."

"Thank you for thinking of me and coming to check." I released his shirt. "Hail."

"Yes, definitely hail."

"My roof. My car. Oh, gosh." Suddenly, the need to check for damage was paramount.

"Relax. There's certainly damage. But it's done now. You'll get it fixed."

"You make it sound like it's not a big thing. Dad did all that stuff before."

"Now *you* will. You'll discover it's a headache, but not something you can't handle. Luckily, you have insurance. I know that much about your father. He wouldn't leave anything like that to chance."

I leaned back against his side. There was something companionable about the shared mud. And the shared kiss. I grimaced. The lingering grit had worked its way into my mouth and felt icky against my teeth. I wanted to spit. But not with Seth here next to me.

"The hose," he said.

"Good idea."

The water was cold. I wasn't inclined to linger in its stream, but within a couple of minutes, the thickest layer of mud was washed off my arms and legs. I left my shoes on the porch and stopped at the back door.

"Want to come inside?" I kept my face carefully neutral. There seemed a world of possibilities in the invitation.

I saw the yes in his eyes but then his hesitation.

He said, "I also came to tell you I accepted the offer from the California PR firm. It came on Wednesday."

"The day of the funeral."

"I put off telling you, thinking the news could wait a day or two, but then you seemed so . . . sad."

"Of course. I understand. That's wonderful, Seth."

"I found out this morning that they want me out there right away."

"You're leaving. Soon. How soon?"

He nodded. "Tomorrow morning." He shook his head. "I'm sorry I didn't tell you when the offer was made. I thought there was time."

I shrugged, but my movements were slow and stiff. I was trying to sort out the correct response. The right words were hiding somewhere in my hurt, if I could find them. "The timing was awkward for you."

"Not awkward. I thought I could give you a chance to breathe first. Then it turned out they wanted me immediately. They'd said *soon.* I was notified about the airline tickets this morning. I could've told them no, but . . ." He trailed off.

A heart could only take so much. Mine broke a little more, even as a part of me wanted to cheer him in his decision.

"I'm glad for you." My voice cracked. I covered it with a cough. "That awful mud," I said.

"Are you okay?" he asked.

"I will be."

He reached toward me, then pulled his hand back. "You're going to have bruises."

Without intent, I said, "I've been bruised before. This isn't anything new."

"Kara," he said. "I'm sorry. I can put them off if you need me to. I can reschedule."

I forced a small smile. "No, you should never put off important things—not truly important things." I shook my head. "If you'll excuse me, I'm going to get cleaned up." But I paused one more time before stepping over the threshold. "When do you fly out?"

"Early tomorrow. They were eager to get me out there."

I nodded. "Have a safe flight. I know you'll do brilliantly."

"Thank you."

I closed the door behind me, then the big door, too, and locked it. It was hard to move beyond that, but I kept my mind carefully blank, grabbed the kitchen towel, and mopped some of the dampness from my face and limbs. Then I heard knocking.

Quickly, I flipped the locks and opened the door. Seth held out his arms, and I folded myself into them.

He said, "I'm not going forever, and those flights work both ways, Kara. I don't want to leave as if something is wrong between us."

I pressed my face against his shirt for a long moment. I felt the beat of his heart against my cheek.

"I'll be back," he said.

I stepped away and nodded.

"Will you be here?" he asked.

"I'm not sure."

He kissed me again, this time with a little less earth from the wildflower field but with a lot more promise.

"I'll be back, okay?"

I didn't say anything. I let him leave. As he walked away from the flowers and toward the path, I watched. He paused and waved as he stepped into the woods, then vanished from sight.

I ran. I ran straight through the mud, trampling the few flowers that remained upright, and headed into the woods. Seth was on the footbridge over Cub Creek. He was standing there, his hands on the wet railing, staring upstream. He sensed me, or heard me, and turned.

He received me in his arms. After a long embrace, I stepped back. I pressed my hands to his face, saying, "I want you to go. But I want you to understand that it's not *because* I want you to go. It's because I want you to come back. You understand that?"

CHAPTER TWENTY-FOUR

I'd let him leave. Encouraged him to go. It had been the right thing to do.

I'd always thought I was independent, but I didn't feel that way and hadn't in a long time. When had that changed? Had it never been true?

Maybe, for me, it was more about being left. Or more correctly, *not* being left. Binding people to me—perhaps with love but also with obligation—so they wouldn't, couldn't leave. It didn't work. They left anyway. So I'd gotten that wrong in a big way.

I was right to tell Seth to pursue his dream while I figured out what mine was. I wouldn't be hard to find regardless. He had my phone number.

Of course, I had to call the insurance company and take care of a few tasks. I couldn't sell a damaged house.

I dropped my muddy clothing in the laundry.

Storm damage aside, this kitchen was still awful. The house needed lots of work.

I could sell it as is. Or I could fix it. At that point, I could then sell it or stay.

But living alone? I didn't mind being alone sometimes, but a solitary life wasn't really my thing on an all-the-time basis.

I was a lot like those wildflowers. Accidental. Hapless. But strong and resilient once I dug in. It had taken a full-out assault by hailstones to bring down my beautiful field of wildflowers.

Whether I chose to stay or go—it would take more than that to stop me.

~

When I awoke the next morning, I felt a strong sense of things left undone. I thought of Seth. He would already be in the air headed to California. I sat on the edge of my bed and stretched my legs and feet, then my arms. All my limbs felt surprisingly good. Many of the red marks on my arms had faded instead of turning to bruises. No great harm had been done, at least not to the physical me. As for Seth, I would miss him. But his departure was temporary. I didn't doubt that in the bright light of a new day. But there was also the nagging guilt over Victoria. I wasn't in the wrong. But I wasn't in the right either. I should've handled it better.

Over coffee and toast, I sat in the kitchen and wrote a short note. Seemed like my subconscious must've drafted the note in my sleep because the words came to me easily. It wasn't a note of apology, but in it I wanted to express my regret over the hard words we'd exchanged. Whether Victoria was innocent or not—and I found it difficult to shake my visceral reaction to those selfies even now—I had handled the confrontation badly. I'd wrapped all my anger, my grief, and my feelings of being left out or left behind into that one ugly encounter. I could almost feel sorry for her.

I wrote,

Victoria, I don't want to deal here with questions or accusations of guilt, but I believe I could have, should have, handled it better.

I sat back and drew in a deep breath. Truly, I didn't want to relive any of that last encounter. It was all history—all of it, including Niles and my friendship with Victoria. I wanted to live in the now.

I ended the note with this:

This isn't an invitation to respond but a hope that we can each put this unfortunate time behind us and that you will move forward with your life as I intend to do.

After I addressed the envelope, I left it on the kitchen table. I'd mail it when I went into town later in the day. For now, I needed a hot shower and a truer, better start to the day.

Given the mud in the yard, shorts were the better choice in clothing today. The long scar on my thigh was visible. It hadn't been exposed to the light of day, except in doctors' offices, since . . . maybe never. Today, that didn't seem to matter.

My wildflower field was a sodden, muddy, trampled mass of bruised, stinking greenery—and that was the kindest thing I could say about it.

I couldn't clean up the mess yet. There was nothing to be done until the mud dried out. When that happened, if I could figure out how to make the machine work, I'd mow the field of yesterday's flowers. Or plow it under, maybe.

For lack of a better place to sit and stew, I swung my leg over the cushioned seat of Dad's mower and tried it on for size.

The wildflowers had given me a lovely greeting the first time I'd seen the house and had shared their beauty with me daily. Until nature had ended it. It was time to let the season move on. It was the least one friend could do for another.

"Kara?"

Nicole stood on the porch. She stared at me. "What are you doing?"

"Finishing Dad's work. The work he started."

She frowned. "Do you mean that literally or metaphorically?" She came down the steps but stayed safely out of the mud area. "If you're being literal and intend to run that mower, you need to wait until the ground dries up."

I nodded. "I know. So where'd you come from?"

"The house. You left the front door unlocked. I brought Mom by. She made you fried chicken and potato salad."

"More food?" I ran my hands around the steering wheel. "Sorry. I appreciate the thought. The effort too."

Nicole shrugged. "She likes to contribute. As to the metaphorical part—or should that be symbolic or subtext? I don't know. I was always better at math than grammar. All that wishy-washy English comp stuff drives me crazy."

She kicked off her shoes and walked barefoot through the mud. It contrasted oddly with her silk blouse and businesswoman skirt. She put a hand on the mower's hood.

"Will you stay?"

"No. There's nothing for me here."

"You have something better waiting for you somewhere else?"

"That's cruel."

"I don't mean to be cruel. I just don't want you to do something you'll regret."

"Like staying here? Pretty sure I'll regret that."

"Give it a few days, and we'll talk it through. I'm a good sounding board. Plus, I can recommend repairmen for the storm damage if you need any names."

At one time, I'd planned to leave when the flowers were past their season. Well, they were finished for this spring; that was for sure. But the grounds, aside from the destroyed flowers, were beautiful in their wild, neglected way. The creek was loud, running high from the heavy rains upstream.

"Kara," Nicole prompted.

"I don't know, Nicole. I don't know where to begin."

Another voice joined in from the porch. "That's what Nicole's good at. She can help. She knows everyone."

"Hello, Mel," I called up to her. "Thanks for the chicken."

"My pleasure."

Nicole said, "You mean you don't know where to begin with the repairs?"

I shook my head. "Not that. Believe it or not, I have some ideas . . . for the house."

"Are you considering the bed-and-breakfast idea?"

I heard the edge of excitement in her voice and answered promptly. "Nope. Definitely not."

Nicole took a step back, waffled a little with her footing, and steadied herself against the mower again. "What then?"

"That retreat idea. A place for small groups to come. Maybe writers. Maybe artists." I pointed at the carriage house, mostly hidden by the foliage. "I could turn that into a studio for artists who want to come here to create. For creative types, generally."

"There's lots of artists and artisans in the area. I can put you in touch with them, help you bring them on board for involvement in those retreats. For instance, Hannah Cooper can talk about pottery. There's a lady over in Goochland who does scherenschnitte."

"Scherens . . . what?"

"Paper-cutting art. You wouldn't believe how cool it is. And there are others. There are local writers who would be happy to work with aspiring ones or host book clubs. And yoga. Did you know there are yoga retreats? All manner of possibilities. I can help you with pulling things like that together."

"Retreats." I reached out, then yanked my hand back. "But I have no idea where to start, how to start. I can afford the work to make the house ready if I do it well and right. I can't afford mistakes. This is a risky enough consideration as it is."

"Nonsense," Mel yelled down. "I told you—Nicole knows people. She'll help you get this going. You can put me to work too. Nicole will work for sales referrals, but I could use a paying job from time to time. Maybe cooking, maybe taking care of guest rooms. I work cheap for the right people."

Could this be my dream? It would also be my risk. Dad, who'd rescued me more than once, was gone. Seth, who might've been willing to step in as a rescuer . . . I'd sent him away. He might be back, but who knew when? People didn't always keep their promises. And it wasn't always their fault. I'd never believed Mom had wanted to leave me. She just hadn't known how to go on as she was. And Niles hadn't intended to fail at marriage when we'd said our "I dos."

This would be on my own. It would be all on me if it failed. The idea was scary and sobering.

Maddie Lyn came from nowhere, running barefoot across the grass chasing an orange butterfly.

Mel yelled from the porch, "Don't get stung by those bees, and stay out of that mud."

I thought about Dad. I heard his voice saying, *We'll be okay, Kara. We'll manage.*

He was right. I could probably manage, especially with a little help from my new friends.

Nothing ventured. Nothing gained.

If fate was ready to spin that wheel for yet another go-around, I was ready to take the ride.

EPILOGUE

I sat in my customary chair. Dad's chair was empty, but the throw pillow was neatly fluffed. I could almost imagine he was simply at work—almost but not quite, because I wasn't in the house I'd grown up in nor in his house on Silver Street. I was here in the house that represented his long-ago past and his future dream. I was alone, and Dad wasn't coming home. I wanted to be okay with that. I wasn't yet, but given time, I would be. I reached into the walnut cabinet and chose the appropriately colored threads.

A fresh cloth was already secured in the hoop. I'd plotted my design on graph paper in advance. No flowers this time, though it was *about* flowers. It was about people, too, children and adults both. For my first project at Wildflower House, and in honor of centuries of women stitching samplers to show off their needlework skills, this would hang in the foyer next to the group photo of those girls and young women who'd attended school here more than a hundred years before.

I threaded my needle and picked a starting square, where I created a small green leaf as a bullet point. I skipped a square, then wrote via needle and thread:

- *Wildflowers are tough. They root in unlikely, often hostile environments, yet they manage to grow and bloom.*

- *Wildflowers are fragile. Careless or deliberate acts can easily destroy them.*

- *Wildflowers grow where the seeds find themselves. They must succeed or perish. If they don't grow, no one notices. It's as if the seed or the flower never existed.*

- *Wildflowers are beautiful for a season. Some may be beautiful for seasons to come. The wildflower will never know the difference because it either is or isn't. Only the bees and the butterflies—or a human heart—may feel the lack.*

—Stitched by Kara Lange Hart at Wildflower House

When I was done, I selected a new cloth and tightened the hoop key until the fabric was taut. This embroidery piece would also hang in the foyer and would have larger, bolder letters. Its message would be clear and simple:

Wildflower House

You are welcome to thrive here.

ACKNOWLEDGMENTS

Many thanks to Alicia Clancy, my editor at Lake Union, for her support, encouragement, and story skills and to all those who worked with me to make *Wildflower Heart* shine, including Kelli Martin, my developmental editor; Stephanie Chou; Nicole Pomeroy; Riam Griswold; and all of the editing team for their dedication.

Also, I'd like to thank Caroline Teagle Johnson for the beautiful cover and all the Lake Union and APub team members whose contributions turned *Wildflower Heart* into a beautiful book and will help it find readers who'll love it.

Thanks to my husband for his patience and support and to my beta reader and Cub Creek expert, Jill, and sincere gratitude to all my readers—past, present, and future. I hope they will continue to travel with me from the Outer Banks of North Carolina to the Blue Ridge Mountains of Virginia—and to all of the beautiful locations in between.

AUTHOR'S NOTE

For my readers and friends in Virginia, especially for those in that beautiful area west of Richmond, including Louisa and Goochland Counties—please note that Wildflower House is fictional. I wish it were possible to visit it in person, but you can visit it here in these pages and in *Wildflower Heart*'s sequel, *Wildflower Hope*, which will be released later in 2019.

QUESTIONS FOR DISCUSSION

1. Many of us had imperfect childhoods—meaning childhoods that were relatively stable and happy but with flaws that stay with us and impact our adult lives. Kara's early family life was imperfect in some obvious ways, but she did her best to fit in and make it work. In doing that, however, what did she give up? What life lessons did she *not* learn because she accepted the imperfections as a necessary part of life and worked hard to disguise them from the outside world?

2. Henry Lange had personal challenges. He was emotionally closed off from his wife and child, but he was a good provider, and Kara never doubted he'd live up to his responsibilities and come to her rescue even when she was an adult. Some people are driven by emotion, some by logic, and some by needs like ambition or the desire for human contact or even to protect themselves from hurt. Knowing Henry's background, what do you think drove him to focus on business? Why would he do something out of character, like marry a woman who was driven creatively and emotionally?

3. No one can truly rewrite history (though some try), but they can rewrite how their history is presented. No one chooses to whom and where they are born, but they have some choice in where they choose to grow as adults and where to invest their lives and hopes and dreams. Henry chose. Did Kara? Did it take the loss of her protector, her rescuer, the dad she modeled so much of her own behavior on, to force her into taking responsibility for her life and her choices?

4. Why was Kara angry at Victoria? Was it really about Niles? Or did Victoria's actions, including her insistence on being part of Kara's life, work on her deepest fears—the ones she internalized as a child and that were reinforced by her relationship with her father and her husband? What were those fears?

ABOUT THE AUTHOR

Photo © 2018 AmyGPhotography

Grace Greene is an award-winning and *USA Today* bestselling author of women's fiction. Her contemporary romances are set in the bucolic reaches of her native Virginia (*Kincaid's Hope*, *Cub Creek*, *The Happiness In Between*, and *The Memory of Butterflies*) and on the breezy beaches of Emerald Isle, North Carolina (*Beach Rental* and *Beach Winds*). Her debut novel, *Beach Rental*, and the sequel, *Beach Winds*, were both Top Picks by *RT Book Reviews* magazine. For more about Grace Greene and her books, visit www.gracegreene.com, or connect with her on Twitter @Grace_Greene and on Facebook at www.facebook.com/GraceGreeneBooks.